CASE OF THE
BAYFRONT MURDER

A MACARONI ON WHEELS MYSTERY

BOOK 1

ENDORSEMENTS

"When avid mystery reader and caterer, Terza Tiepolo, decides to help solve her client's murder, it could have been a recipe for disaster. But since she added plenty of family, friends and faith with a dash of caution to the mix, the result is a culinary masterpiece. This is a delicious cozy mystery with plenty of Italian flare."
—**Gretchen M. Garrison**, author of *Detour Nebraska*, and more.

"With humor and moxie, Derban weaved a mystery that had me gasping with surprise one moment and laughing the next, as love for God and big-family shenanigans warmed my heart."
—**Rebecca Trump**, author of *At Last My Love*.

"Terza Tiepolo, amateur sleuth and caterer, is on the case. Readers will love this cozy mystery filled with Little Italy charm, and romantic chemistry that keeps you guessing. Enjoy with a cup of espresso and lemon gelato!"
—**Tica Winston**, author of the upcoming novel *On the Way to Cotillion*.

CASE OF THE
BAYFRONT MURDER

A MACARONI ON WHEELS MYSTERY

BOOK 1

S.K. Derban

COPYRIGHT NOTICE

Cover Design: Mariah Sinclair | www.mariahsinclair.com

Interior Design: Derinda Babcock

Logo Design: Adam Ramirez

Editor(s): Leslie L. McKee; Proofread by Jessica Sisneros

PUBLISHED BY: S.K. Derban, https://www.childofthecarpenter.com, San Diego, CA, 2024

Library Cataloging Data

Names: Derban, S.K. (S.K. Derban)

Case of the Bayfront Murder: A Macaroni on Wheels Mystery, Book 1/ S.K. Derban

276 p. 23cm × 15cm (9in × 6 in.)

ISBN-13: 978-1-963188-00-4 (paperback) | 978-1-963188-02-8 (trade paperback) | 978-1-963188-01-1 (e-book)

Key Words: Cozy mystery with cats; female detective; food and recipies; beaches; Italian cozy mystery; murder and mayhem

Library of Congress Control Number: 2024902029 Fiction

WITH AFFECTION

to
Antonino Mastellone
of
Buon Appetito
San Diego Italian Restaurant
in
Little Italy
Grazie mille
for the many
Magnificent Meals
and
Marvellous Memories

ACKNOWLEDGMENTS

Thank you to Jesus, the Author of Salvation—El-Shaddai.

How do I find the time to write? All because of my wonderful, Godly husband who takes amazing care of me. Thank you, Mario!

How do I have the energy to write? All because of my fantastic family and friends. What a comfort to know you are always by my side.

God has blessed me with the very best in the publishing industry:

ADAM RAMIREZ, I adore your artistic talent! Thank you for the cute Macaroni on Wheels noodle.

LESLIE L. MCKEE, you are a jewel! Thank you for your attention to detail, and for entertaining me throughout the editing process. Now that's a miracle!

ASHLEY CARLSON, your second-round editing review made my manuscript shine. Thank you very much!

JESSICA SISNEROS, you are a blessing! Thank you for proofreading with such care.

MARIAH SINCLAIR, your cover design is marvelous! I am thrilled and grateful for all you do.

DERINDA BABCOCK, you are a gift from Heaven! Your interior design skills are exceptional. Thank you for always being there to answer my many questions. I smile just thinking about you!

Thank you to authors, GRETCHEN M. GARRISON, REBECCA TRUMP, and TICA WINSTON. I am extremely grateful for your support, encouragement, and time. Your endorsements filled my heart with joy. I wish you continued success as authors extraordinaire!

SAM RHODES, of Sam's Smokehouse, you are a smoking, grill master! Thank you for sharing one of your many delicious recipes.

TRIBUTE TO CHARLEY

A very special young lady named Charley has touched my heart. I heard her story when I first began writing my Macaroni on Wheels series. Charley's bravery inspired me to name one of my characters after her:

It began on June 27, 2016, when Charley and her friends were swimming in a neighbor's pool. They laughed and played, enjoyed popsicles, and celebrated the beginning of summer vacation. The following morning Charley woke up with small, strange bruises over her entire forearm. Charley's parents took her to the doctor, who in turn ordered precautionary blood work. Hours later Charley's parents were informed their precious little daughter had cancer. They were both in shock. At the tender age of just three and a half, Charley was diagnosed with B-cell acute Lymphoblastic Leukemia. Overnight, without warning, their lives dramatically changed.

Unstoppable love created a strong family bond as Charley began her treatment. Her initial hospital stay lasted for two weeks, with numerous additional overnight stays. Charley remained joyful and strong, fighting hard for more than twenty-seven months. She completed her treatment in September of 2018. Charley never lost her sense of humor, and was honored as the Leukemia Lymphoma Girl of the Year. Her dedicated parents also helped with the man and woman of the year campaign, by fundraising and increasing awareness of blood cancers.

Charley's parents were willing to share her story as their way of providing hope to others. Their beautiful daughter is spunky, and has a strong personality. Charley loves her family and friends, and adores playing softball. The five-year mark has passed, meaning Charley is considered cured!

SPECIAL MESSAGE FOR THE READER FROM S.K. DERBAN

Thank you for selecting this book to read. I sincerely hope you find it fun and entertaining. If you enjoy reading about Conner Reeves, one of the characters in Case of the Bayfront Murder, you should read *Uneven Exchange*, where Conner Reeves was first introduced.

But please do not worry. There are no spoilers. Reading this book before reading *Uneven Exchange* is perfectly fine.

Stay until the end! After the Epilogue of each Macaroni on Wheels mystery, Terza Tiepolo shares a cooking tip straight from the **Macaroni on Wheels Kitchen.** Enjoy!

TABLE OF CONTENTS

PROLOGUE

Summer. Terza nestled comfortably in a leather swivel chair and stared out the expansive office building windows. The time neared 7:00 p.m., yet the sun remained an hour above the skyline. Although a summer day had the same twenty-four hours, the extended daylight always made Terza feel as if she had extra time.

"What are you thinking?" Moheenie tapped her on the shoulder. "You seem far away."

Terza blinked hard and then turned her attention to her best friend. "Lost in thought, I guess. The ocean water looks beautiful with the sun sparkling on it. I was thinking how summer might be my favorite season."

"No, it isn't," Moheenie responded with confidence. "Autumn is your favorite season. All of the tourists have gone home, the weather is still fantastic, and there is room at the beach."

"You're right." Terza chuckled. "How could I forget?"

"Because your mind is probably also on the murder mystery," Moheenie said while swiveling her chair from side to side. She lifted her eyes. "This view is incredible. I can see the Coronado Bay Bridge."

"Yes, the view is gorgeous," Terza said. "Plus, it's so nice we get to meet in this boardroom." She looked out toward the bridge and then shifted her gaze to Moheenie. "The fact that

Barnaby owns the law firm makes sense," Terza whispered to prevent the other book club members from hearing.

Moheenie nodded. "I'm sure you're right. Too bad it is not a criminal law firm. He might be able to clue us in on some cases."

"That's probably why Barnaby facilitates this murder mystery book club. I bet practicing corporate law can be pretty boring."

"Maybe." Moheenie turned to her right. "Look, here he comes now."

Knowing what would come next caused the corners of Terza's mouth to curl into a smile.

"Good evening, ladies and gents. For those of you who are new to our club, my name is Barnaby Paddington."

Terza adored his British accent. *He also looks the part.* Most days, even on the warmer ones, Barnaby dressed in a long-sleeved shirt and tie. His overall appearance could be classified as *distinguished*, with the added touch of graying temples and horn-rimmed glasses.

Barnaby continued, "I would like to welcome you to this July meeting of the San Diego Murder Mystery Book Club. Now, shall we introduce ourselves? Miss Brickman"—Barnaby gestured toward Moheenie—"will you please begin?"

"Of course I will." Moheenie stood to introduce herself and then returned to her seat. Terza pushed the hair from her face and also stood. The nineteen other attendees followed suit.

When the introductions were finished, Barnaby continued, "I would like to especially welcome those who are new attendees this evening. I am hopeful you will enjoy this wonderful book club. If you like solving mysteries, you have come to the right place." He motioned to his left. "On the credenza you will find coffee, tea, soft drinks, and water. This is an informal gathering, so please pop up to partake of refreshments whenever you desire." Barnaby then nodded to Terza. "You will also notice a lovely assortment of Italian cookies, compliments of our resident chef, Miss Terza Tiepolo." He smiled. "Thank you very much, Terza."

Terza nodded. "You're welcome. It was my pleasure."

"Now, speaking of mysteries," Barnaby said, "while on holiday Christmas past, I found an amazing whodunnit mystery book. This delightful treasure was buried beneath a stack of other mysteries in a little shop just north of London." Barnaby lifted the faded hardbound book for all to see. "Of course I purchased it, and when I returned home, I went on to do a bit of research. The book is an obvious antique, but I checked to see if it had been reprinted."

Terza smiled as she listened to Barnaby tell the familiar story. *Just listening to him speak makes me happy.*

"Due to the age of the book"—Barnaby adjusted his glasses—"I discovered there were no references online and no newer editions. Meaning, of course, only *I* know who did it!" he said with a mischievous grin. "There are over thirty short mystery stories that I will photocopy for you each month. Since we are only on our fourth story, we shall be able to have fun for another two years!" Barnaby's blue eyes sprang to life. "Now, these short stories are separate from the mystery book we are currently reading together as a club. The whodunnit is meant to be solved on your own. Each month I will provide a deadline for emailing your guess." He looked directly at Terza. "From the email submissions I received for the last story, Terza was the only one who guessed correctly. Congratulations, Miss Tiepolo. You regained the lead."

Terza's smile beamed. "Thank you very much." She had won in February and March, was beaten by Ramsey in April and May, but she had now taken the lead with the mystery Barnaby selected for their June meeting. Terza winked at Ramsey. He ran a hand through his thick, chestnut hair before clenching his fist. Ramsey laughed, pretending to air punch Terza.

3

"I don't know how you and Ramsey always seem to get it right." Moheenie spoke aggressively with her hands. "I really thought I had it this time."

From around the room, Terza could hear a chorus of "Me, too," and "Congratulations, Terza."

"Thank you," Terza responded again.

"Remember," Barnaby said, "not only do you have to name the murderer, but you also have to explain how you knew who committed the murder. Most of you did name the correct person, but only Terza could pinpoint how she knew. Would you like to explain who committed the murder and how you knew he did it?"

"Certainly." Terza stood, lifted the story pages and began her explanation. When finished, she received a round of applause.

"Now, let's move on to our current murder mystery novel. Has everyone completed reading through chapter ten? Please let me see a show of hands."

Each member of the group raised a hand.

"That is fantastic. I realize it was a lot of reading for those who are new, and I appreciate the effort. Has anyone read more than the ten chapters?"

Moheenie raised her hand.

"How far along are you?" Barnaby stepped closer.

"I'm finished." She placed her palm on the closed book.

"Good job. Please remember not to give anything away, especially to your partner in crime."

Moheenie laughed. "My partner in crime? You must be referring to Terza."

"Of course I am." Barnaby smiled.

"Don't worry." Moheenie pretended to zip her mouth closed. "My lips are sealed."

The group discussed the first ten chapters for the next hour and then speculated on solving the crime. Moheenie remained silent during the discussions. At 8:15 p.m., Barnaby distributed a three-page handout to each member. "Ladies and Gents," he said, "on these few pages you will find a short story involving a murder. Your challenge is to solve the murder and to delineate just how you did. My email address is located at the top left corner of the first page. In order to participate, you must send me your answer within three weeks. Are there any questions?" Barnaby looked around the room.

"Is there a prize?" Ramsey asked, his smile infectious.

"He's joking," Barnaby announced, especially for the new members. "The prize is the same as always. It is bragging rights and nothing more." Barnaby checked for other questions. "Right-oh, we are off then. Please remember our next meeting on the twenty-second of August. Drive safely."

Terza stood and walked toward Barnaby. She held out her palm. "What a fun meeting. Thank you, Barnaby."

"It was." He shook her hand. "And thank you again for the delicious cookies."

"You are so welcome. It's the least I can do. Thank you for always letting us invade your offices."

"It is nice to have the conference room filled with friendly faces instead of stuffy corporate officers."

Moheenie stepped up. "Aren't you the one who helped Terza with her corporation?"

Barnaby chuckled. "You've got me there. But I must say Terza is not my typical corporate client."

"I'll take that as a compliment," Terza said. "Thanks again, Barnaby. We'll see you next month."

"Yes, thanks Barnaby," Moheenie added.

"Goodbye, ladies."

As they rode the elevator down twenty-four floors to the parking garage, Moheenie quizzed Terza on how she had solved the murder. "I don't know, Mo. It just came to me."

"I have an idea." Moheenie sounded excited. "Let's become detectives."

"Become detectives? Change professions just like that?"

Moheenie's brown eyes twinkled. "Why not? We are young enough to change careers."

"Mo, you have got to be kidding! I spent years in culinary school, and you went to State for your bachelor's degree. Do you really want to start over?"

Moheenie shook her head. "Not in the least. I'm sick of school."

"Well, we can't automatically become detectives because it is a fun thing to do," Terza told her. "Let's be content with solving the murders in our Murder Mystery Book Club, okay?"

"I guess." Moheenie sighed. Her demeanor suddenly brightened. "No, really, I am happy doing what we do. You're right. We can be detectives by solving book crimes instead of real-life ones."

"I think it's safer that way, too."

CHAPTER ONE: DEAD BODY

LITTLE ITALY, SAN DIEGO, CALIFORNIA

Thursday

Sunlight flooded the Macaroni on Wheels catering company, forcing Terza to duck behind her desktop monitor to avoid the glare. She looked toward the open blinds, considered closing them, and then changed her mind. Terza had one last call to make before she returned to their catering kitchen.

She located her customer's number from the client list on her computer tablet and then lifted the receiver of her office telephone to dial. After two rings Doctor Mitchell McCool answered.

"Doctor McCool speaking."

"Hi, Doctor McCool. It's Terza Tiepolo. I called to confirm our meeting for tomorrow afternoon. Does one-thirty still work for you?"

"Hi, Terza. Yes, it's perfect. I'll see you then."

"Are there any changes to the menu?"

"No, I think everything we planned will make for a fantastic party. I'm really looking forward to it."

"Great. I will see you tomorrow. Goodbye."

"Bye, Terza."

Terza disconnected the call and stood, smiling at the thought of her next job. Doctor Mitchell McCool had hired

Macaroni on Wheels for a party of thirty people. Since he lived in a home along the bayside boardwalk, Terza easily imagined the guests enjoying her food while lingering on the front patio with a picture-perfect view of the water. Although her catering company was doing well, Terza felt confident she would receive many referrals from this noteworthy party. She planned on making it a Saturday night the guests would remember.

Saturday

In the Little Italy community of downtown San Diego, three caterers gathered in their Macaroni on Wheels kitchen. Terza, owner of the small company, stepped back to survey their jammed rolling cart. Clear plastic food containers filled both shelves, leaving just enough room to grasp the chrome handle. Using one hand, Terza held her computer tablet with the checkoff sheet in view, and she used her other hand to brush the hair from her face. Several curls from her long, full hair had fallen across her left eye.

"Do we have the antipasto?" she asked them.

The Hawaiian-born Moheenie answered by placing a delicate hand on the top tub. "Yes, it's in this one."

"Perfect, Mo, and how about the bread?" Terza looked on top of Moheenie's tub.

A light crackling of paper signified Ranger had remembered the bread. "It's right here." He held two baguettes in each hand and waved them high before placing the four loaves on top of the bins.

Terza reached down to the lower shelf and touched the two largest containers. "These bins are filled with both the lobster ravioli and the meat ravioli." She looked at Moheenie. "What about the cannoli?"

Moheenie's head bobbed. "Yes, it's in this bin, next to the antipasto salad."

"Great job." Terza straightened. "How about everything we need for the coffee?"

"Ranger and I checked." Moheenie looked to her husband for confirmation. When he nodded, she said, "It's all in the van."

"And Ranger?" Terza reviewed her notes. "Is your bar all set?"

"It's ready to go, and yes..." He paused. Ranger's lake-blue eyes revealed merriment. "I have the ice and plenty of it."

Terza's weight shifted to her back foot as she crossed her arms in front. She pretended to take offense. "And how did you know what I was going to ask?"

"Because." When the tanned blond used his muscular arms to pull Moheenie close, the difference in their height made it easy for Ranger to rest his chin upon the top of her head. "You and Mo are always worried that we don't have enough ice. You ask me every single time."

With Moheenie's back still to Ranger, she widened her circular-shaped eyes and spoke directly to Terza. "Ask him if he has at least five bags of ice."

Ranger playfully pushed Moheenie away. "You see! One of you always has to ask." When Moheenie turned to face her husband, Ranger's gaze captured hers. "Yes, my sweet wife." He then directed his attention to Terza. "And yes, my sweet boss. I have more than five bags." His chest visibly puffed. "I have a total of seven bags of ice."

Terza and Moheenie nodded their approval and exchanged a smile. "Then it sounds like we are good to go," Terza announced.

Ranger pushed the cart at a slow, steady pace while Terza and Moheenie each manned opposite sides.

Moheenie winked at her husband. "I think we should keep him around, don't you?"

"He *is* a pretty good catch." Terza agreed. She then teased her friend by saying, "Too bad you stole him away from me."

Ranger grunted an abrupt "Ha" sound as he maneuvered their cart through the doorway. "As I remember it, *Miss* Tiepolo, weren't you the one who introduced us?"

"I was." Terza tilted her head a notch and winked at Moheenie. "But now, maybe I'm jealous. All the good ones seem to be taken."

Moheenie laughed loudly. "Terza, you're so full of it. After all these years I know you far too well." She reached out to pat Ranger's shoulder. "Surfer boys have never been your type. Not with your hot Italian blood!"

Ranger chuckled as he unlocked the back door of the white company van. It was painted with stripes of red and green, and featured the Macaroni on Wheels noodle logo. "Mo does have a point, Terza." He hopped inside.

"So, what do I do?" Terza passed the baguettes to Moheenie.

Moheenie relayed them to Ranger. "We're going to have to find you someone who is tall, dark, and handsome," she said.

"And mysterious," Terza added. "Don't forget that he has to be mysterious."

The girls methodically handed the plastic bins to Ranger, who in turn placed them into the van. After he secured the final bin, Ranger then loaded the cart. He jumped down and closed the double van doors. "Are you ladies ready?"

Responding to Moheenie's nod, Terza said, "Yes, it's a go. Let's get this party started."

After less than a twenty-minute drive through the typically congested Mission Beach traffic, Ranger guided the catering van into the cramped visitor's space next to the owner's single car garage.

"Are we taking everything through the garage?" he asked.

"I wish we could," Terza told him. "There is a door in the garage that leads directly into the kitchen, but I don't think we can fit alongside Doctor McCool's car. I'll go around to the front and tell him we're here."

Terza's black tennis shoes first touched down upon the cement walkway, then guided her toward the bayside patio. She leaned over the short, white slatted gate, undid the latch, and pushed it open. After crossing the patio, Terza walked up to the front door and pressed the bell. Terza heard the singsong chime through the open front window.

"Are we too early?" Moheenie asked as she stepped up next to Terza. "I thought Doctor McCool was expecting us."

"Yes, he was. He is," Terza said while creasing her forehead. She turned her wrist to check the time. "When we were going over everything yesterday, I am certain I told him three o'clock. That gives us several hours before the guests begin to arrive."

Ranger joined them on the crowded step. "Hey, what's up? Isn't anyone home?"

"It doesn't look like it." Terza again pressed her finger to the doorbell and allowed it to chime repeatedly.

"Did you try the door?" He asked while turning the knob. It opened.

"Doctor McCool?" Terza called out as she peeked around the half-opened door. "Mitchell? Are you home?"

Terza stood in the threshold with her hands on her hips. "Now what do we do?" She looked up at Ranger.

"Maybe he left you a note," Moheenie suggested.

"But wouldn't he have left it on the *outside* of the door?" Terza questioned.

"Not necessarily," Ranger stated. "If Doctor McCool did have to leave, he wouldn't want to advertise it to everyone walking along the boardwalk. Most likely he left the door unlocked just for you and also left a note inside."

Terza looked to Moheenie. "What do you think? Should I go in and check?"

Moheenie shrugged. "I think it makes sense. Why don't we stay here, and you just take a quick look around?"

"All right." She entered the beach house with measured steps, rounded the corner to the kitchen, and instantly saw her client lying flat on the kitchen floor.

"Doctor McCool!" She screamed. Terza rushed to his side, knelt, and nudged his shoulder. "Doctor McCool, Mitchell, are you alright?" Shock rippled through her system.

Moments later Ranger was next to her. "Terza, oh my gosh!" Ranger dropped to his knees. "Please move aside so I can check his pulse."

Terza watched Ranger as he expertly placed two fingers against the vein of Doctor McCool's neck. She then looked up after hearing Moheenie's loud gasp. Moheenie's face registered complete disbelief, and her opened mouth formed a perfect 'O.'

"Is he dead?" Mo choked on her words.

"We don't know yet," Terza answered.

"Yes, he's dead," Ranger said, still staring at the body. "Is this our client?"

"Yes, this is definitely Doctor Mitchell McCool," Terza told him. "Are you positive he's dead?"

Ranger nodded.

Moheenie screamed. "What do we do?"

"We call the police," Terza and Ranger spoke in unison.

Ranger stood to remove the phone from his back pocket. "I'll call them," he said while moving away from the body.

Terza clenched her fists. "Maybe we should check the house. What if he was just murdered, and we caught them in the act?"

"Ranger, hold on!" Moheenie's trembling hand reached out for her husband. "Terza's right. What if he *was* murdered and they're *still* in the house? We need to check it first."

"You two stay here. I'll be right back."

"Be careful," Terza said.

"Very careful," Moheenie added.

They waited in silence for Ranger to return. Moments later he entered the room with his thumb up. "You can take a breath.

The house is clear. Now I really need to call the police." Ranger walked toward the front door to make his call.

"What do you think happened?" Moheenie asked.

"I have no idea. This is so sad, Mo. Just look at the way Doctor McCool is dressed." Terza motioned to McCool's print madras Bermuda shorts and salmon-colored polo shirt. "It looks like he is ready for his party."

Moheenie shielded her eyes. "I feel sick." When she moved away from the body her loud sigh sounded like a punctured beach ball. "Terza, this is horrible!"

Terza walked over to Moheenie and reached for her hand. "This is devastating. I can't imagine having to tell his poor family. Plus, what about all of the people scheduled to arrive this evening?"

"Can we call them?" Moheenie asked.

Terza nodded. "I think we should. After the police arrive, maybe we can look for a list or something. We have the head count but no names or phone numbers."

"He's a guy, Terza. It was probably an e-vite, or maybe he just sent a group text."

"Well, the police will know what to do." Terza rubbed her palms together. "Maybe they will just post an officer at the door."

"What about all of the food? Who is going to eat it?"

"That is definitely the least of our worries," Terza responded. "Let's hear what Ranger has to say."

Ranger ended his call and motioned for the ladies to join him. "The police are on the way. Let's wait outside."

"Good idea." Terza looked out the window.

"I hate to say this, but we really should bring in the food," Ranger told them.

Moheenie's face contorted. "You mean take it into the house with the dead body?"

"I think he's right," Terza agreed.

13

"But why?" Moheenie paced between them and the front door. "We *certainly* aren't having a party."

"Of course we're not, but we are going to be here a while," Terza explained. "I'm certain the police are going to have lots of questions. We don't want everything to go to waste."

With nervous fingers, Moheenie twisted the end of her waist-length braid. "Isn't that like messing around with a crime scene?"

"We won't touch anything but the fridge. Let's just bring in the minimum and forget about the ice," Terza spoke to Ranger as they progressed toward the van. "We can leave it in the coolers, and if it melts, it melts."

"Okay, but there were a couple of loose bags that wouldn't fit in the two coolers."

"Well, you can try the freezer, but I don't think you'll find any room. When I was here making the arrangements, I checked the refrigerator and freezer to see how much space was available. The refrigerator was practically empty, but the freezer was another story. I swear it looked as if half a cow was in there."

Moheenie lifted the bin of cannoli. "That seems odd, especially for a bachelor."

"I think it was left over from when they were married," Terza explained. "From what I understand, Mrs. McCool loved to cook. Since this beach house was their second home, she probably used the freezer for extra storage space."

They entered the house, each carrying a load, and avoided walking near the corpse while storing the perishables. Terza even used a dish towel to open the refrigerator. Then, the trio paced the front patio's perimeter as they waited for the police. The squawking sounds from the officers' radios announced their arrival before they rounded the corner and came into view.

"Is that Ranger Brickman?" One of the officers instantly recognized the San Diego lifeguard. He extended his hand. "I assume you're the one who confirmed the death?"

"I definitely couldn't find a pulse," Ranger stated. "He was a client of *MOW*, Miss Tiepolo's catering company. The full name is Macaroni on Wheels. Terza found him when we arrived."

The officer addressed Terza. "Did you touch him?"

Taking a step backward, she nodded her head. "I just pushed on the side of his arm to try and wake him. I'm sorry. I had no idea he was dead."

"That's okay," the officer said. "Don't worry about it."

"I touched him, of course," Ranger added. "Just to check for a pulse."

The officer moved toward the door. "I take it he's in the house?"

"Yes, right between the dining room and kitchen."

"Okay, let us first check this out. Can the three of you stick around?"

Their heads bobbed in harmony.

"Good. We need to ask you some questions for our report, but I know the detective will also want to speak with you."

"That's what we figured," Ranger responded.

Terza, Moheenie, and Ranger watched the police activity increase from their seats at a concrete patio set. While they waited for the unknown detective in charge, three pairs of elbows rested upon the round, mosaic tabletop. Then, moments later, a slight and unexpected tap from Moheenie's foot caused Terza to look sideways at her friend. Without speaking, Moheenie used her earth brown eyes to guide Terza's vision. A new and very handsome man had just joined the group.

Terza strained to look uninterested and then checked her watch. "If that is the detective, I wish he would hurry. I really don't want to be here when the guests begin to arrive."

Moheenie took a quick, audible breath. "Oh no! I forgot about the guests. How awful for them. I thought we were going to ask the police about contacting them?"

"We were. We still are. They just haven't come out yet."

"Isn't there anyone we can call?" Ranger rubbed his forehead. "I mean, what a way to find out. Can you imagine coming to a party just to be informed that your host is dead?"

Terza shrugged. "I know. It's terrible. But unfortunately, I don't know any of the guests. Heck, I don't even know their names. Moheenie and I were hoping to talk with one of the officers about it."

"I doubt if he sent any type of formal invitations. It was most likely something electronic," Moheenie told Ranger. "Terza and I planned to offer our help if the police can retrieve his phone and email."

Ranger nodded. "I think you're right, but at this point in their investigation, his party guests are probably the last thing on their minds."

Moheenie focused on the new addition. "Maybe this detective will find a guest list or something."

"How do you know *he's* the detective?" Terza rubbed her right eye.

"Because he looks like a detective," Moheenie told her. "Besides, isn't that a badge clipped onto his belt?"

Terza's gaze zoomed in on the handsome man's waistline. And while scanning for the badge, she couldn't help but notice the solidity of his body. Beneath the denim shirt and tan cords, there didn't appear to be any wasted curves.

Ranger suddenly cleared his throat loudly. "Are you still looking for his badge, Terza?"

Instantly, her face flushed. "Okay, cut it out you two. This is a murder scene, remember?"

"Murder?" Moheenie exclaimed. "I thought he just fell or something."

"I'm sure, Mo," Ranger said. "That guy was whacked! Didn't you notice the blood?"

"Of course not! I tried not to even look at him." Moheenie tossed back her braid. "Plus, how creepy. That means you touched a dead body."

"May I join you?" The nearness of the detective startled Terza. "My name is Detective Garza. Nicolas Garza."

Ranger shot to his feet. "Please, Detective Garza." He pointed to the empty, concrete bench seat. "Yes, feel free."

Terza watched as Garza surveyed each of their outfits. As typical for a catering event, they wore tan khaki pants and black Macaroni on Wheels golf-style shirts. The detective moved closer toward the logo on Ranger's shirt. "*MOW*," Garza read aloud. "What does *MOW* mean?"

"Macaroni on Wheels," Terza told him.

"Nice macaroni noodle. I like the wheels," Garza said. "I take it you three are the caterers?"

"What gave us away?" Ranger joked.

The detective half-smiled while glancing at his pocket-sized spiral notepad. "Ranger Brickman, I assume?" He extended his hand.

Ranger shook it firmly. "You assume correctly." He sat down.

Detective Garza remained standing as he leaned toward Moheenie. "And you must be Mrs. Brickman."

Still seated, Moheenie reached out her hand. "Yes." Her reply sounded sweet. "Moheenie Brickman."

"It is very nice to meet you."

She smiled warmly. "You may call me Moheenie."

"Moheenie," Garza repeated, then turned his focus to the right. "You must be Terza Tiepolo?"

Her name seemed to roll right off his tongue. Terza smiled inwardly as she perceived just a hint of an Italian accent. "I am pleased to meet you, Detective Garza."

When their palms locked, Terza had a close-up look into his eyes. Their deep-brown color appeared black, almost like strong coffee. Only the reflection of light seemed to withdraw the vibrant specks of cocoa.

"Now that we've all met," Garza said while sitting. "I am just sorry it's under such unfortunate circumstances." He directed his question to Ranger. "I understand you're a lifeguard?"

"Yes, for the city of San Diego. I am a lifeguard by day and a part-time bartender by night. I help out Terza whenever I can."

"And did you know the decedent personally?"

Ranger slowly turned his head. "No. I didn't know him personally or professionally. I've never met Doctor McCool, nor have I even seen him on the beach."

Garza looked at his notebook. "I am told you only checked for a pulse, is that correct?"

"That's correct. Although, I did notice he still felt warm."

Garza again glanced down at his notes and then said, "As it stands right now, the time of death is estimated between eleven in the morning and one this afternoon."

"Too bad we didn't come earlier," Moheenie said.

"Yes, maybe we could have saved him." Terza pushed her palms together.

Garza added his own word of caution. "You also might have gotten hurt yourselves." He rechecked his notes. "Do you know exactly what time you arrived?"

As the wind increased, Terza brushed the hair from her eyes. "Three on the dot," she said. "When Doctor McCool didn't answer the door, I checked my watch. He was expecting us right at three o'clock."

While recording her words on paper, Terza caught Garza watching her flyaway locks.

"The front door was unlocked, is that correct?"

"Yes." Terza removed the red elastic from her wrist. In two precise moves, she pulled her hair back and secured it with

18

the band. "Ranger thought Doctor McCool might have left us a note," she added. "First we rang the doorbell, but when no one answered, Ranger checked the door."

"Since it was unlocked," Ranger added, "I thought Doctor McCool may have left a note in the house."

"Who went inside the house first?" Garza asked.

"I did." Terza raised her hand. "I went in to look for a note, but I found Doctor McCool instead."

"I came in when I heard Terza scream," Ranger added.

"Did you also go inside the house?" Garza asked Moheenie.

"Just for a moment, then we waited outside," Moheenie answered.

"Oh, but we did go back inside to use the refrigerator," Terza explained. "We are really, really sorry, but we didn't want all the food to spoil. We placed a few small plastic bins in the refrigerator and other containers of food, but we steered clear of the body, and I even used a cloth to open the door."

"I see," Garza said, writing in his notebook.

Terza looked anxiously at Moheenie as the detective's pen continued to move. *What the heck is he writing?* She moved her lips silently.

Moheenie shrugged.

"Do either of you know why Doctor McCool was having this party in the first place?" Garza asked. "Did he say?"

Terza volunteered to answer by lifting her hand. "Doctor McCool said his friends had been giving him a hard time about getting out and moving on with his life. He thought a party at his beach house would be a way of appeasing them and kind of breaking the ice."

"Getting out? Moving on with his life? Were those his words exactly?" Garza asked.

Terza nodded. "I think almost word for word."

"Why would his friends want him to get out?" Garza asked. "Why did he need to move on with his life?"

"Because Doctor McCool is recently divorced. Hey," Terza added, "maybe his ex-wife did it."

"What makes you say that?" Garza pressed.

Terza shook her head. "No special reason. I thought you always suspected the spouse?"

Garza ignored her question. "Have you ever met the ex-Mrs. McCool?" he asked the group.

"Well, kind of, but not really." Terza sighed audibly. "When I was over here yesterday Mrs. McCool rang the bell. Then, when Doctor McCool opened the front door, she obviously could see me sitting at the dining room table."

"How do you know that? What did she say?" Garza asked.

"At first, I heard her demand to know who I was. It was so rude. I could tell that Doctor McCool was extremely embarrassed. Even though he lowered his voice, I heard him try and explain that I was just the caterer. But then"—flustered, she waved her hands—"she completely freaked! I heard her accuse him of having a party to celebrate their divorce."

"Did you ever see her face?" Garza asked.

Terza turned her head. "No. I didn't even catch a glance. I could see one arm, and that's about it."

"So, she never entered the house?"

"Not while I was there. After Doctor McCool mentioned the party, she stormed off."

"Maybe she returned this afternoon to apologize," Moheenie suggested.

"Yeah, right." Ranger grunted. "It's more like she returned to whack her husband over the head!"

"But she's the one who wanted the divorce," Terza explained while looking at Garza. She noticed a look of amusement in his eyes. "Oops! I'm sorry. I guess we should leave the detective work to you."

Garza laughed. "It's fine. Of course we're going to check out the wife, but tell me what you know about her wanting the divorce."

"I don't know. I only suspect because of Doctor McCool's embarrassment. I think he felt the need to explain her actions." Terza rubbed her fingertips over the colorful mosaic tiles set within the table. "First, he apologized for her rudeness," she continued. "He told me she's had a hard time this year."

"In what way?" Garza asked.

"I don't know as he didn't really say. Doctor McCool said he was originally shocked when his wife asked for the divorce, and he told me he had tried to make things as easy for her as possible. He let her choose whichever house she wanted, and he said he continues to pay for everything."

"For not knowing you, it sounds like Mitchell McCool really opened up about his personal life."

"Right now, when I was listening to myself talk, I just thought the same thing," Terza commented, looking down. "But yesterday, when he was telling me, it really didn't seem that way. It just seemed natural."

"I bet she regrets the divorce," Moheenie commented. "He sounds like such a nice man."

Terza looked up. "I agree, Mo." She then leveled her gaze at Garza. "I don't want to read anything into it, but I got the distinct impression that Mrs. McCool, for whatever reason, decided she wanted to try it single. Even though he didn't understand, her husband hoped to make things as easy for her as possible. Then, she began to realize her mistake and tried to gradually inch her way back into his life. But, although he still loved her, he had already started to make a life without her."

"And she couldn't stand the fact that he was able to live without her!" Moheenie quickly added.

Terza pumped a fist at Moheenie. "Exactly."

Garza jotted something in his notebook. "I know he was a doctor," he said. "Do you know if his guests were colleagues, personal friends, or both?"

"I think he invited mostly colleagues and maybe a few friends, but I am not positive," Terza answered. "That is definitely the impression I got, but Doctor McCool didn't say it specifically."

A voice sounded from the front door. "Nico?"

Garza turned toward the man wearing army green pants with a rust-colored T-shirt. "We're ready when you are," he said.

"Thanks, Gordy," Garza said. "We're wrapping it up now. I'll be right there."

"He's with the crime scene unit," Garza explained. "Well." He closed his notebook. "I thank you for all your information." Garza shot Terza a smile. "And for your insights," he added.

"Do you really think Rose McCool could have done it?" Terza asked.

"Time will tell," Garza said. He stood to stretch his legs. "This was a crime of passion, not a robbery. So, of course the ex-Mrs. McCool is a suspect. But, we haven't even started with his colleagues. Who knows? There could be something going on at the hospital."

Terza tilted her head in interest. "Will you ever let us know?"

"I'll do my best. It's not standard operating procedure, but you did find the victim. Thank you again," he said before pivoting toward the house. After taking a few steps, Garza turned back. "If you can give us just about fifteen minutes more, it will be clear for you to remove your food from the refrigerator."

"What about the party guests?" Terza asked. "Are you planning on notifying them?"

"Do you have a list?" Garza tilted his head.

"No, but what about his computer?" Terza suggested.

"Or you could check his phone," Moheenie added.

"We don't have time for that right now. I'll make sure that an officer remains at the door."

"Would you like us to call them for you?" Terza offered.

"That's okay, but thanks," Garza said with a slight smile.

Terza noticed how it never reached his eyes.

"Thanks, Detective," Ranger called.

"Thank *you* for your patience. I'll give you the heads up when we're ready." He walked away.

"Maybe Mrs. McCool came back and –"

"Maybe what, Mo?" Ranger interrupted. "Maybe that's when she killed him?"

"Well, it's possible," Moheenie insisted. "And don't think I can't tell you are laughing at me."

"Or what if she never even came back," Ranger offered.

"We need to get a look at his guest list," Moheenie told Terza.

"I agree," Terza said. "It just might give us a clue as to who was in the house."

This time Ranger's laughter rang loudly. "Ha! Give *us* a clue? When did you join the force?"

Terza couldn't help but grin. "Stop teasing me, Ranger. You know I'm not going to let this go."

"Then who's going to warn Detective Garza about the two of you?"

"Speaking of Detective Garza," Moheenie added. "I heard that other guy call him Nico."

Terza's eyes sparkled. "I heard it too."

"Let's see," Moheenie said. "He's tall."

"About six-one," Ranger informed them.

"Dark," Moheenie added. "*And* handsome."

"But is he mysterious?" Ranger teased.

Terza released her hair and shook out the curls. "I'm taking the fifth on this one."

"No need to answer," Moheenie told her. "The twinkle in your eyes says enough."

"Okay, enough already. We need to talk about all of the food. Since tomorrow is our family dinner day, I will bring it over so my mother can take the night off from cooking. Would you and Ranger like to join us?"

"For family dinner at the Tiepolo house? We wouldn't miss it, but are you positive it's okay?" Moheenie asked.

"Yes, I am more than positive. Are you kidding, Mo? You know how much my mother loves to have company. When it comes to family dinner, it's the more the merrier to her."

"Okay then, we'll be there." Moheenie looked to her husband, who nodded his approval.

"Good, because I need to call my mom and tell her not to cook." Terza reached into her bag and retrieved her phone. She then pressed the contact button to call her parents' house.

"Hello," Terza heard her mother answer.

"*Buona sera*, Mom, it's Terza."

"*Buona sera*, my love. How was your day?"

"My day was interesting." Terza rolled her eyes. "I'm calling to say you can have a day off from cooking tomorrow. My catering job for this evening was canceled, and we have tons of food!"

"Why was your job canceled?" Benedette Tiepolo asked.

"Why was my job canceled?" Terza repeated while looking to her friends for an explanation. Moheenie shook her head in a signal not to mention the dead body. "It's a long story, Mom. I'll explain later."

"Oh, my love, I don't want you to lose all of that money. Your papa and I will pay you for it."

"Mom, you don't have to pay me for the food. The catering job was paid for in advance."

"Aren't you going to return the money?"

"Well, Mom, we usually don't offer refunds after the food is made."

"But what if there was a good reason for canceling?"

"Mom, I understand." Terza once again looked to her friends for help. Moheenie smiled knowingly, and Ranger was obviously trying not to laugh aloud. "Besides, the man is gone, so I have no way to return his money." Terza instantly regretted her choice of words.

"Gone? Where did he go? Who would leave before an event?"

"Like I said, it's a long story. I will explain everything tomorrow. Okay?"

"Okay, but shall I make dessert?"

"No, I have everything. It will be fun for you to have a Sunday off."

"Thank you, but I love to cook."

"I know you love to cook, Mom. That is why I love to cook too. But this Sunday will be a proper day of rest for you. Plus, Ranger and Moheenie are joining us."

"What a lovely treat. Please tell them I cannot wait."

"Of course, I will. On second thought I'll put my phone on speaker, and you can tell them yourself." Terza pressed the speaker button and placed her phone on the mosaic tabletop. She leaned in to talk. "Okay, Mom. Ranger and Moheenie can hear you."

"Hi, Mrs. Tiepolo," Moheenie and Ranger said in unison.

"Who is Mrs. Tiepolo? You are supposed to call me Beny," Benedette told them.

"Hi, Beny," Moheenie replied.

"Hi, Beny," Ranger repeated.

"Hello, you two! It is so nice to hear your voices. How are you?"

"We are doing great," Moheenie said.

"That is wonderful to hear. Terza tells me you are joining us for family dinner."

"Only with your permission," Ranger said.

"Don't be silly. I am thrilled you are coming over. You two are family, and Sunday dinner is our family dinner. You are welcome tomorrow and every Sunday thereafter."

"Thank you very much, Mrs. Tiepolo, Beny," Moheenie quickly corrected herself. "Ranger and I are excited to see you."

"It is always a joy to see the both of you."

"Yes, thank you, Beny," Ranger said in agreement.

"You are welcome."

"We have to go now, Mom. We'll see you tomorrow at four."

"See you then. Arrivederci, my love."

"Ciao, Mom."

After ending the call, Terza looked to her friends. "See, I told you. The more the merrier at the Tiepolo residence."

"What does arrivederci mean?" Moheenie asked. As she spoke, one brow raised higher than the other.

"You know it means goodbye," Terza told her.

"But I thought ciao meant goodbye."

"It does," Terza said. "Arrivederci is just more formal. My mom prefers arrivederci to ciao, but it's just too late for all of us kids to change. We grew up saying ciao instead of arrivederci.

"Are you fluent in Italian?" Ranger asked.

"No." Terza laughed. "I'm fluent in food and family Italian. I would probably get by if you dropped me off in Italy, and I had no choice. But for the most part, I just know the basics."

"How did I not know that about you?" Ranger asked.

"I guess it never came up," Terza told him.

"I knew it," Moheenie teased.

Ranger smiled at his wife. "That is because the two of you are thick as thieves."

CHAPTER TWO: WHAT A NIGHT

The time neared 5:00 p.m. when the caterers had permission to retrieve all of their food and catering supplies. An officer stood at the door watching as the trio made their way to the kitchen by walking close to the living room walls.

"Look at the outline, Terza," Moheenie whispered. "Doesn't it look like a movie?"

"It does, plus I see lots of blood." Terza turned into the kitchen before finishing her thought. "Although I don't think he bled out. There just isn't enough."

"Maybe he died from a brain hemorrhage," Moheenie offered.

"Would you two stop it?" Ranger asked. "Bled out, brain hemorrhage. You both are watching too many mystery movies."

"It's not the movies, Ranger." Moheenie removed a bin from the refrigerator.

"It's our Murder Mystery Book Club," Terza added, reaching for another bin. "You know we only read murder mysteries."

"Well, whatever it is, let's speed this up. We're getting dirty looks from that officer."

After filling their arms, Ranger, Moheenie, and Terza walked single file out the door. They loaded everything into the Macaroni on Wheels catering van and then drove straight to their Little Italy catering company.

"I'm exhausted," Moheenie said after Ranger finished parking the van. "It's barely six o'clock, and I feel like it's midnight." She hopped down from the van and walked to the rear.

"I agree," Terza said, following her.

"It's the adrenaline," Ranger told them. "When your adrenaline peaks, you grow tired afterward."

"Well, whatever it is, I feel like going to bed."

"I do too," Terza added. "Let's get this food put away."

"Load and reload," Ranger said as he returned the bins to their catering cart.

"Isn't that the truth?" Terza brushed the loose hairs from her eyes.

Ranger pushed the cart again, and Moheenie and Terza guided it straight through the Macaroni on Wheels side door. They continued rolling until the cart stood directly in front of their two refrigerators. Terza opened one of the doors. "Let's just hurry and get this finished."

In less than ten minutes, the trio stood around a large island in the generous-sized kitchen. They leaned in and rested their elbows on the concrete counter.

"I'm hungry. What's for dinner, Mo?" Ranger asked.

"Dinner? How can you be hungry after a day like this?"

Ranger creased his forehead and looked sideways at his wife. "Maybe because I haven't eaten all day? Plus, you eat like a bird anyway."

"I do not!" Moheenie argued. She looked at her friend. "Terza, do I eat like a bird?"

"Mo, how much do *you* weigh?" Terza asked.

"Why do you ask?"

Terza laughed. "Just answer the question."

After a long sigh, Moheenie answered, "Just a tad over one hundred."

"And you are how tall?" Terza pressed.

"Five-one."

"You eat like a bird," Terza said flatly.

"How much do you weigh?" Moheenie asked Terza.

"A girl never tells," Terza responded as she watched Moheenie's dark eyes shoot arrows at her. "Okay, I clock in at about one hundred and ten."

"Then we are even because you are two inches taller than me. You should weigh more."

"Of course I should, but that has nothing to do with how little you consume."

"I'm not too skinny!" Moheenie whined.

"I never said you were too skinny," Ranger assured his wife while sliding an arm around her slender waist. "I think you are perfect, but you do eat like a bird."

"Moheenie, I agree with Ranger. We are not saying you're too skinny. You are beautifully petite, and you do not require much food, except dessert, of course. But please give your husband a break. The poor guy is hungry!"

"Then what are *you* having for dinner?" Moheenie asked, looking eye to eye with her friend.

Terza met the gaze and returned it. "I'm not really hungry."

"Ha!" Moheenie grunted.

"Don't *ha* me. I didn't say I wasn't going to eat. I said I'm not really hungry. Good grief, we just saw a dead body! I'll probably just heat up a can of soup or something."

"You should walk over to your parent's house," Ranger told her.

"Oh no, today has already been long enough. The last thing I need right now is a doting mother and father."

Ranger turned to Moheenie. "Are you ready? We can stop for tacos on the way home."

"Tacos? Yum!" Moheenie's countenance brightened.

"Now you're hungry?" Ranger asked.

"Of course I want a taco!"

"Are you ready to go, Terza?" Ranger asked. "We can walk you home before we head out."

"Thanks, Ranger, but there's no need. It's still light out."

"You're right," Ranger agreed. "Typically it's dark after our gigs."

"That's because we don't usually find a dead body!"

"Right again." Ranger wrapped his strong arms around Terza's back and squeezed. "Have a good night. We'll see you tomorrow."

Moheenie took Ranger's place and hugged Terza. "Bye, honey!" She squeezed tightly. "Love you."

"Love you, too, Mo. Sleep well."

Terza walked her friends to the door.

"Say hi to Olive for me," Moheenie said while sliding into their car. "We both know how much your gorgeous cat adores me!"

"Quit rubbing it in," Ranger teased. "I don't think Terza's cat likes any male."

Moheenie laughed. "You may be right, but she definitely doesn't like you."

"Doesn't like me? We've never even met," he complained. "She refuses to show her face whenever I'm there."

Still smiling, Moheenie waved goodbye to Terza.

After watching them drive away, Terza double-checked to make sure all the perishables were properly stored. She then exited through the front door and secured the deadbolt. She raised and lowered her shoulders while expelling a loud breath of air. "What a day!"

Typically when leaving her catering company, Terza took the scenic route to her Little Italy condominium. It was two blocks longer but enabled her to walk along the main boulevard lined with restaurants, coffee shops, Italian markets, and more. She knew most of the workers and loved saying hello as they served the outside diners.

Tonight, she took the shorter route, electing to walk along the residential side streets. Moving at a casual pace, Terza easily covered the five blocks in less than ten minutes. She did not feel like talking. Instead, Terza wanted to be alone with her thoughts. An idea about the murder simmered within her mind, and she needed quiet time to let it rise to the surface.

When Terza reached her burnt orange, four-story condominium building, she punched her code into the keypad. A click sounded as the lobby door unlocked. Terza pushed the glass door open and walked directly to the elevator. *Perhaps I'll skip dinner altogether.*

Terza exited the elevator on the top floor and counted the eighty steps to her front door. She unlocked the deadbolt, opened the door, and called out, "I'm home and I'm alone!" Terza knew what to expect next. Olive would wait at least five minutes before showing her furry face. Olive had to make certain Terza did not have company.

After Terza opened one of her kitchen cupboards and stood looking at her soup assortment, she heard a single meow.

"Uh oh," Terza said. She selected a can and closed the door. Looking down at her Siamese cat, she spoke lovingly. "A single meow always means you are mad at me, but Olive, I am not late." Terza knelt to caress the top of Olive's head. As she massaged the chocolate brown fur, Terza could hear Olive purring. She smiled. "I was going to be home much later tonight. You know I had a catering event. Now, I am home extra early, just in time to give you a treat." The purring intensified as Terza rubbed the fur behind Olive's ear.

Terza reached for Olive's crystal bowl, stood, and moved to another cabinet. Olive instantly weaved in and out of Terza's legs, practically dancing at the sound of Terza popping the pull-tab lid. She opened it, and Olive's meows increased. After scooping two generous portions of the wet food into the bowl, Terza carefully placed it upon the ground. Olive would be busy long enough for Terza to heat up her soup. She planned to eat, shower, and go to bed. Any ideas about the murder would have to wait. Terza was officially too tired to think.

CHAPTER THREE: BOARDWALK ADVENTURE

Sunday

Terza got up to attend the early church service. When she returned home, instead of going to her condo, Terza parked her red Fiat in the garage of her complex. She sat for a moment, reflecting on the morning message before exiting her car. Terza pressed her key fob to lock the doors. "Thanks, Cab," she said as the car lights flashed. After saving for what felt like an eternity, Terza's very first car was a used Volkswagen Beetle. She had spent hours waxing her black beauty and decided to name him Coal. When Terza purchased her brand-new Fiat, she selected an Italian red color, and named him Cab, as in Cabernet.

Terza exited the parking garage, grinning as she thought about her only two vehicles. *I wonder why I consider them male?* She shrugged, her smile intact, and walked to her favorite Little Italy coffee lounge for her first cup of the day. The time neared 9:30 a.m., and she felt the caffeine withdrawals kicking in. Terza took her place in line and tried to patiently wait her turn. She was fifth.

One of the three baristas greeted her. "Good morning, Terza. Buon giorno." He was busy backing up the main barista by fulfilling the pastry orders.

Terza looked up and smiled. "*Buon giorno*, Romano. How's your morning going?"

"Hectic," he said while using tongs to capture a cranberry muffin from the pastry case. "Would you like something to eat this morning?"

"That sounds wonderful, but I need coffee first. I'm kind of desperate," she said while stifling a yawn."

"Long night?"

"Not really, just a very busy day yesterday. It feels good to have a day off."

Terza stepped closer to the front of the line.

"Well, hang in there. Your coffee will be ready in no time. Would you like the usual?"

"Yes, please!"

By the time Terza moved to the head of the line, Romano had prepared her usual order of a Grande Americano. "You're the best," she told Romano, then paid the cashier. "Thanks, everyone. Have a great day."

"Give me a wave if you want something to eat," Romano said. "I'll get it for you, and you can pay me later."

"Sounds great. Thanks again." Terza added cream and sugar at the prep station and then took her cardboard cup of coffee around the corner to a quieter table in the courtyard. She enjoyed several satisfying sips of coffee before reaching for her phone.

She sent Moheenie a text:

Are you up?

Moheenie responded:

Drinking coffee and reading the paper.

Terza sent another text:

Is Ranger next to you?

Moheenie responded:

Yes, why?

Terza's text followed:

Call me when you are alone.

Moheenie replied:

Okay.

Terza relaxed and enjoyed her coffee. She was contemplating getting something to eat when her phone vibrated on the wrought iron patio table.

"Hi, Mo."

"What's up?" Moheenie asked.

"Where's Ranger?"

"He's in the shower."

"Good. I have an idea I need to run by you," Terza told her.

"What is it?"

"It's about the e-vite list. You know how people respond by either saying yes, no, or maybe? And then some even make comments?"

"I'm with you," Moheenie said.

"Well, if Doctor McCool did use an e-vite list, and *if* we can get a copy, maybe the comments will give us something to go on."

"I agree, but how can we get a copy even if he did send out some sort of invitation?"

"I had a thought about that," Terza said. "Do you suppose Doctor McCool invited any of his neighbors?"

"Yes, I do. People always invite their neighbors, so no one complains about the noise. He probably invited the neighbors on each side."

"Exactly. So what if I go over to Doctor McCool's house and kind of hang out on the boardwalk right in front? I'm guessing the neighbors are all pretty curious by now. Perhaps I can talk to one of them."

"But they might ask what you're doing," Moheenie cautioned. "What will you say?"

"I don't know," Terza responded. "Maybe something about how badly I feel for Doctor McCool, and I just felt like walking by his house."

"I don't know, Terza. That sounds kind of lame," Moheenie chuckled. "Why don't you explain how you left some of your catering supplies and hoped to retrieve them?"

"That's good, Mo! I can say I was hoping an officer would let me in."

"Oh no!" Moheenie blurted out. "What if an officer is already there?"

"That won't matter. If I am seen I will give the officer my same story."

"But we didn't leave anything."

Terza drummed her fingers on the table. "They don't know that. I will pretend to look around."

"Then what will you say when nothing is found?"

"That's simple. I'll just say I was mistaken."

"Okay, so when are you going to do this?"

"Now," Terza told her. "I was thinking about driving over in a few minutes. Do you want to go with me?"

Moheenie hesitated. "I better not. Ranger has the day off."

"I understand. Besides, it's better if he doesn't know."

"That's for sure." Moheenie whistled. "Good luck though. It's Sunday and it's summer. You are going to be stuck in beach traffic. Plus, where are you going to park?"

"I was planning to park in Doctor McCool's extra spot," Terza said.

"Okay, but please keep me posted."

"I will. Remember now, do not tell Ranger. He already thinks we're nuts."

"That he does. Your secret is safe with me."

"What do you mean *my* secret? We are in this thing together!"

"Okay then, *our* secret is safe with me. Be sure and call me before we arrive for family dinner. You won't be able to tell me in front of everyone, and I will go crazy not knowing."

"Will do. Bye, Mo.

"Bye, Terza."

Terza disconnected the call and quickly decided against breakfast. She was anxious to get started on her new plan. She race-walked back to her parking garage and retrieved her car.

Terza slid behind the wheel and started the engine.

Moments later, the sporty Fiat exited the garage. Terza drove to the on-ramp, entered the freeway, and smiled. *Could it be? A summer Sunday without traffic?* Her smile ended when she hit the beach freeway heading west. Terza's car also came to a complete stop. "Oh well." She turned on the radio and cranked up the volume. "Time for some music," she spoke aloud. Terza tapped her steering wheel in time to the beat and sang along with the Beach Boys to *Surfin' Safari*.

What should have been a twenty-minute drive took Terza almost an hour. She parked next to Doctor McCool's garage, turned off the engine and got out. Terza casually walked to the front of the house and stood at the patio gate. Tempted to reach over and free the latch, she paused to look through the front window. All appeared quiet and surprisingly normal. It was then she noticed the tape alongside the front door. It was yellow, approximately four inches wide, a foot long, and with black writing. It read: *Crime Scene—Do Not Enter*. Although not large in size, Terza realized the position of the tape prevented the door from being opened.

Hoping to see someone, Terza looked toward the house on the left. It was a Spanish-style adobe home, different from the McCool's white-and-blue beach cottage. A front window was open, but there was no sign of the occupants. The gray, box-style house on the right side appeared even quieter. No windows were open, and the curtains were drawn. It seemed too quiet for 11:00 a.m. on a beautiful Sunday morning. Even if the neighbors slept in, Terza concluded they should be up by now. The rest of the boardwalk buzzed with activity. Stalling, Terza began walking along with the carnival atmosphere. Rolling apparatuses of all kinds traveled by her. "On your left." She heard a male's voice before a beach cruiser bicycle passed her. The cyclist moved to his right as a trio of skateboarders approached from the front. Terza then heard a symphony of pinging bells. She turned to see a duo of the cutest toddlers on tricycles. Their parents were peddling close behind.

Terza walked to the first side street then turned around to head back. She moved extra slowly when passing in front of the adobe-style opened-window home and still saw no signs of life. By the time Terza strolled north a few more blocks, the time neared noon. She circled around and walked back toward the McCool home. Finally, the neighbor was outside!

Terza waved.

"Hello," the woman said, smiling as she walked toward her front gate.

"Hello," Terza responded. *She seems friendly.* The neighbor looked to be very active, possibly in her late fifties. Terza instantly noticed her suntan and well-toned legs. She wore white Bermuda shorts and an orange and brown San Diego Padres T-shirt.

"Terza!"

Hearing the sound of her name, Terza turned toward the water. Sammie, a friend of Moheenie, waved from a stand-up paddleboard. Terza returned the wave.

"Is Mo working with you today?" Sammie asked.

"No, Sunday is our day off." Terza turned her head from side to side.

"When you see her, please say hi for me!"

"Will do," Terza called out and waved goodbye. She quickly returned her attention to the neighbor.

"I like your name," the woman said. "Terza, is it?"

Terza reached over the low gate and offered the neighbor her hand. "Yes, my name is Terza. It's nice to meet you."

"I'm Caroline Mann." Their palms connected.

"It's nice to meet you, too, Ms. Mann."

"It's Mrs., and please call me Caroline. I saw you drive up. Were you coming to see Mitchell McCool?"

"Well..." Terza hesitated and then lowered her voice. "Do you know what happened?"

"I do. My husband and I were invited to his party yesterday. How do *you* know?"

Terza's deep sigh caused her shoulders to lower. "I'm the caterer. I found him yesterday."

Caroline instantly opened the iron gate and wrapped an arm around Terza's waist. "You poor child. I am so sorry. Please come in and let me make you some tea."

"That's okay," Terza said. She tried to politely object while not believing her good luck.

"I insist!" Caroline opened her front door and practically pushed Terza through. "Let's sit here at the kitchen table. You do like tea, don't you? I call it my cure for everything."

"I do like tea, but I'm a bit hot. How about just a glass of water?"

"Would you prefer a glass of iced sun tea?" Caroline walked toward the refrigerator. "I made a large batch yesterday."

"Sun tea sounds delicious. Thank you."

Terza sat perfectly still and watched Caroline pour the tea into a tall, ice-filled glass.

"Would you like sugar?"

"No, thank you."

"Then here you go. Enjoy." Caroline placed the glass onto a coaster in front of Terza.

Terza took a long, satisfying drink. "Thank you again. You are very sweet." She returned the glass to its coaster, then placed her palms upon the skirt of her blue-checkered sundress.

"I feel so badly for you. It must have been awful!" Caroline told her.

Is she trying to get information out of me? "It definitely wasn't pleasant."

"Do you have any idea what happened?" Caroline pressed.

She is trying to get information!

"What did the police tell you?" Acting casual, Terza drew a circle in the condensation on her glass. *Two can play this game.*

39

"Only that Mitchell was dead. We don't know if it was from natural causes or what. I mean, it could have been murder."

"I have no idea. I found Doctor McCool on the floor. He had obviously hit his head, but I guess it could have been from a fall."

"Was there any blood?" Caroline asked.

Terza nodded. "Yes, quite a bit."

"It's probably murder then. But who would kill poor Mitchell?"

"And why?"

"This is all so troubling. I wish you could stay to meet my husband. He had a golf game this morning."

"Perhaps another time," Terza suggested.

"That would be nice. I wonder if the police told Rose."

"Do you mean Rose McCool?"

"Yes. Even though they are divorced, I am positive it will be a great shock. Poor Rose."

"Do you know her well, Caroline?"

"No, not very well. Alan and I bought this home around Thanksgiving time two years ago. From what I understand, Mitchell and Rose also own a home in La Jolla. They only used their beach house as a weekend and vacation getaway. That is until Mitchell moved here full time after the divorce in March. I spoke with Rose a couple of times in December during her Christmas break and then once or twice in February. I know she was quite busy at work."

"What does she do?" Terza sipped her sun tea.

"Rose is an elementary school teacher in La Jolla. I believe she teaches first grade, but don't quote me on that."

"This is such a tragedy," Terza said.

"That it is. So why are you here today?" Caroline asked.

"I was hoping someone would be here to let me in. I think I left a box of catering supplies."

"Oh dear, I wish I could help, but I don't have a key."

"You probably wouldn't be able to use it if you did. There is crime scene tape securing the door," Terza said.

"Oh, I didn't know."

Before speaking it, Terza quickly thought about her next comment so it came off as caring, not nosey. "I am so sad we were not able to notify the party guests before they arrived. It must have been horrible."

"Alan and I were shocked! I mean, we live right next door and never suspected a thing!" Caroline pointed to the side of her house. "As you can see, we do not have any windows on the side facing Mitchell's house. We can see toward the back, and of course, we have our beautiful bay view, but none to the side. Alan and I were busy getting ready with no knowledge someone had just died!"

Terza gaped at Caroline. "How did you find out?"

"Not before we went over to the party. There was an officer waiting by the front door. He told us."

"I was hoping to find some sort of invitation list so I could at least forewarn his guests. I am sorry you had to find out like that."

"That was very thoughtful of you. It's too bad I didn't know. I actually have the e-vite list."

Bingo! "You do? Wow, that would have been extremely helpful."

"I guess it's too late now."

"Probably so." Terza stalled, wondering how to ask for the list. She finished her tea and got up to leave. "Thank you very much for the tea. It was delicious."

"You are most welcome. I hope you can retrieve your catering supplies."

"I will. I have the detective's card. Speaking of the detective," Terza added, "I'm certain he would love a copy of that e-vite list. Would you mind printing it for me so I can give it to him?"

"Certainly, but I'm positive he already has a copy. It must have been on Mitchell's computer."

"Just in case he doesn't," Terza said. "But only if it's not any trouble."

"It's no trouble. Wait here. I'll be right back." Caroline walked down the hall and entered a back room.

Moments later Terza heard the sounds of a keyboard and then a printer. Shortly thereafter, Caroline returned holding at least a dozen sheets of paper.

"I printed everything for you, including the comments."

"Thank you very much." Terza accepted the papers and walked toward the front door.

"When you speak with the detective, you might suggest he look into Henry Follett, Mitchell's neighbor on the other side. He's the one with the bland, gray house."

Terza's ears perked. "Why is that?"

"When I was printing the e-vite sheets, I noticed he was supposed to be out of town. And yet, last night I saw him looking out the window. It was strange because when I saw him, I naturally waved. But instead of waving back, he quickly moved away from the curtains."

"That *is* strange," Terza commented.

"It is. I told Alan, but he thinks I was seeing things. All the lights were off with the curtains drawn as if he was away. But I know what I saw."

"Perhaps it was a guest staying in his home?" Terza suggested.

"No, it was Henry," Caroline stated. "I'm positive. You will tell the detective, won't you?"

"Of course I will." Terza knew she planned to investigate first. She reached out to shake Caroline's hand.

Caroline cupped Terza's hand within her own. "I am sorry you were the one to find Mitchell."

"Thank you. It is a hard image to forget."

"I can imagine." Caroline released Terza's hand.

"It was nice meeting you."

"I agree. It was nice meeting you as well, Terza. Goodbye."

"Goodbye."

Caroline remained at the front door while Terza left through the patio gate. She retraced her steps through Doctor McCool's front patio to her car. With her fingers laced around the door handle Terza stood, contemplating her next move. She opened her door and slid in. Unsure of her plans, Terza stared out her windshield. She fought the urge to sneak another peek at Henry Follett's house. At this point, she didn't know a thing about him. Terza also suspected that Caroline would probably see her, and it was not the time to press her luck. Terza placed the e-vite list into her straw bag and counted her blessings. *I can always come back again.* Terza also made a mental note not to use the McCool's parking space. *Caroline could be watching me now.*

The drive home took half the time, and within thirty minutes, Terza stood alone in her condo, wondering what to do next. Having skipped breakfast, her hunger pains screamed for attention. Her curiosity screamed just as loudly when she thought about mentally devouring the e-vite list. Terza knew she had to eat something, but her family dinner was less than three hours away.

She opened the refrigerator door to peruse the contents. On this sunny afternoon, not even the sound of the opening door caused Olive to stir. Without looking, she knew her beloved cat would be stretched out in a place where the sun touched. Most likely Olive was asleep on the back of Terza's sofa.

Once Terza checked the date on the milk, her decision came instantly. She enjoyed a bowl of cereal at the counter while looking over the e-vite list.

Terza spooned a bite into her mouth and read the names as she chewed. "Henry! Here it is. Henry Follett." She looked at the box where Henry Follett checked *NO* for his RSVP. Terza then read his short, terse-sounding comment. *Out of Town.* The other comments were much friendlier. Guests able to attend added comments like *Can't wait to see you!* or *Looking forward to your party!* The guests unable to attend seemed genuinely sorry, with comments like *So sorry we can't make it. Hope you have a great time!* Henry Follett's comment seemed to express more than just three words. Terza had some work to do.

Once finished, Terza rinsed her bowl and placed it into the dishwasher. She looked down after hearing a scraping sound. As typical, even after eating, Olive stood in front of her empty crystal bowl. Olive pushed the bowl a few inches to the left using her right paw and then switched paws to slide it back.

"You already ate," Terza told Olive, knowing her cat would continue to slide the empty dish around. "Go back to the sun." Terza returned to the kitchen counter.

She opened her laptop and placed her fingers on the keys. *Who are you Henry Follett?* Terza typed his name into her search engine. Several Follett names appeared, but nothing to jump-start her investigation. She then logged into her Facebook page and completed a search. She could not find an account for him. Terza considered her options before logging into the county tax assessor's website. Once in, she entered his beach house address. Henry Follett had a homeowner's exemption credit on the beach house, and his property tax bills were being sent to the same address. This information let Terza know the beach house was his residence and not a second home. Terza closed her laptop. It wasn't much, but it was a beginning.

Terza looked toward her sofa and smiled at the sight of Olive stretched out in the sun. She then picked up her phone and dialed Conner.

"Terza Tiepolo," Conner said when he answered.

"Conner Reeves, where have you been?"

"Ah baby, you missed me?"

"Of course I missed you," she told him. "Where did you go?"

"How do you know I went somewhere? Did you call? Did you text?"

Terza hesitated before pushing forward. She didn't mean to take advantage of their friendship, but she often ended up reaching out only when it would benefit her. "No, but you're always the one to call. That's just how it is. Since you didn't call me, I assumed you were out of town."

"But you're calling me now. I bet you need something."

"I didn't say anything. Plus, quit changing the subject. Where have you been?" Terza pressed.

"I think you're the one changing the subject, Miss Tiepolo. But, to answer your question, I have been on assignment," Conner told her.

"Would that be a DEA assignment?"

"That would be a yes."

"Were you undercover?" Terza asked.

"Another yes."

"Wow, Conner! Did you go somewhere exciting?"

"If you consider Mexico an exciting place, then yes. I spent some time in Cozumel first and then Cancun."

"What a nice place to work undercover."

"It's not like we went diving. I was working," Conner told her.

"You said *we*, so that means you weren't alone. Who'd you go with?"

"A partner, and no I will not give you a name."

"Can you tell me anything about your assignment?"

"What do I say every time you ask me that question?" Conner asked.

"You always tell me no," Terza said.

"The answer is still no, my sweet. It is confidential DEA business."

"DEA secret business," she added.

"That it is. So, when do I get to see you, Miss Tiepolo?"

"That depends." Terza looked down at her notes on Henry Follett.

"It depends? You mean on how much I help you?"

"I only need a little tiny favor, Conner," Terza spoke sweetly.

"I knew it. This relationship of ours is very one-sided."

"Conner, you know we are just friends," she reminded him.

"Friends call each other," he countered.

"I called you today."

"Yes, and only because you want something. Am I right?"

"That's not true. Now, are you going to help me or not?" She heard him chuckle. "Are you laughing at me?"

"No. I'm laughing at the situation. What do you need?"

Terza knew she was taking advantage of Conner but also knew she had no choice. She made a mental note to make it up to him. *How? She had no idea.*

"Did you hear about the murder in Mission Beach last night?"

"No, I didn't. What happened?"

Terza recounted the entire episode of being hired for the catering job, finding the body, and waiting for the police. "Terza, I am sorry you had to experience this. Are you okay?"

"I'm fine. It was creepy, but I'm not the one dead."

"That's a good thing. Okay, now I feel sufficiently worried about you. How can I help?"

She smiled. "I need some information on Henry Follett, one of McCool's neighbors."

"Why?"

"I think he might be involved."

"Well, then tell the police! What do you mean that you think he might be involved? What business is it of yours?"

"I'm just doing a tiny bit of my own investigating. I spoke to one of the other neighbors, and she was very nice."

"Terza Tiepolo, you better stay out of this. It could get dangerous," Conner warned.

46

"Conner, all I want is some information."

"You know I can't use DEA resources to share information with you."

"I just need to know a couple of things," she pleaded.

"Like what?"

"Like where he works, or if he's married. You know, just simple facts that one can find online."

Conner laughed. "Ha! Did you look online?"

"Yes, as a matter of fact, I did."

"And did you find anything?"

"Not much. That's why I need you. Please, Conner. It's just one little favor. I'm sure it won't take you very long."

"Terza, you drive me crazy. Tell you what..."

She held the phone closer, hoping for good news.

"I will complete a quick check on Henry Follett."

"And then what?" Terza pressed.

"Then, I don't know. If there is something I can share with you, I will. But there are no guarantees."

"I understand, and that's good enough for me. Are you going to do it now?"

"No, I'm not. It is bad enough I'm doing this, let alone on a Sunday. I can't run the check from home. If I go into the office today it will look too suspicious. I need to slip this in somehow."

"Can you get into trouble?"

"Of course," he told her.

"Then forget it, Conner. Seriously, I don't want you to get into any trouble. Really, I would never forgive myself."

"Let me look tomorrow. I'll get back to you, one way or another. If it's a simple check, then I'll proceed. Deal?"

"It's a deal." As always she could tell he wanted to please her. "I really appreciate it, Conner. Thank you."

"You're welcome. But remember, Terza, you owe me."

Terza giggled. "I don't owe you right now."

"But you may."

"Okay, if I owe, I'll pay up. Is that a deal?"

"It's a deal. I have to go now. I'm meeting Mando. Do you remember him?"

"Armando De la Cruz, right? Of course I do." A thought flashed through her mind. "Hum, you work with Armando, who I recall speaks fluent Spanish, and you went to Mexico. Is he the one who went with you?"

Conner laughed. "I'm still not telling. Your questioning is relentless, Miss Tiepolo. Maybe you should have become a detective instead of a chef."

"Are you hiring?" Terza chuckled. "Moheenie talked about us changing jobs."

"Well I hope she was teasing. I'm sure Ranger feels more comfortable with Moheenie using a spatula instead of a gun."

"Yes, we're staying put, safely in our company kitchen. By the way, where are you guys going?"

"Believe it or not, we're going bowling," he said. "There's a new place downtown."

"Yes, I've heard about it. They have food too, right?"

"They do, and it's pretty good," Conner said.

"Have fun, and thank you."

"Don't thank me yet. I'll be in touch."

"I'll be waiting." Terza ended the call and rested her phone on the counter. *Now what?* She could go early to her parents or keep scanning the e-vite list. Settling on the latter, Terza carried the list to her dining room table. She sat and tucked one leg beneath her on the chair. As she read each name one at a time, none sounded familiar or sounded like it belonged to a killer. *How would I even know!*

Terza decided to focus on those not attending the party. That didn't help either, as all of the responses sounded nice. *Except for Henry Follett's.* Feeling a bit frustrated, she started preparing for their family dinner.

CHAPTER FOUR: FAMILY DINNER

Since all of the food was stored in the Macaroni on Wheels kitchen, Terza planned to stop at her catering company first. She brushed her teeth, touched up her makeup, and paused to check her image in the full-length mirror. Terza smoothed the fabric of her checkered sundress while she considered changing her clothes. It looked to be a warm summer evening, so she added a red, short-sleeved sweater instead. She looked down at her navy-blue espadrilles and calculated the amount of walking ahead. She then replaced them with red, high-top tennis shoes. After brushing through her curly hair, she grabbed her purse and headed for the door.

When Terza arrived at work, she unlocked the front door and headed straight for the kitchen. It seemed pointless to load her catering van with the food, then drive the few blocks to her family home just to unload again. Instead, Terza rolled one of her carts directly to the refrigerator.

She lifted the large bin of lobster ravioli and placed it on the lower shelf of her cart. The container of meat ravioli fit perfectly next to the lobster ravioli. Terza added the bin of antipasto salad to the middle shelf, along with the container of cannoli. She reserved the top and final shelf for the baguettes and her straw purse. "Ready, set, go," she said, taking a glance at her vintage black-and-white cat kitchen wall clock. She had an hour to spare before Ranger and Moheenie arrived at 4:00 p.m.

"Oh darn," Terza spoke aloud, watching the cat's tail sway back and forth. She had forgotten to call Moheenie. Terza removed the phone from her purse and pressed Moheenie's number.

"It's about time," Moheenie whispered.

"Can you talk?"

"Not really."

"Okay," Terza said. "Then don't ask any questions, and I will tell you quickly."

"That sounds perfect."

"I met the neighbor—more on that later, and she gave me the e-vite list. And yes, I have the comments!"

"Good job, Terza. See you soon."

Terza disconnected and stowed her phone. She wrapped her hands around the handle of her catering cart and carefully maneuvered it between the doorjambs. Terza pushed hard to make the right turn through the door and onto the sidewalk in front. She slowly removed her hands to ensure the cart would not roll and then left it while she locked up. Grateful for her decision to wear tennis shoes, Terza pushed the cart along the sidewalk as she progressed toward the main boulevard and then dug her rubber soles into the concrete as she negotiated another right-hand turn.

As she pressed forward, Terza walked directly in front of the Tiepolo Mercato, her family's butcher shop and market. She smiled at the sign that read *Closed — Spending Time with Family*, knowing how important the Sabbath day was to her parents. For as long as she could remember, the Tiepolo family first went to church on Sundays and then spent the entire day together eating and playing games.

Terza passed by several restaurants jam-packed with diners. She smiled and nodded as she made eye contact with several of the familiar servers. When Terza reached the driveway of her favorite pizza restaurant, the parking attendant rushed toward her.

"Here, let me help you," he said and grabbed the front.

"Thank you very much, Stephen."

"I can help you across the street. Are you going to your parents?"

"Yes. I really appreciate it."

They looked toward traffic on the one-way street. "I think we're good," he told her.

"I think you're right. Let's hurry."

Terza pushed while Stephen pulled and guided her cart safely across the street. He then helped her up the driveway of her family home, and stopped the cart in front of their gate. "I better go," Stephen said while looking across the street.

Terza followed his sight pattern and saw one car trying to exit the driveway at the same time two others tried to enter. "Oh my, yes, go! Thanks, Stephen," she called out as he raced to take control.

He stopped momentarily and waved. "No problem. It's always like this!"

She waved goodbye and tried the front gate. It was locked. Terza looked at her purse, considered reaching for the keys, then rang the bell instead. She definitely needed help unloading.

While waiting, she looked at the red front door of her family home and felt a sense of security. This was the only home Terza had ever known, as her parents had moved in just after she was conceived. At that time, Little Italy only existed for the fishermen and their families. Now it was just the opposite. Only a few other single-family houses occupied the urban area. The one-story Tiepolo home looked dwarfed by the four-story condominium projects on either side. But her parents stood firm. Their land value alone could be an abundant source of retirement income if they ever decided to sell. Terza understood though. Her parents were not yet sixty. They owned a beautiful home and could walk to work. Who could ask for more?

Terza heard the front door open. "There you are, my little gnocchi!" Her father quickly covered the five-foot distance from his door to the front gate. "Where's your key? Did you lose it?" He unlocked the gate.

"No. It's in my bag. I rang because I knew I needed the help."

Ezio Tiepolo opened the gate and grabbed hold of the catering cart. "This looks like a lot of food, even for the Tiepolo family."

"Yes, that does!" Terza's mother, Benedette, walked out to the porch.

Terza looked up to the front porch. "*Buona sera*, Mom. You look pretty today." Her mother wore black cropped pants and a black-and-white striped boatneck top. "I like your new haircut."

"Thank you, my love. I think I like it too." Benedette turned her palms up to touch the bottom of her short, blunt cut.

"Did Rain style it?" Terza referred to her sister-in-law.

"Of course. There is none better."

Terza nodded. "I'm glad she didn't talk you into one of her wild colors!"

Benedette laughed. "She knows better than that. The vibrant colors look great on Rain, but definitely not on me."

"What do you think, Papa?"

Terza watched her father look to her mother. She could see his brown eyes smiling.

"Your mother will be beautiful no matter what, but I still like her hair longer."

"Oh Ezio, you are so old-fashioned," Benedette told her husband. "The long hair makes me look older."

"You will never look old," he assured her.

Benedette laughed. "Your father will be saying that when I'm ninety!"

"Yes, he will, and that's because you are the love of his life."

"And he is mine." Benedette smiled lovingly at her husband while fingering the gray hairs resting upon his ear. "Speaking of haircuts, my dear, you need to see the barber."

Ezio shook his head. "I know, I know. I am going sometime this week."

Benedette walked over and hugged Terza. When Terza felt the familiar comfort of her mother's arms, she thought about her future. Terza hoped to have a loving relationship just like her parents. As she snuggled in, she imagined holding her own daughter one day. Terza straightened up and said, "You do look beautiful, Mom."

"I thank you, my love." Benedette held on to one of Terza's hands and took a step back. "Now, aren't you the fashion setter today? I really like this look of red tennies with your sundress."

"Thanks, Mom. I needed comfy shoes to push this cart."

"Oh yes, the cart," Ezio said. "I don't think we can make it up the stairs. Let's just unload out here." He picked up one of the largest bins and asked, "Do you think we have enough food, Terza?"

She knew her father was being sarcastic. "Didn't Mom tell you? I made it for a catering party. If I don't finish preparing it today, the food will go to waste."

The upward curve of her father's mouth inverted to a simulated frown. "We don't want that to happen!"

They took turns carrying everything into the kitchen. When they finished, Ezio looked at the crowded kitchen counter. He laughed and said, "I don't think we are going to finish all of this no matter how hard we try."

"Then each person will go home with a doggy bag," Benedette told him. "Come on, honey," she said to Terza. "Let's get busy while your father rolls the cart into the garage."

"Well, don't send *all* of the food away! You know how much I love Terza's cooking."

Terza watched her mother look directly at her father. She placed both hands on her hips. "Now tell me, Ezio Tiepolo, exactly why you love Terza's cooking."

"Did you marry a fool, my sweet wife?" Ezio's laughter filled the kitchen. Terza could not help but laugh along with him. She also knew her mother would join them any second. "I love Terza's cooking because she cooks just like you!"

Benedette's smile grew until she finally laughed out loud. "You are one smart man, Ezio Tiepolo. And just for that, I will send you home with a doggy bag, too. Now please, go take care of the cart. We have work to do."

"Work? I thought dinner was already made."

"We have to cook the pasta, dress the salad, and make the garlic bread," Terza told him.

"Okay. I get it and I'm gone."

"I love you, Papa!"

"I love you too, my little gnocchi!"

Terza and her mother worked together like identical twins as they completed the preparation for their family dinner. Before her arrival, Benedette had set the table, and as always, her father was in charge of the drinks.

Terza heard a car door slam. "We have guests." She peeked out the front window. "The little ones are here!"

"It's nice to know your brother is on time," Benedette said with a smile. She wiped her palms on a colorful kitchen towel. "I'll go see if they need any help."

Minutes after her mother left, Terza heard the kitchen door open. She grinned as her brother's little girl ran toward her.

"Hey, you! Get over here and give me a hug." Terza leaned down to capture the six-year-old in her arms and squeezed hard. "I missed you, Charley! We haven't seen each other all week."

"Hi, Auntie Tee. Did you bring Olive?"

"No, honey. You know that Olive doesn't like to go out."

Charley scrunched her petite nose. "I don't think Olive likes to do anything," she said with a giggle.

"She likes to eat and sleep. And she also likes you," Terza told her.

"Can I come over and see her sometime?"

"Yes, you *may*," Terza answered.

Charley beamed. She looked down at Terza's tennis shoes. "Your shoes are pretty."

Terza looked at Charley's pink princess tennis shoes. "Why thank you. Yours are pretty, too. Shall we trade?"

Charley rolled her eyes. "You're silly."

Terza brushed Charley's button nose with her fingertip. "And you're cute! Where is your brother?"

"He's out with Daddy and Grandpapa."

"Let me guess. They are looking at the old truck!"

Charley nodded.

"What about your mommy?"

"She's with Grandmama. They are picking flowers for the table."

"Well that's nice. I am certainly glad you didn't wait to come see me. Hey, guess who's coming to family dinner?"

The little girl's eyes opened wide. "Who?"

"Moheenie and Ranger will be our special guests this evening."

"Moheenie? She's so beautiful. I just love her hair."

"What are you talking about, silly girl? Your hair is just as beautiful." Terza reached out to caress a lock of Charley's lustrous brown hair.

"It's all curly."

Terza touched her own hair. "Mine's all curly, too. Don't you like my hair?"

"It looks like mine," Charley responded flatly.

"Yes, it looks *exactly* like yours! We have beautiful hair if I do say so myself."

"But Moheenie's hair is nice and straight," Charley explained.

"I'm going to let you in on a girl secret, okay?" Terza whispered.

Charley moved closer to Terza.

"If a girl has straight hair, she will try and curl it. If she has curly hair, she will try and straighten it. It's just the way of the world."

"Have you ever tried to straighten your hair?"

"Of course I have, and Moheenie has tried to curl hers, too," Terza answered. "In fact, Moheenie had her hair curled just for their wedding. Ask her to show you a photo."

Charley lifted her bright eyes in interest. "Did Moheenie like it?"

"Yes, and I liked mine straight. But we both realized it was just too much work. God's way is the best way. So you and I are going to be happy with the wild and crazy hair He gave us. Is that a deal?" Terza extended her opened hand.

Charley shook Terza's hand and giggled. "It's a deal!"

"What are you two making deals about?" Benedette asked as she entered the kitchen.

"Nothing special," Terza answered just as her sister-in-law joined them. "Hi, Rain! It's so nice to see you."

"You, too, Terza." Rain leaned in for a hug. "Thank you for bringing all the food today."

"It's my pleasure. Plus, you will be taking some home."

"Sounds good to me. You know how your brother likes to eat!"

"Do I ever."

"Mommy," Charley spoke up, "Moheenie is coming today."

"That's great. Does Ranger have to work?" Rain asked.

Terza chuckled. "No, he's coming too. But once I mentioned Moheenie, Charley thought of nothing else."

The Tiepolo kitchen instantly filled with noise as Terza's brother Damiano entered. His son Caleb and their father followed closely behind. "Hey, sis!" Damiano hugged her aggressively.

"Hi, Dom." She knelt to be face to face with four-year-old Caleb. "How's my special boy?"

Instead of answering he reached forward with his hands. Terza wrapped her arms around his body and hugged tightly. "I made you a special dessert," she told him.

Caleb's hazel eyes sprang alive. "What kind?"

"Do you have a favorite?"

Caleb nodded.

"What is it?"

"Cannelloni?" Caleb guessed.

"Cannelloni?" Terza asked, laughing.

"Not cannelloni, Caleb," Charley told him. "You like cannoli!"

Terza watched Caleb's face brighten.

"Chocolate cannoli?"

"Of course, it's chocolate," Terza told him.

When Terza heard the loud chime of the gate doorbell she walked to answer it, but her father beat her to the knob. She placed her palm lovingly around his elbow as Ezio opened the door.

"Moheenie, Ranger, welcome," Ezio said, stepping down to unlock the gate.

"Hi, Mr. Tie," Moheenie said. "Hi, Terza."

"Hi, guys," Terza said, walking out to meet them. "Welcome!"

Ranger held his hand out to Ezio. "Thanks for having us."

"It's our pleasure. Plus, someone has to help eat all this food."

Ranger and Moheenie entered the house and joined the rest of the family in the dining room/kitchen area. When the Tiepolo's remodeled, they focused on creating a large kitchen with an open floor plan to the dining room. The only divider consisted of a wide counter, perfect for seating an additional five people.

As Terza listened to the family welcome her friends, she watched her sister unlock the front gate. "Hey, Ange," she called from the opened door.

"Tee, how's it going?"

"Good." They greeted each other with a loving hug.

"Am I the last?" Angeline asked as she entered the house.

"Yes, but not the least." Terza grinned.

Angeline grinned back. "Aren't you the funny one?"

The next fifteen minutes looked like organized chaos as plates were packed with food and glasses filled with an assortment of beverages. Musical chairs came next to accommodate the little ones. Charley wanted to sit next to both Moheenie and Terza, and Caleb just had to sit by Ranger, a real lifeguard. When all backsides finally settled, Ezio held out both hands.

"Shall we?" he asked, taking the hand of his wife to the right and Terza's to his left. When all of the hands connected, Ezio began, "Dear Lord. Thank You for my beautiful family. Thank You for our special friends, and thank You for blessing us with good health and with this meal we are about to eat. Please bless this food in Your Holy Name. Amen."

A chorus of "Amen" sounded, followed by a single delayed response from Caleb. "Amen," he said.

"Good job, Caleb," Ranger told him.

Caleb's precious smile was enough to silence the table. Of course, in a household of Italians, the silence quickly ended, and food, fun, and laughter filled the Tiepolo home.

"Terza, have you seen that nice young man lately?" her mother asked.

Terza lifted her eyes suspiciously. "Which nice young man?"

"You know, the one with the police."

Moheenie instantly looked at Terza. "Is your mom talking about that detective from last night?"

"No, of course not." Terza looked to her mother. "Do you mean Conner Reeves, who works with the DEA?"

"Yes, that's his name."

"I just talked to him today, in fact."

Ranger turned toward her. "You talked with Conner today?"

"I called to say hi." She tried to sound nonchalant.

"You called him, or he called you?" Ranger pressed.

"I called *him*," Terza said. "Why? What's wrong with that?"

"The problem is that you only call Conner when you want something." Ranger looked at Moheenie and then back at Terza. "You called him about the case, didn't you?"

Terza could feel her face flush with guilt.

Damiano's dark eyes narrowed. "What case?"

Terza motioned toward Charley with her head. "I'll tell you about it later."

"Well, tell me about Conner," Benedette continued. "Are you planning to see him?"

"I don't know, Mom. I really hate to lead him on."

"Ha!" Ranger laughed. "Except when you need his help."

"Ranger, be nice," Moheenie told him.

"I *am* being nice," he said, smiling. "I just know you two, that's all."

Damiano reached his arms out to stretch. "Not to change the subject but we need to talk bocce ball. When we are finished with dinner, how about if Ranger and I go check out the courts? If there is a waiting list we can add our names and then come back to help."

"You have bocce ball courts around here?" Ranger asked.

"Yes, just up the street at Amici Park," Damiano explained. "Didn't we play the last time you came to family dinner? We always do. It's our tradition."

"It was raining," Terza said.

"That's right. I remember it *was* raining," Ranger said. "Wow! I love bocce ball."

"I'm finished," Damiano told Ranger. "Are you?"

Ranger stood. "I'm ready." He looked to his wife, "I'll be right back, Lakalaka."

"Lakalaka," Charley squealed. "What's a Lakalaka?"

"Lakalaka, Lakalaka," Caleb repeated.

"What a funny word," Charley said.

"Tell me about it," Moheenie answered. "Lakalaka was my last name I had before I married Ranger."

"I like saying Lakalaka," Caleb told them. "Lakalaka, Lakalaka."

Both children giggled loudly.

"It *is* a funny name." Moheenie looked up at Ranger. "See you soon."

Damiano leaned over to kiss his wife. "Ciao, honey. We'll be right back."

Rain smiled lovingly. "We'll be waiting."

The rest of the family started cleaning up. In Tiepolo tradition, everyone did a little so one person did not have to do a lot.

Less than a quarter-hour later, Damiano returned with Ranger. Terza had just finished serving chocolate cannoli to Charley and Caleb, the only two left at the table.

"How did you do?" Terza rested a fist on her hip.

"We're good to go. There is one team playing on court two, and we're next. We should be up in about half an hour. The team on court one is almost finished, but there is another team waiting to play. All in all, we should have both courts within the hour."

"That's perfect. Thanks, Dom."

Damiano scrutinized his two children. "What do we have here? I thought we were having dessert *after* bocce ball?"

Caleb looked at his father with a chocolate-filled mouth while Charley explained. "Auntie Tee said this was just a snack. We are having dessert later."

Damiano shot Terza a brotherly smile. "She did, did she?"

Charley and Caleb purposefully filled their mouths with gigantic bites. Terza could see their little shoulders moving with the giggles.

"And I suppose you two cannot talk because your mouths are full?"

The giggling continued.

"Well, since it is family day, I will let Terza win just this once."

"Thanks, bro. But remember, we still have bocce ball. I will be winning there, as well!"

Damiano followed her into the kitchen. "Ha! I have Ranger as my secret weapon."

"You might have Ranger, but I have Moheenie."

"We'll see, little sister," Damiano said. "We'll see."

The team finished the cleanup in record time, and Benedette started the dishwasher almost as a final gesture.

"I like having Ranger and Moheenie here," Angeline announced. "You two are fantastic in the kitchen."

"Thanks," Ranger said.

"It's because of all the catering jobs," Moheenie added. "The faster we clean up, the faster we get to go home."

"That's for sure!" Terza looked around the kitchen. "Are we ready to go?"

"I am!" Charley clapped her petite hands.

"Then let's get out of here," Damiano said while reaching for Caleb. He lifted his son high into the air and rested him on the back of his neck. "What about you Caleb?"

"Ready!" Caleb raised both hands.

With Caleb holding tightly to his father's neck, Damiano and Rain walked with each holding one of Charley's hands. Angeline and her parents followed, with Ranger, Moheenie, and Terza in the rear. Terza watched with amusement as Charley lifted her legs to swing from her parents' arms.

"I cannot believe the bocce ball court is so close," Ranger commented.

"I know," Terza said. "Isn't it fun? They've been here since the beginning when Little Italy was only a fishing community."

"Oh, I forgot to tell you." Ranger slapped the side of his leg. "When we brought all of the food from the McCool house I accidentally left five bags of ice."

"You did?" Terza scratched her head. "I don't understand. Where did you leave them?"

"In the freezer, of course."

"You left them in the freezer, Ranger? I thought there wasn't any room."

"Yes, I remember you said something about it being full. But when I checked, the freezer was completely empty."

"It was empty?" Terza turned to face him. "That's so odd. When I went to Doctor McCool's home on Friday afternoon I purposefully checked his refrigerator and the freezer space. The freezer was packed with white packages of meat."

"That *is* odd," Moheenie agreed. "Where did all of it go?"

"Maybe Doctor McCool took the meat somewhere else," Ranger guessed. "He probably figured we would need the freezer space."

"I don't know," Terza said, sounding doubtful. "It looked like more than half a cow. Plus, there was a huge bone. It went from one side of the freezer to the other."

"The bone wasn't wrapped?" Moheenie asked.

"Maybe with just some plastic."

Ranger stopped walking and stared at Terza. "I can literally see the gears of your mind working." He then focused on his wife. "I can see yours too, Mo. Both of you had better stay out of police business."

Moheenie and Terza looked at each other with non-committal stares.

Around 9:00 p.m., Terza headed back to her condominium. They all had great fun playing bocce ball, followed by dessert and coffee. Although she cherished every moment, she needed time to think. Hopefully Conner would have news for her tomorrow about Henry Follett. *But, what about the missing meat? It had something to do with the murder.* Terza could feel it in her bones. *And the bone!* Where was the bone?

CHAPTER FIVE: NEW DAY—NEW DISCOVERIES

Monday

The early morning sunlight flooded into the room, waking Terza earlier than desired. She stumbled out of bed, quickly closed her curtains, and returned to the comfort of her cushiony mattress. Moments later Olive began kneading Terza's chest.

"Not now, Olive." Terza pushed her cat away. After Olive began to meow, Terza pulled her close and caressed her back. They both slept until 8:15 a.m. when Terza finally decided to begin her day.

Although Terza typically went to work on Mondays, Macaroni on Wheels was closed to the public. As a result, she decided to take her time and make coffee at home. Mug in hand, she opened the door of her fourth-floor balcony and placed her coffee on a small, round patio table. Terza then retrieved her Bible from her nightstand and settled into one of the two chairs. Olive jumped onto Terza's lap and rotated until comfortable.

After she finished reading, Terza refilled her coffee mug and brought her laptop out to the balcony. She dropped a catnip treat onto the floor and watched Olive come to life. With Olive busy playing, Terza enjoyed her morning coffee while searching for additional information on the names from the McCool e-vite list. She hoped Conner would call soon, but first she decided to check in with her mother. Terza went into her bedroom to make the call.

"Tiepolo Mercato," Benedette answered.

"*Buon giorno*, Mom. Are you busy?"

"*Buon giorno.* I am not at the moment. It is still early for the market. How are you, my love?"

"I'm fine. I'm trying to decide how much work I should do today."

"Why don't you take the day off?" Benedette suggested. "Macaroni on Wheels can survive one day without you."

"I know. There is just so much to do. I like to get caught up when the company is closed."

"And there will always be. It is important to relax your mind."

"You are funny!" Terza laughed. "This coming from the woman who is already at work?"

"That is only because it's Monday. You know I do not work on Wednesdays or Saturdays, and of course, we are closed on Sundays. Really, I only work four days a week."

"Okay, you've got me there. I'll let you go. Have a wonderful day."

"You as well, my love."

"Ciao, Mom."

"Arrivederci."

Still feeling the familiar warmth after a conversation with her mother, Terza brought her telephone into the bathroom and rested it on the sink. She did not want to miss Conner's call while getting ready. He did call right before 9:00 a.m. while Terza was squeezing toothpaste onto her toothbrush. She balanced her toothbrush onto the edge of the sink before answering.

"Good morning, Conner."

"How are you doing?"

"Good. How was bowling?" She sat on the edge of her bed.

He laughed. "It was a hoot. You'll have to come with me sometime."

"I will. It sounds like fun. So?" She stretched out the word.

"I did a little checking this morning," Conner told her. "Did you speak with a Caroline Mann?"

Terza momentarily hesitated. She did not remember giving Conner Caroline Mann's name. "Am I in trouble?" Terza's voice squeaked.

"Did you speak to her, yes or no?" Conner demanded.

"Yes," Terza finally answered. "But I don't remember ever telling you her name."

"You didn't," Conner told her. "Listen, Terza, you have to promise to stay away from that house."

"Did she complain about me?"

"No, but I did some checking on my own."

"But I wanted you to check on Henry Follett, not on Caroline Mann."

"Here's the deal," Conner said. "You told me you visited one of the McCool's neighbors, right?"

"Yes, that's right."

"So, when I checked on Henry Follett, I also decided to check the neighbor on McCool's other side. It seems that Alan Mann was forced into an early retirement by Doctor Mitchell McCool," Conner said.

Terza jumped to her feet. "Are you kidding? Tell me! What happened?"

"Mann and McCool were both doctors. Alan Mann was working on a clinical trial when he lost his funding. It seems that Mitchell McCool served on the board responsible for pulling it. When it all happened, Mann had to be escorted from the building. After that, he just quit."

"Now that is what I call a motive," Terza said.

"Exactly. So don't go over there again."

"I looked up Alan Mann's name but nothing like that

showed up," Terza explained.

"My resources are a bit different than yours," Conner told her. "The police had to file a report on the incident."

"What about Henry Follett?" Terza asked.

"He appears to be just a kind, sweet teacher."

"Did you say teacher? Rose McCool is a teacher. Where does he work?"

"I don't know. Let me look."

As Terza waited, she walked into her kitchen for a notepad and pencil. She wrote *Alan Mann*, followed by the word, *motive*.

"He works in La Jolla," Conner said, interrupting her thoughts.

"Rose McCool works in La Jolla! These people are just too cozy for a normal neighborhood. When did Alan Mann lose his funding?"

"About a year ago," Conner answered.

"Then the Mann's were already living next door to the McCool house when it happened. Caroline told me they bought the home approximately two years ago."

"Since they were both doctors maybe Mitchell McCool told Alan Mann about the house," Conner suggested.

"Maybe. But what about Henry Follett? When did he buy?"

"I suppose you want me to look that up, too?"

"Yes, please. Or I can just walk down to the county administration building."

"Okay, since I know you can get the information on your own, I will save you the trip."

Terza struggled to wait while Conner searched for information on Henry Follett. After several minutes he finally spoke.

"It looks like Henry Follett bought his house around ten years ago, and the McCool's bought theirs nearly eight years ago."

"So Henry and Rose McCool were having a work romance,

and Rose decides to move next door to him," Terza announced.

Conner laughed heartily.

"Or," she continued. "Follett got the wrong impression when the McCool's moved in. He thought Rose was in love with him. Then, when they got divorced, Henry decided to take care of Mitchell and free Rose."

"That doesn't make any sense," Conner said. "Rose was already freed by her divorce."

"You're right. The killer must be Alan Mann. I just can't believe how casual Caroline spoke. She acted as if they barely knew each other."

"She could be one dangerous woman, Terza," Conner asserted. "I mean it. Do not go over there again."

"I won't, Conner. Thank you so much for all of this information."

"I don't know what good it is going to do you. It's not like you are investigating this case."

Terza's mouth formed a knowing smile. "You know how I like a good mystery."

"I do know you owe me now. When do I get my home-cooked meal?"

Terza liked Conner as a friend but not romantically. She knew Conner wanted more than she was able to give. If she invited him to an intimate dinner, Terza was afraid he would get the wrong impression. "Why don't you come to family dinner next Sunday?"

"Family dinner?" He sounded disappointed. "I thought you were going to cook just for me."

"My mom keeps asking about you. Check with Ranger. My mom asked about you just yesterday. Besides, I need you on my bocce ball team. We got smoked last night."

"Who was on your team?"

"It was the girls against the guys. I cannot believe how good Ranger plays!"

"He should. The lifeguards have tournaments all the time."

"But Ranger didn't even know about the courts in Little Italy."

"That has nothing to do with whether he is good or not. I'm telling you, he usually wins."

"I know that now," Terza whined. "I thought for sure we were going to take it. Moheenie and I walk down to practice whenever we have the time."

"Are you sure your mom asked about me?" Conner pressed.

"Yes, I promise."

"Alright, I'll come.

"You're the best, Conner. Thank you."

"I hope you mean that, Terza."

"I do. I really do. Ciao, ciao. Thanks again!"

"Bye."

Terza ended the call and dropped her phone on the bed. "Oh my gosh!" *Alan Mann or Henry Follett? Which one did it?* She pumped her legs and then paced the perimeter of her bedroom. Terza exited the bedroom and began circling the living room. She then walked to the refrigerator, opened the door, and looked for a snack. As she reached for a yogurt, Terza strained to will the answers to her brain. She exhaled loudly. Nothing. Her mind felt empty.

She leaned onto the counter stool, and spooned small amounts of the peach yogurt into her mouth. Terza knew she had to meet again with Caroline. She also realized it would be wrong to go alone. She sent Moheenie a text. *We need to talk!* Her phone rang seconds later.

"Mo!"

"Why didn't you just call instead of texting me if we needed to talk?"

"I don't know. I'm probably not thinking straight. We just have to get into the McCool's house."

"But why?"

"Because I really need to talk with Caroline again," Terza

explained. "If we go to Doctor McCool's, it will give me an excuse to visit her. I can tell Caroline we were already there and wanted to stop by and say hello."

"There's a problem with your plan, Tee. I bet the police still have the scene blocked."

Terza groaned. "Then I need to call the detective and get permission to go inside."

"Ha! Like *that* is going to happen! What reason are you going to use?"

"I've got it!" Terza pumped her fist. "I'll ask if we can go and get our ice. It's perfect, Mo."

"It's far from perfect and sounds kind of lame, but who cares. Maybe the police will fall for it."

"Tell me, what are *you* doing today?"

"Well, since it's my day off, boss, I was planning on running errands."

"Phooey." Terza almost spit out her words. "Run errands another time. You can go during the week when we're not busy. I need you, Mo."

"You don't even know what time," Moheenie said.

"I will know soon. Hang tight and I'll call the detective."

"Nico? You are going to call Nico?"

Terza ignored Moheenie's teasing. "I'll call you right back."

She disconnected and then dialed the telephone number listed on Nicolas Garza's business card.

"Garza here."

"Detective Garza, this is Terza Tiepolo."

"Hi, Terza. How are you doing?"

"I'm good. Thank you. I was wondering if you were going to be at the McCool house today."

"I'm not, but there should be a couple of crime scene techs there right now. Why? What's up?"

"It's silly, but we left all of our ice in the freezer. May I go get it?"

"Sure thing. Are you planning to leave now?" Garza asked.

"I can."

"Okay, go ahead. I'll call and tell them to expect you."

"Great. Thank you very much."

'You're welcome. Have a good day."

"You too. Thanks again."

Terza's smile widened as she disconnected. She instantly called Moheenie.

"We're set. I'll pick you up in ten."

"What did you say?"

"I'll tell you in the car. We have to hurry."

"Okay, okay," Moheenie relented. "I'll wait outside."

"Bye."

Terza quickly rinsed her yogurt container and dropped it into the recycle bin under her sink. She tossed her phone into a tote bag, grabbed her keys, and rushed out the door. After retrieving her car from the parking garage, she drove southeast to the downtown area where Ranger and Moheenie lived. As promised, Moheenie was waiting on the curb in front of her high-rise building. Terza stopped curbside and unlocked the passenger door. Moheenie got in.

"Hi there!" Moheenie reached over to touch the material of Terza's skirt. "This is cute! Is it new?"

Terza lifted the bright orange fabric to show off her matching shorts. "It's a skort! Can you believe it? I got it at the big box store for $9.99."

"Get out! Do you know if they have any other colors?"

"Purple, bright-green, black, aqua, and... I think that's it."

"Cool. I'm going tomorrow," Moheenie announced. "Now, catch me up! You talked to Conner, didn't you?"

"Did I ever!"

As Terza drove to the McCool's, she replayed her conversation. She finished by saying, "So now we have two possible suspects, and the missing meat remains a mystery."

"Maybe Alan Mann stole the meat, and Doctor McCool

caught him in the act."

"Why would he steal the meat?"

"Your dad is a butcher. Isn't meat expensive?"

"Well, yes," Terza responded, sounding doubtful. "But nobody is going to steal frozen meat."

"I know. I was just hoping to tie everything together."

"Rose McCool might have taken it when she came over," Terza offered.

"True, but how can we know that?"

"I can go over to pay my respects."

"Terza Tiepolo, you had better not," Moheenie warned.

"Let's not worry about that right now. We have to focus on the Mann family first and then Henry Follett. Does that sound like a plan?"

"Yes it does."

"Oh darn," Terza said when she pulled into the alley behind the McCool home. The police car occupied the lone parking space. "We'll have to park elsewhere."

"Do you want me to wait here with the coolers?"

"Thanks Mo, that's a great idea." Terza turned off her engine and opened the back door of her four-door Fiat. "You get this cooler, and I'll get the one from the trunk."

After placing the two coolers next to the fence Terza jumped back into her car. "I shouldn't be long." Fortunately, she found a parking space less than two blocks away.

"That was fast," Moheenie commented as Terza walked toward her.

"You can tell it's a Monday. There's plenty of parking." Terza rolled one of the coolers while Moheenie followed behind with the other. They opened the front patio gate and walked up to the door. Terza knocked.

When the door opened, Terza found herself staring at a fascinating looking woman. She had bright red hair, obviously dyed. Her haircut was short and jagged, with longer pieces in the front. Purple highlights added to the colorful medley. The woman wore huge yellow glasses. Her smile turned out to be just as bright. "You must be Terza. Come in, my friend. Your ice is waiting. In fact, I could say it's chilling!" Her shoulders shook with laughter.

Terza and Moheenie both laughed. "My ice is chilling? Good one," Terza said while extending her hand. "It's nice to meet you."

"No can do," the woman said, referring to her gloved hands. "I don't want to contaminate the scene. It's nice to meet you too, Terza. My name is Melody, as in a song."

"Hi, Melody. This is my friend Moheenie."

"Hello," Moheenie said. "If you don't mind me saying, I think you are about as feisty as a jalapeno pepper!"

"Why, thank you. I don't mind at all. I will take that as a compliment," Melody announced with obvious pride. "Well, don't just hang by the door. Come on in, but let's leave the coolers out front. Okay?"

"Of course," Terza said. They left the coolers and followed Melody to the kitchen.

"Help yourselves to the freezer," Melody told them. "We have already cleared this area."

Terza opened the door, and they both grabbed a bag of ice. They hurried to the coolers, deposited their ice bags, and returned to the freezer. After storing all of the ice, Terza returned to the kitchen. "Thank you very much, Melody. We'll get out of your hair now."

"It was my pleasure, ladies." Melody grinned. "Enjoy this lovely day."

Terza stopped to look at Moheenie after they finished rolling the coolers out the front gate. She placed a hand on her right hip. "Feisty as a jalapeno pepper?"

With a shrug of her delicate shoulders, Moheenie squeaked

74

out her response. "I thought that was a great line! I read it in a book and have wanted to use it for a long time now."

Terza rolled her eyes. "You're such a goof!"

"But you still love me," Moheenie said.

"Yes I do!"

"Now what do we do?" Moheenie rubbed her hands together.

"Well, I don't want to drag the coolers next door. Why don't we take them to the car and walk back?" Terza suggested.

"Good idea. Let's go."

When they reached Terza's car, they failed to realize how heavy the coolers had become. "Hold on!" Moheenie strained to pick up her side.

"On three," Terza said. "One, two, three." They lifted the first cooler into Terza's trunk. "Once again on three. One, two, three." They lifted the second cooler into her back seat.

"You're going to need help when you get back to *MOW*," Moheenie told her. "If you like, we can drop the coolers off before you take me home."

"Thanks, but I can ask my dad. He's always happy to help." Terza pumped her eyebrows. "Are you ready for phase two?"

Moheenie laughed. "Yes, indeed! I am as ready as ever."

Terza led the way as they walked through the back alley and then onto the boardwalk without passing in front of the McCool's home. When they reached Caroline's front gate, Terza waited a few moments in hopes Caroline would see her. She then reached over to unlock the latch and opened the gate. They walked to the front door, and Terza pressed the doorbell. She heard a faint ringing inside the house, followed by the sound of footsteps. When the door opened, Caroline greeted them.

"Well hello, Terza. It's so nice to see you again."

"Hi, Caroline." Terza smiled. "I hope you don't mind me stopping by without notice. I was at Doctor McCool's house and just wanted to say hello." Terza looked toward Moheenie.

"I also wanted to introduce you to my friend, Moheenie. She works with me at Macaroni on Wheels, my catering company."

Moheenie extended her hand toward Caroline. "It's so nice to meet you, Mrs. Mann. Terza told me how sweet you were to her."

"It is also nice to meet you, Moheenie," Caroline said while they shook hands. "Please call me Caroline."

"I will. Thank you, Caroline."

"Would you ladies like a cup of coffee?"

"I would love a cup of coffee," Moheenie told Caroline. "I got so busy this morning that I barely had time to enjoy any."

Caroline stood aside so they both could enter, and then directed the duo into the kitchen. "Let's sit here." She motioned to the cloth-covered table. The brilliant oranges and reds matched the hacienda-style home.

Terza and Moheenie sat on the same side of the kitchen table and watched Caroline pour three mugs of coffee from a carafe.

"Would you like cream or sugar?" She looked at them while bringing the mugs to the table.

"Both for me," Terza said.

"Me too," Moheenie agreed.

Terza watched Caroline withdraw a carton of half-and-half from the refrigerator. She poured some into a white ceramic pitcher and then placed the pitcher and matching sugar bowl onto the table. She sat across from them.

Terza felt on coffee overload but dutifully added cream and sugar to the aromatic liquid. Her taste buds surged with the first sip. "Wow! This is amazing."

Caroline smiled warmly. "Isn't it? Our friends just got back from the Big Island of Hawaii. It's from the Kona region, my absolute favorite."

Moheenie rushed to taste hers. "Wow, Mrs. Mann, I mean

Caroline. This is wonderful, but I feel bad that you wasted it on us."

"Nonsense. The pot was already made, and Alan does not appreciate good coffee. When he returns, I can always brew him something else."

"Well, thank you very much," Terza said.

"Yes, I agree," Moheenie added.

"It is my pleasure." Caroline looked at Terza. "Did you retrieve all of your catering supplies?"

"Yes. Bags of ice turned out to be the only items we left. We just finished taking them out of the freezer."

"Oh dear, won't they melt?" Caroline asked.

"No, we brought coolers," Terza said. "We didn't know how long it would take us to drive home. Summer beach traffic is always an adventure."

"You can say that again," Caroline said before changing the subject. "I still feel so badly about Mitchell."

"I can imagine," Moheenie commented. "I didn't even know him, and I feel just awful."

"Did your husband and Doctor McCool used to work together?" Terza asked boldly.

Caroline's expression grew stern. "I have a suspicion you already know the answer to that question. Did you do an online search? Is that why you're here?"

"Of course not," Terza squeaked out.

"I don't believe you," Caroline spoke harshly.

"Please, Caroline," Moheenie quickly said. "Terza is not like that. She wanted me to meet you. That's all. She told me how nice you were."

Terza watched Caroline's shoulders relax. *Thanks, Mo.*

Caroline suddenly grew animated. "You know that Internet is filled with lies! Nothing about what happened between Alan and Mitchell is correct. Absolutely nothing!"

"I'm not sure what you mean," Terza spoke softly.

"I mean the funding. Didn't you read about how Alan lost his grant? They blamed Mitchell, but Alan knew it was not his fault. Plus, Alan was so tired of the project. He wanted a way out. Even though his early retirement was forced, in the end, it turned out to be a relief."

Terza had her answer and now needed a way to change the subject. Fortunately, Moheenie took the lead. "Your husband sounds like a wonderful man. How long have you been married?"

Caroline finally smiled. "Thirty-two years. Are either of you married?"

"I am," Moheenie said. "My husband Ranger and I got married just last year. Terza, on the other hand, is still waiting for Mr. Right."

Terza moaned. "I think I might be waiting forever."

"You are a beautiful young woman," Caroline told her. "The right man will come along when you least expect it."

I didn't expect to meet Nicolas Garza. "Thank you," Terza said. "I know it will happen one day."

Moheenie finished her coffee and looked to Terza. "Are you ready to head out?"

"Give me a second." Terza downed the last mouthful of coffee and stood to carry their mugs.

"Please, just leave them," Caroline instructed.

Terza returned her mug to the table. "Thank you again, Caroline. The coffee was delicious."

"It was extremely nice to meet you, Caroline," Moheenie said as they walked toward the front door. "I agree. The Kona was amazing. Thank you very much. It reminded me of home."

"Did you live in the islands?" Caroline asked.

"I sure did. My father was in the service, so we lived in Oahu. I came here just in time to begin high school in San Diego."

Terza placed an arm lovingly around Moheenie's waist.

"And the perfect time for us to become best friends. Mo and I went to the same school."

"I still have several girlfriends from my high school," Caroline told them. "We get together once in the summer to celebrate our birthdays and then once during the Christmas season."

"That's wonderful," Moheenie said. She stepped out the front gate.

Terza followed her then turned to face Caroline. "Thank you again. Have a wonderful day."

"You, as well. Goodbye, ladies."

Terza and Moheenie walked along the boardwalk and distanced themselves from the Mann's house. Neither one spoke until they were more than a block away. Terza then stopped and screamed in a whisper. "Oh my gosh, Mo! Thanks for the save. I thought she was going to kick us out."

"I think I literally saw smoke coming out of her ears!"

"I know. But what do you think about Alan? Was she telling the truth, or covering something up?"

"My gut says she was truthful, but I don't know, Tee. What do *you* think?"

"I tend to agree with you, but I'm not a hundred percent positive." Terza shook her head. "I need time to think this through."

Moheenie nodded. "I also think we need to research the link between Alan and Doctor McCool. I'm sure there's more to the story."

"Isn't that always the case?"

They returned to the car, and Terza drove Moheenie back to her downtown condominium. She pulled alongside the curb. "Thanks for coming with me," Terza said.

"No problem. Thanks for including me. Plus, it's not even noon so I still have time to run errands."

"Does that mean I don't owe you a day off?" Terza teased.

Moheenie held onto the car door and leaned in. "No." She smiled. "You still owe me." Moheenie closed the door and waved.

Terza returned the wave and drove off. On the drive to her catering company she thought about each possible suspect. Alan and Caroline Mann had moved to the bottom of her suspect list, with Henry Follett remaining at the top. She had no evidence, only a feeling she couldn't shake, all from his one-line comment on the e-vite list. Terza considered how to initiate contact with him and what excuse to provide when she did. *Maybe I could somehow mention his name to Rose McCool? But then what excuse would I use to meet her?* Terza lightly tapped the side of her head. The next suspect was the person who had the missing meat. She had no name, nor any ideas. Just missing meat and a gut feeling that would not quit gnawing at her. Terza mentally outlined the facts. She knew the freezer was crammed with white butcher paper packages on the afternoon she met with Doctor McCool. Since the freezer was empty the following day, either McCool moved the packages, or someone came and got them. If the latter proved to be true, then someone else was in the house. That person could be the killer.

After parking in one of the spots reserved for her catering company, Terza sat in the car and placed a call to her father's direct butcher's line.

"Ezio, the butcher," her father answered.

Terza giggled at the way her father always answered. "Hi Papa, it's me."

"Hello, my little gnocchi."

"Are you with a customer right now?"

"No. Your mother is helping someone, but I am free for a moment."

"Can you come over and help me with two coolers? They are in my car, and there is no way I can lift them by myself."

"Certainly. I'll be right there."

Terza got out of her car, walked around to the back, and heard footsteps. She looked up to see her father walking toward her. He wore a white butcher's apron and a large smile. "What did you do? Fly?"

"I came out the back. It's faster." Ezio kissed her on the forehead. "Did you read your Bible this morning?"

"I did." Terza knew the next question.

"Did you call your mama this morning?"

"I did." Terza smiled, knowing the upcoming response.

"Then you are my favorite daughter."

"Why thank you, Papa." She laughed heartily. "I just love being your favorite daughter."

After they finished carrying the coolers into the kitchen, Terza thanked her father and hugged him goodbye. Ezio returned to his market through their adjoining doors, and Terza rapidly filled the freezer sections of both refrigerators with ice. She then opened one of the refrigerators in search of desperately needed food. A little salami, some cheese, and a crusty chunk of bread instantly did the trick.

After fueling her body and brain, Terza sat behind her desk and powered up her computer. She withdrew the e-vite list from her bag and placed it on top of the desk.

"Henry Follett," she spoke aloud. "If Alan Mann is not the killer, then maybe it's you." Terza struggled to come up with some idea for a reason to visit Henry Follett. Nothing seemed to work until she finally thought of housekeeping. "That's it!" She pumped both fists. "Yes!"

Terza immediately opened the program for her desktop publishing and selected the artwork for business cards. Since she printed her own catering company cards Terza had a box of blanks on hand.

She quickly designed a business card perfect for a

housekeeping service, and named her business *The Speedy Vacuum*. Now she was stuck for a telephone number. She had a landline for Macaroni on Wheels. When not at work she forwarded the number to her cell. Terza always answered "Macaroni on Wheels" in case a customer was calling. What to do? She stood and paced the small office perimeter. Finally she decided to check and see if Mo was okay with having her number on the card. Terza retrieved her phone from the desk and dialed.

Moheenie answered, "Hi there."

"I have another idea."

Moheenie chuckled. "Should I be worried?"

"Ha! Not in the least. I do need to use your telephone number though."

"For what?"

"I'm making some business cards for a fake housekeeping service. But I need to use a telephone number on the off chance he calls."

"In case *who* calls?" Moheenie asked.

"Henry Follett," Terza answered. "Doctor McCool's next-door neighbor."

"You're going over there?"

"Not really. But kind of. I'm going to knock on his door and see if he needs any housekeeping services."

"Oh no!" Moheenie screeched. "What if he says yes?"

Terza froze. "I didn't think of that. Yikes! What would we do if he really does?"

"I guess we could clean his house just once and then quit," Moheenie suggested.

"Well, I certainly hope he doesn't say yes." Terza groaned. "We don't have time to clean any houses."

"So explain to me what you have planned for my number?"

"I'm putting it on the card. I can't use mine because I always answer, 'Macaroni on Wheels.'"

"You're right. Of course, you can use my number. When are you going?"

"I'm not sure, but maybe even later this afternoon."

"I better go with you, Terza. It might not be safe."

"All I'm going to do is knock on his front door. I will not go inside."

"Do you promise?"

"I promise."

"Okay, then text me before you go and after you're done," Moheenie told her.

"It's a deal. Thanks!"

"No problem. Bye."

Terza ended her call, and then finished designing the business cards. She smiled at her ingenuity of using a cartoon vacuum caricature. The lines and dust cloud made the vacuum appear to be racing around the room. Terza then inserted the perforated sheet of white, blank cards into her color printer and watched her new business come to life. Now she needed an outfit. Terza thought about what she should wear.

CHAPTER SIX: ONE DOWN TWO TO GO

Catering events kept Terza busy as she waited for the perfect time to drive over and knock on Henry Follett's door. She had no idea whether he taught summer school or not, but she figured that 4:00 p.m. would be a perfect time. Terza planned to leave an hour before. When she was ready to head out the door Terza's phone rang. *Nico Garza* flashed across the screen.

Terza answered. "Hello, Detective."

"Miss Tiepolo," he spoke sternly.

Terza sighed. "Uh oh, this sounds serious."

"It *is* serious," Garza told her. "I just left the home of Alan and Caroline Mann."

"Oh." Her voice squeaked.

"I cannot believe you went to their house."

"I didn't mean to," she argued. "It just happened. I was walking along the boardwalk, and Caroline came outside."

"On Sunday, am I right?"

"Yes, on Sunday. Why do you ask?"

"What were you doing in front of the McCool's house on Sunday?"

Terza's mind raced for an answer. "I stopped by, hoping someone would be there. I wanted to pick up the ice."

"I'm not buying it," Garza told her. "You called me about the ice this morning. If you wanted to pick it up yesterday, why didn't you call me then?"

"I just didn't want to bother you. Then, when I was not able to retrieve it on Sunday, I decided to check in with you first."

Terza waited through a long pause before Garza spoke again. "I understand," he said. "But I do not understand why you returned to the Mann home."

"That one is harder to explain," Terza said.

"I'm listening."

"Well, I..." She stammered. "I did a bit of research and discovered that Alan Mann and Mitchell McCool previously worked together."

"And so with this new information you decided to interrogate Caroline Mann about it?"

"I didn't interrogate her!" Terza shot back. "I just casually mentioned it."

"But why? I don't understand. How is it your business?" Garza pressed.

"It's not. I guess I just felt so bad for Doctor McCool." Instead of waiting through another long pause, Terza rushed to say, "I am really sorry, Detective Garza." She hoped to soften his disposition.

"You don't have to apologize," he responded, sounding less stern.

Good. It worked. "Thank you. I won't do it again."

"Have a nice day, Miss Tiepolo."

"You can call me Terza, if you like."

"Maybe next time," he said. "Goodbye."

"Goodbye."

After ending the call Terza allowed her smile to grow. *Next time? So there is going to be a next time.* She felt her face flush and wiped the perspiration from her palms. Something about Nicolas Garza made her heart pound, and Terza had not felt a reaction like this since her high school sweetheart. There was a hint of attraction between them. It felt good, knowing she was once again capable of even considering a future relationship.

It also frightened Terza as she was bound and determined to never fall in love again. Or so she once thought.

When in high school she just knew that one day Yale would ask her to marry him. She was positive he loved her as much as she loved him. Everyone in high school knew they would get married after graduation. Almost everyone also knew he was seeing Ellie, one of the other cheerleaders, behind Terza's back. She remembered the look of shock on Ellie's face when Terza peered into the back window of Yale's car. Ellie had screamed, and Yale jumped up, hit his head, and scrambled to zip his pants. *"It's not what you think,"* he had told her. *"I love you!"*

Terza also remembered hearing Ellie shout, *"I thought you loved me!"*

Yale ignored Ellie and ran after Terza. As she recalled the incident Terza truly felt sorry for the way Yale had deceived Ellie. A part of her felt responsible. No less than a dozen times Yale had tried to win Terza back. "I couldn't help it," she remembered him saying. *"If you truly loved me, you would have slept with me."*

"If he truly loved you, he would have waited for you," Terza's mother had said. She nodded her head in agreement with the memory of her mother's words. Ellie stayed with Yale, but he never married her. He just used her for sex and then moved on. Yale was now divorced after being married for less than a year. His wife left him when she came home from work early only to find Yale and her best friend in bed together.

"Lucky me," Terza said aloud, returning to the present. But it still hurt, and Terza continued to have feelings for her first love. She would never act on them, no matter how much Yale pleaded. *Mama didn't raise a fool.*

Before leaving to meet Henry Follett Terza stood in front of her bedroom door mirror and considered her outfit. She had selected black pants, black tennis shoes, and a white T-shirt.

She moaned, thinking how she looked more like a waiter than a housekeeper. Terza considered not going at all. She definitely did not want Nicolas Garza to find out.

"Let's just do this," she finally told the mirror. Without further hesitation, she left.

Terza drove to the beach and parked a few blocks from the Follett home. She then sent Moheenie a quick text that read:

I'm here.

Moheenie replied:

Good luck. Text me when you're through. Remember, don't go in!

Terza typed the thumbs-up emoji and then progressed along the boardwalk. Hoping to see movement inside, she slowed when she reached Henry Follett's home. All looked quiet but at least the front window was open. She took a deep breath, exhaled loudly and opened the front patio gate. Terza closed it, walked to the front door, and rang the bell. She waited more than a minute and rang again. The door finally opened.

"I heard you the first time," a man answered. "What do you want?"

She instantly recognized Henry Follett from her online research.

"I would like to offer you our housekeeping services." Terza extended a card which Follett ignored.

"You're a housekeeper?" he asked. "I doubt it."

"Excuse me?"

"Please don't tell me that you're a caterer one day and a housekeeper the next. Listen to me, young lady. I don't know what you're up to, but I don't want any part of it."

Terza stood dumbfounded until the adrenaline got the best of her.

"I thought you weren't home," she accused.

"I don't know what you mean," he shot back.

"You declined Doctor Mitchell McCool's invitation because you were going to be out of town."

"I declined Mitchell McCool's invitation because I don't like the man, and what business is it of yours?"

"Plenty, if you must know. Whether you liked him or not, I had the complete displeasure of finding him dead."

Follett softened. "I am truly sorry. It must have been awful."

"It was." She faked a sniffle.

"How did he die?"

Shock rippled through her system. "You don't know?"

"Of course I don't know. How would I?"

"I don't know either. He either fell or was hit on the head or maybe even poisoned. All I know is that Doctor McCool was down on the ground with a head wound."

"Please tell me why you are at my door pretending to be a housekeeper," Follett pressed.

Terza instantly felt foolish. "I don't know," she said, her shoulders slumping. "I guess I just wondered why you didn't come to his party, when you were obviously home."

"All I can say is that Rose McCool is my friend. Mitchell was not. And with that, I shall say goodbye." He closed the door.

Terza breathed a sigh of relief, turned around, and hurried out the gate. When she reached her car, she sent Moheenie another text:

All done. I'm safe in my car.

Moheenie responded:

What happened?

Terza still felt shaky, and needed time to calm herself. She sent a reply text:

Tell you tomorrow.

Terza was officially through with her detective work for the day. She needed a brain break and a delicious meal. Terza drove home and changed into a tan sundress, along with a black belt and a pair of black espadrilles. While tying the ribbons, she thought about her choice of restaurants. There were so many good ones, but Terza was in the mood for risotto, and only one had the absolute best. Today was her day off and a perfect day for someone else to cook. She left home and walked the few blocks to Buon Appetito. Without even looking at the menu, Terza ordered the Risotto Alla Piemontese. The menu described her favorite dish as an Italian Arborio rice with porcini mushrooms and asparagus tips, drizzled with truffle oil, and served in a parmesan nest. Terza felt her mouth begin to water at the thought of her fork digging into the delicious creation.

CHAPTER SEVEN: BACK TO BUSINESS

Tuesday

Ready for a full day of work, Terza walked into the Macaroni on Wheels catering kitchen a few minutes before 9:00 a.m. Moheenie would arrive within the next half hour. As typical for a Tuesday morning Terza used the calendar notes from her computer tablet to write on the kitchen whiteboard. It made their preparation progress easier as they could quickly see the catering jobs for the week ahead.

Terza finished writing Sartù Di Riso under the Friday column just as Moheenie entered the kitchen.

"Sartù Di Riso?" Moheenie read. "Are you kidding?"

"I know. Tell me about it," Terza said. "The hostess saw it on an Italian cooking show and wanted to try it." She noticed Moheenie's new black skort. "I see you made it to the store. How many did you buy?"

Moheenie held up two fingers. "Just two. This black one and the aqua color. I decided to go yesterday afternoon instead of today. Now, about this Sartù Di Riso the hostess would like. If she wanted to try it, did you ask why she doesn't just make it herself?" Moheenie teased.

"No I did not! Especially since she is paying us to make it for her."

Moheenie nodded. "That was smart." She reached for her red-and-white striped apron.

"It really isn't hard to make, Mo. There are just a lot of steps. Plus, what else are we going to do?"

"Exactly," Moheenie said while tying her apron. "We are here to cook, so let's cook. But only after you tell me what happened yesterday."

"I will, I will. There's plenty of time. I did have a thought. What are you doing on Saturday night?"

Terza watched Moheenie look at the whiteboard. "I don't know. I usually keep it open for work, but it doesn't look like we have a job that night."

"Then let's prepare an extra pan of Sartù Di Riso. We never make it for ourselves. I say we make it and have dinner together Saturday night."

"That sounds fantastic. I know Ranger is going to love it."

"Good. Now let's figure out a few things."

Moheenie and Terza rested their elbows on one side of the large kitchen island while reading from the whiteboard on the opposite wall.

"We have a late afternoon board meeting downtown tomorrow. They only want Salumi E Formaggi with bread, olive oil, and balsamic."

"All they want is a meat and cheese board?" Moheenie folded her arms in front of her. "Will that be their dinner?"

"I don't think so. The secretary called and said her boss wanted a little something in case the meeting went late. So, when we're finished here I'll run over to the market and pick out a selection."

Moheenie's arms dropped to her sides. "What are we doing Thursday afternoon?"

"That is an office bridal shower. It's a coed luncheon. Fortunately, it is also downtown."

"Salad and lasagna look pretty easy."

"It will be. We are preparing antipasto salad, chicken lasagna, meat lasagna, and garlic bread. They are having a cake, so we will not be making dessert."

"Shall we prepare the sauce today, get everything else ready tomorrow, and cook the lasagna first thing Thursday morning?"

"My thoughts exactly. Especially since Friday is going to be a bear."

"What is the entire menu for Friday evening?" Moheenie angled her head.

Terza lifted her computer tablet and read, "We start with petite salad wedges. The hostess does not want any meat because the Sartù Di Riso is loaded."

"I agree. How many people are invited?"

"Ten. It's a sit-down dinner party." Terza added, "We are also making tomato, mozzarella, and basil bruschetta as an appetizer."

"Won't we need two pans of Sartù Di Riso?"

"Yes. That means we're making a total of three," Terza said.

"We can do this." Moheenie raised her palm.

"Yes we can." Terza and Moheenie slapped palms for a high five. "Oh, and we are also preparing dessert for Friday," Terza announced.

"Let me guess. We are making Tiramisu."

"Of course! We are making chocolate Tiramisu to be exact."

Moheenie exhaled loudly. "Okay then. We better get started."

"I agree. Do you want to begin preparing the marinara sauce?" Terza asked.

"That sounds like a plan."

"I'll be right back." Terza went out the door to her kitchen and directly into the Tiepolo Mercato. She could see her father behind the meat counter helping a customer, and her mother on the opposite side of the market, straightening the spices.

She waved to her father and walked up next to her mother. "Hi, Mom. *Buon giorno.*"

"*Buon giorno*, my love." Mother and daughter hugged each other tightly.

"I need to select some meats and cheeses when Papa is finished," Terza told her mother. "One of our clients requested the Salumi E Formaggi board for their meeting."

The market phone rang loudly. "He shouldn't be long," Benedette said while walking toward the register. "I'll be right back."

Terza followed her mother to the register and heard her answer, "Tiepolo's Mercato."

"Your sister is on the phone," Benedette spoke to Terza.

"Tell Ange I said hello."

"Terza says hello."

When the customer finished paying for his selection from the butcher's counter, Terza walked toward her father. "*Buon giorno*, Papa. How are you today?"

"Hello, my little gnocchi. Did you read your Bible this morning?"

Terza smiled brightly. "I certainly did. And yes, I called Mom first thing."

"Then you, Terza Tiepolo, are my favorite daughter. Now, what can I do for you this fine morning?"

"Ezio, Angeline is on the telephone," Benedette called out to her husband.

"Take your time, Papa," Terza told him. "I want to look at the Salumi E Formaggi. I'm not sure how much I need."

Ezio lifted the receiver of his black wall phone. "Hello, my little cannoli. Did you read your Bible this morning?"

Terza smiled. She imagined her sister saying yes.

"And since you just called your mother, you are officially my favorite daughter."

"Hey!" Terza spoke up. "I thought *I* was your favorite daughter."

Ezio acknowledged Terza's comment with a smile and continued speaking into the receiver. "Your sister thinks she is my favorite daughter, but I have news for you both. I have two daughters, and so I have two favorites."

Terza watched her father listen to Angeline's response.

"How can I have two favorites, you ask?" Ezio winked at Terza. "Because I am the father, and I say so."

Terza laughed. "Good enough for me."

She listened to her father finish speaking with Angeline. He ended his call by saying, "Have a wonderful day." Ezio then turned his attention to his youngest daughter. "Now, what type of Salumi are you thinking?"

"Before we talk deli meat, I have a question. How come Angeline gets to be a dessert, and I'm just a potato?"

Ezio laughed heartily. "When Angeline was born, she was long and skinny, just like a cannoli."

Terza lowered her brows in preparation for her father's next answer.

"You, my little gnocchi, were round and chubby, like a potato."

"I was?"

"Yes, but don't have a heart attack. You are not round and chubby any longer," her father told her.

"That's a good thing!"

"Plus, you must also remember that gnocchi is not always made from potatoes," Ezio explained.

"You are right about that," Terza said while leaning toward the deli case. "Okay, Papa. I am open for suggestions. I need to make a Salumi E Formaggi board for an executive meeting in one of the downtown office buildings. I think a selection of three meats and three cheeses would be perfect."

"I know just what to do." He immediately began pulling deli meats from his case. "How many people will you be serving?"

"Six or maybe seven people total."

"I can handle that easily. Would you like to wait, or shall I bring it over?"

"I can wait. Thanks, Papa. You're the best."

Terza chatted with her father as he sliced the meats to perfection. She decided to leave the cheese in blocks until closer to the event. As typical, her father did not want to charge her, so she insisted he record the purchase in the Macaroni on Wheels account book. Once a month, Terza and her mother settled the account with an agreed amount.

With six white packages in hand, Terza returned to her kitchen where Moheenie was busy washing tomatoes for the marinara sauce.

"Welcome back," Moheenie said. "Did you find what you needed?"

"Yes. Papa had a wonderful selection today. Shall I start with the onions?"

"That would be great."

Terza opened the bin and selected three large brown onions. Within seconds, she removed the outer layers and started chopping.

"I can't believe how fast you can chop an onion, Terza."

"Culinary school," Terza responded. "By the end of the first month, I think I must have completed more than a thousand."

"That's a lot of onion," Moheenie said. "Okay, now that we're on a roll tell me about your meeting with Mr. Follett."

"Well"—Terza looked up from her cutting board—"He recognized me."

"What?" Moheenie squealed.

"Yep," Terza groaned. "He knew I was the caterer."

"That is unbelievable, Tee! What did you do?"

"Believe it or not, I fought back." Terza waved her butcher knife.

Moheenie gasped. "Not with that knife I hope!"

Terza looked at the large blade and laughed. "It might have helped." She sighed. "No, I guess I just got a rush of adrenaline when he found me out. Instead of apologizing, I actually asked him why he lied about being out of town."

"You did?" Moheenie's eyes were as wide as saucers.

"I did. He basically told me he was friends with Rose McCool and not Mitchell. Then he practically closed the door in my face."

"Ouch. So, do you think he did it?"

Terza exhaled loudly. "I haven't a clue, Mo. He certainly could have, and we still don't have any leads on the missing meat. I really want to know who took it."

Moheenie rubbed her chin. "Have you mentioned it to Nico yet?"

"Cute, Moheenie, cute. No, I have not mentioned it to *Detective Nicholas Garza*," Terza emphasized his full name. "Besides, he is not too happy with me right now."

"What makes you say that?"

"Not what, but *who* makes me say that. Caroline Mann told him about our visit."

Moheenie placed a hand to her mouth. "Oh no, she didn't!"

"Oh yes, she did. Detective Garza called and essentially told me to stay out of police business."

"So are you?" Moheenie's dark eyes questioned. "Are you going to stay out of police business?"

"Heck no, of course I'm not," Terza stated firmly. "And neither are you! In fact, I think it is about time I had a little talk with Detective Garza. Before he finds out, I plan on telling him about my visit with Henry Follett. Maybe if I am up-front with the detective, he will be more inclined to drop us a little breadcrumb about their investigation."

While listening, Moheenie's eyes questioned. "Why would he? Don't get me wrong. It would be fantastic if Detective Garza shared anything with us, but I doubt he will."

Terza bit her lower lip. "You're right, of course, but it never hurts to try."

"Whatever you do, keep him on your good side." Moheenie grinned. "Maybe he will ask you out."

Terza looked out their small kitchen window. "I thought about Yale yesterday," she said softly.

"Yale is a pig, Terza!"

"Wow, Mo! Why don't you tell me how you really feel about him?"

"I really feel like he's a pig," Moheenie repeated. "I know he was your first love, Tee, but don't you dare go soft on me. It's been over five years."

"I know, I know." Terza waved her hands. "I would never, ever let Yale back into my life, Mo. But, I cannot believe he still breaks my heart."

"You need a boyfriend, big time."

"That's for sure, but who?"

"When the time is right, you'll know it."

"Thanks, Mo. You're such a great friend."

They worked at a rapid and steady pace until four in the afternoon. Lunch consisted of some fresh fruit and Greek yogurt. When they finally finished cleaning the kitchen, both girls removed their aprons and dropped them to the counter.

"What a day!" Terza exclaimed.

"At least it's still early."

"That it is. Shall we begin at eight tomorrow? I know it's earlier than usual, but I think we will need the extra time."

"Yes. Eight it is." She gave Terza a quick hug. "See you tomorrow."

"Ciao."

CHAPTER EIGHT: GETTING TO KNOW NICO

After Moheenie left, Terza walked through the kitchen door and into the front office. She sat down and propped her feet onto the side return of her desk. *Should I or shouldn't I?* She considered calling Detective Garza, changed her mind, and threw her hands into the air. "Yes," she said loudly before pressing the button for his contact number.

"Garza."

"Detective Garza, it's Terza Tiepolo."

"Miss Tiepolo. It's so nice to hear from you."

Is he being sarcastic? "How about just Terza?"

"Okay, Terza. Then what are you going to call me?"

Is he flirting? "What do you want to be called?"

"How about Nico?"

He is flirting! "Nico, it is," Terza said sweetly. "So Nico, do you have time to talk about something?"

"Right now, I do. What's on your mind?"

Right now, you are on my mind, and I'm not sure why. "I have some more information about Doctor McCool."

"Shall I come over so we can talk?"

"Now?" Terza asked, panicking. *He wants to come over!*

"Why not? The station is downtown. I can be there in less than ten minutes."

Ten minutes! I look like crap! "Well sure. I'm at Macaroni on Wheels. Do you still have my card?"

"I'm looking right at it. See you in a few. Ciao."

Ciao? He said ciao? He speaks Italian, too? "Uh, yes, ciao."

Terza ended the call, grabbed the makeup bag out of her purse, and raced into the bathroom. She looked in the mirror and groaned. It was a busy workday, and Terza's makeup was almost nonexistent. She brushed her teeth, refreshed her mascara, and applied a rose shade of lip gloss. Terza then removed the hairband of her ponytail and brushed out her long hair. She looked down at her blue denim skirt and matching Converse tennis shoes. It was not a first-date look, but at least her red T-shirt was free from flour. *This will have to do.*

She waited in her small front office until she saw him walk past the window to her front entrance. He rang the obnoxiously loud doorbell just as she turned the knob. Terza opened the door and said, "Hi. Come on in. That was fast."

"It would have been faster, but you were a little hard to find," Nico admitted.

Terza flashed him a grin. "It took all of your detective's skills, did it?"

"I even had to show my badge," he announced proudly. "It was to your father, of course."

"Ha!" She threw her head back. "That sounds like my pop. Did he also give you the third degree?"

Nico nodded. "Oh yeah. When I looked at the addresses I thought your business was in the back. So I went into the butcher shop, and when I asked, the butcher turned out to be your father–"

"And he made you prove your business with me before he would tell you how to find me," Terza interrupted.

"That he did," Nico replied. "I like protective fathers, so I was happy to oblige."

Terza noticed a tenderness to his crooked smile, and it pleased her to know he had treated her father with respect. In the Tiepolo family, respect for your elders came without question.

"I'll let you in on a little secret," she offered. "My space originally belonged to our family market. My mother and father wanted to expand, and I needed a place to rent. So, they took over the entire space on the opposite side and reconfigured this side just for me. If I ever don't answer this front door you can find your way into the kitchen through the Tiepolo Mercato."

"Only with permission from your parents, of course," Nico said.

"Of course."

"So where is your catering kitchen?"

Terza pointed. "It's through that door. I rarely get walk-in traffic," she explained. "Most of my business is completed over the phone. In fact, I only unlock this front door when I'm in here working in the company office. The buzzer is extra loud so that I can hear it from the kitchen. Would you like a tour?"

"I sure would," Nico said, stepping closer.

Terza inhaled the scent of his woodsy cologne and felt her face begin to flush.

"Lead the way," he told her.

Grateful to be in front, Terza quickly walked through the arched doorway leading into her catering kitchen and stopped next to the sizeable island. She spread out her arms. "Here it is."

"Wow, Terza. This is the largest kitchen island I have ever seen!" He rubbed his fingers over the surface. "Is this concrete?"

She smiled brightly, noticing his manicured nails. "Yes. Isn't it wonderful? I wanted an island big enough so I could work on one side while Moheenie worked on the other. It is five feet wide and nine feet long."

"I'm impressed, plus I really like the smooth surface."

"Thank you. A friend of the family gave me an amazing deal on all my counters. I almost passed out when I priced the granite for such a large island. Then, one thing led to another, and I thought about concrete. I never planned on getting such a great value."

"That is one nice friend," Nico commented.

"I'll say. Jasper and my father go way back. Fortunately, I have been able to spoil him and his family by catering a few events at no charge." Terza walked toward her stove. "Shall we start at this corner and work our way around?"

"One, two, three, four, five, six burners."

"Plus, we have a grill in the middle. Sometimes we have all six burners working at the same time."

"I can believe it." He leaned over to look into her oven. "But is this one oven enough?"

"Not in the least." Terza pointed to her left. "We have three. This stacked double oven and the one with the stove."

"You're making me hungry just thinking about all the food that has been cooked in here."

"That's funny because sometimes I don't even get hungry after tasting everything," Terza told him.

"I can imagine." Nico continued past the ovens to a counter filled with machines. "Some of these I have never even seen before." He pointed to an industrial-sized electric mixer. "What is this?"

"It's just a mixer."

Nico moved in for a closer look. "But it has a hook."

Terza laughed. "It's for kneading bread, silly. I'm sure you would recognize the beater attachments." She turned the corner to her triple sink and then stopped. "Check this out. We have one sink for washing produce and two others for washing dishes."

"I'm surprised you don't have a dishwasher," Nico said.

"Of course we do. Look, it's at the end of this counter. But frankly, most of our dishes are pots and pans. It is much easier to wash them by hand."

Nico peered into the sink. "It is nice and deep. You could probably take a bath in here."

"Almost, but not quite." Terza walked over and opened one of her two refrigerators. "Last but not least, the refrigerators."

"They are good-sized too. But do you have enough freezer space?"

"Yes and no. We really don't freeze much, but when we do need more room, I use the freezer at the market." Terza closed the refrigerator door.

"That's nice and handy."

"It certainly is." She held her palms out. "Well, this is my home away from home. What do you think?"

"That your kitchen is amazing." He looked up at the vintage cat wall clock and laughed. "I think my grandmother had one of those."

"Mine did, too!" Terza said. "That's exactly why I bought it. If I remember correctly, my grandmother's clock was red."

"My grandmother's clock might have been yellow," Nico told her. "Where did you find it?"

"At one of those novelty shops in downtown Palm Springs," Terza said. "The moment I saw that cat tail moving back and forth, I just knew we had to have it for our kitchen."

"It fits perfectly in here," Nico said, studying the whiteboard containing their catering schedule for the week. "It appears you are going to be busy this week. What is Sartù Di Riso? I don't recognize that dish."

"I bet you've tasted it though. Have you ever seen a Bundt pan?"

Nico slowly nodded his head. "I think so. Is it round with a hole in the middle?"

"Exactly. A Sartù Di Riso is made in a Bundt pan with a combination of rice and different meats. I like to use hot Italian sausage and ground sirloin, and of course, there are tons of other ingredients. Then, after a gazillion steps, the mixture is pressed into the Bundt pan, baked, and inverted onto a serving plate. You cut it just like a cake."

"A gazillion steps, huh?" Nico laughed. "I take it the Sartù Di Riso is hard to make?"

"It's not hard," Terza explained. "There are just many, many steps. It actually looks harder to make than it is. The hostess of the party we are catering saw a chef prepare it on one of the cooking shows. She thought about trying it herself and then gave up and hired Macaroni on Wheels."

"That's a great way to get business."

"Isn't it though? I am always happy to secure new customers." While talking with Nico, Terza noticed the precision cut of his deep brown hair. *He's very good-looking.* "Now that I have described a Sartù Di Riso, do you remember ever trying one?"

"I believe I have. The rice was almost like a coating around the filling, right?"

"You are correct. Now, for the most important question, did you like it?"

"I don't remember, but I must have. I am a big eater, but only when I enjoy the food. I remember eating it all, so I must have liked it."

Terza eyed his taut waistline. "You don't look like a big eater," she remarked.

Nico tapped his stomach. "Why thank you. I try to burn what I eat." He narrowed his eyes before asking. "Why are you smiling?"

"I like your golf shirt," she said. "The softened yellow color reminds me of lemon gelato."

"It does, does it?" He smiled broadly. "And do you like lemon gelato?"

"It's my favorite." Terza leaned against the counter of her kitchen island. "How about you? Do you like lemon gelato?"

Nico shrugged. "I don't know that I've ever tried it."

Her eyes widened. "You've never tried *lemon* gelato, or you've never even tried gelato?"

104

"I'm Italian, so of course I've eaten gelato. I just have never tasted lemon."

"Then what's your favorite?"

"Pistachio, without a doubt. It is the best gelato flavor ever made!"

Terza placed both hands on her hips. "You have never even tasted lemon, so how can you possibly make that claim?"

Nico straightened his stance. "Have you ever tasted pistachio?"

"Of course, and I must admit it is delicious. But pistachio is not as good as lemon."

He held out his hand. "Then let's go now."

"You want to go right this minute?"

"Sure. Aren't you finished for the day?"

"Yes, but gelato before dinner?"

"Tell me why not," Nico said. "You need to live a little!"

Terza hesitated.

"I would love to take you to dinner, but I have to get back to the office," Nico explained.

"Oh no, please don't misunderstand me. I wasn't trying to invite myself to dinner."

"Terza don't worry, we can talk about dinner later. Now is the time for gelato. Are you in or out?"

"I'm in. When it comes to gelato, I am definitely in." Terza walked toward her desk. "Let me just grab my bag."

Nico followed Terza into her office. "You don't need a bag. It's on me."

She returned the bag to her desk and opened the top. "Okay. I'll just get my phone and keys."

"Yes on the keys so you can lock up, but no on the phone."

Terza looked up at his smiling face. "No phone?"

"Aren't we planning on having a quality gelato moment?"

She straightened. "And what is that mobile device attached to your belt?" Terza argued.

Nico placed a palm onto his cell phone. "I know, and I promise not to answer unless it is police business."

"Do you realize that you sound like my mother? There are absolutely no phones allowed at the dining room table."

"What are you talking about? I sound like *my* mother. She barely allows telephones in the house!"

"Are your parents local?" Terza opened her front office door and motioned for Nico to pass through.

"They live closer now than when they lived in New York." Nico stepped out the door and onto the sidewalk. "My parents originally relocated from Italy just before I was born, and then approximately five years ago, my mother and father moved to California."

"They must still speak a lot of Italian. I can hear a slight accent."

"That's very perceptive," Nico told her. "Yes, they speak Italian all the time."

"Where did they move to in California?"

"Napa, of course," Nico said, laughing.

Terza pulled the office door closed. "An Italian family in Napa sounds perfect. Please do not tell me they opened a winery." She locked the door.

Nico chuckled. "Okay, I won't."

Terza turned to face him. "I was kidding! Did they really open a winery?"

"Yes, they did."

Terza slid the key ring into the front pocket of her skirt. "Wow, I love it! That is so cool."

Nico extended a bent elbow to Terza. "Shall we?"

She smiled and slid her palm along his bicep. "We shall." Terza instantly felt the strength of his muscles. "You seem very strong, Nico. I'm impressed."

"Thank you," he said while glancing her way. "Right or left at the corner?"

"Turn left. So how do you stay in shape?"

"Besides going to the gym, I'm on the police rugby team."

"The rugby team? Now I'm doubly impressed. That is one tough sport."

"Tell me about it." Nico exhaled loudly. "What about you?"

They turned the corner, and Terza looked up at him. "I go to the gym too, but I also paddleboard with Moheenie."

"Moheenie seems nice. How long have you known her?"

"Since high school. We were cheerleaders together."

He laughed. "I could have guessed that."

Terza stopped walking. She took a step back and shot him a pretend death stare. "What is that supposed to mean, Detective Garza?"

"Don't worry, it's nothing bad. You are just the perfect cheerleader type. You're cute–"

"I'm cute?"

His smile was infectious. "Yes, you are cute, and you know it."

Terza lost the fight to suppress her amused grin.

Nico continued, "You have long, beautiful hair." When he paused, Terza saw his glance shift to the side as she tried to control several strands of hair flying with the wind. "You have long, beautiful, and *wild* hair," he added. "And you're spunky. You just look like the cheerleading type."

"Hmm," she mumbled. "Then I shall take that as a compliment."

"Good, because it *is* a compliment. Now, let's get moving before I get called back to work."

"We are almost there. It's the next restaurant."

As Nico and Terza walked through the opened front door of Solunto, she pointed to the gelato case. They stepped closer to the glass and gazed at the frozen delights.

"They all look delicious. What do you think? Shall I order two lemon gelatos?" he asked her.

Terza shook her head. "No, you should order one lemon and one pistachio. That way we can switch if you do not like the lemon."

"Or I can sneak bites out of yours," he teased.

"Yes, that you can," Terza said, suddenly feeling euphoric.

Nico ordered their gelatos while Terza selected a table by the window. After paying, he joined her and placed the cardboard cup of pistachio gelato directly in front of her. Nico then lowered the cup of lemon gelato to the table in front of his empty seat. He slid onto the chair and held his cup of gelato into the air. "Here goes nothing." Nico scooped the lemon gelato with his square plastic spoon, carefully placed it into his mouth, and closed his eyes.

"Well?" Terza pressed. She watched Nico open his eyes and spoon another bite.

"It is very good, but..." He reached over to steal a bite of hers. "I need to try the pistachio before making a decision." Terza kept her eyes on Nico as he tasted the pistachio. "Oh my, now that is amazing!"

"Do you really think it is better than the lemon?"

Nico angled his head. "I don't know. They are both excellent."

"I'm sure you know there are many restaurants that make gelato in Little Italy, but personally I think Solunto is the best. They make their gelato fresh every morning."

Nico took another bite of his lemon gelato. "I can tell." He showed his cup to Terza. "Look at the fresh lemon zest in here."

She in turn showed her cup to him. "I can see them. Look at all of the pistachio pieces in mine. They are even roasted and chopped."

Nico leaned forward for a better view, and then he smiled with his spoon hovering closely above her cup. "Do you mind?"

She laughed. "No, not at all." Terza pushed the cup closer to him. "Shall we trade?"

He took a moment to consider the lemon gelato before placing the cup in front of Terza. Nico then accepted the cup of pistachio. "Thanks. I like the lemon, but the pistachio still wins."

"And I like the pistachio, but to me, the lemon remains my favorite." Terza bit her lower lip while thinking about how to begin her confession.

"Uh oh," he said. "You suddenly look serious."

"I went to see another neighbor yesterday," Terza quickly announced. She waited for his reaction.

Nico arched a brow. "And?"

"And that's it. There is nothing else to tell. I just went to see him."

"Why don't you go into a bit more detail," Nico suggested. "I've got an idea. Maybe you should start from the beginning?"

Terza raised and lowered her shoulders. "Did you by chance read the e-vite list for Doctor McCool's party?"

"I did," Nico answered. "Why, did you?"

Terza folded her arms. "That would be a yes," she squeaked out. "I got a copy from Caroline Mann."

"Ha! That must have been before you accused her husband of murder."

"We're not on that subject right now," Terza playfully warned.

"Okay, go on. What about the e-vite list?"

"Doctor McCool's neighbor on the other side is named Henry Follett. He responded *no* to the invitation because he was supposedly going to be out of town. But he wasn't out of town. Caroline Mann told me that she saw Henry Follett on the day of the murder."

"I don't understand the big deal." Nico shrugged. "Maybe his plans changed."

"Then why were all of the lights off in his house?"

"Terza, I have no idea, but that doesn't automatically make

him a suspect."

"He also works with Rose McCool," Terza stated.

"We already know that," Nico said.

"Maybe he's in love with her and wanted Doctor McCool out of the picture."

Nico arched a brow. "He was already out of the picture. They're divorced."

"Men." Terza rolled her eyes. "Don't you remember what I told you about Rose McCool? She was upset about his party and mad about me being there in the house. It's obvious that she was still in love with him, meaning Doctor McCool was still in the picture."

"Is that why you went to Follet's house?" Nico asked.

"No, silly. I knocked on his door and pretended to be with a housekeeping service. I planned to just casually mention the crime scene tape on his neighbor's house." Terza could tell Nico was having a hard time suppressing his laughter. "It's not that funny!"

Nico finally hooted loudly. "Yes, it is! Did you actually think Follett would then confess to murder?"

"No, I just wanted to see how he responded," Terza said calmly.

"Did he need a housekeeper?" Nico asked through his continued laughter.

"No."

"I'm curious. What would you have done if Follett said yes?"

Terza sighed. "I made some cards, and I would have given him one. Moheenie and I already decided we could clean his house once and then quit."

"This gets better and better. You actually made housekeeping cards?"

"Yes, now stop laughing." Terza reached across the table and slapped at his hand.

Nico rubbed at his forehead. "Okay, go on with your story. I'm dying to know what happened."

"Henry Follett recognized me as the caterer. That's what happened!" Terza squirmed in her chair. "So when he snapped at me, I snapped back. Then he finally slammed the door."

"Terza, all kidding aside, you have to be careful," Nico warned. "What if Henry Follett really did murder Mitchell McCool? He could have dragged you into his house and killed you too."

"I know," Terza said sincerely. "I just wanted to follow-up on a hunch."

Nico's smile accentuated the dimples on his face. "Maybe you should trust us, trust me, to follow-up?"

"But are you?"

"Am I what?"

"Are you following up? I know you spoke with Caroline Mann, but what about Henry Follett? Why haven't you spoken with him?"

"We have, Terza," Nico shot back. "I met with Henry Follett yesterday."

"Oh." Terza lowered her eyes.

"I am good at my job."

"I'm sure you are," Terza softly replied, looking up.

"Your logic is good though," Nico told her. "If something comes to you, why not call me and I will check it out? That way I can keep you safe."

"Okay." Terza nodded. "Let's start with this then. When I went to Doctor McCool's home on Friday afternoon, I checked his refrigerator and freezer to see how much space was available. Unfortunately for us, Doctor McCool's freezer was packed. It was filled with white packages. You know that my father is a butcher, and the packages looked exactly like packets of meat. There was also a very large bone."

"I don't understand the problem. It's not unusual to have a freezer full of meat," Nico told her.

"I agree, Nico, but now it's gone."

"How do you know that?"

"I found out on Sunday after our family dinner. As you know, we used Doctor McCool's refrigerator on Saturday after we found him and called the police."

"Yes, and you took your food home, right?"

"That's right. I knew Doctor McCool's freezer was full, so I assumed Ranger left the ice in our coolers."

"I take it he didn't?"

"No. While we were walking to the bocce ball courts on Sunday evening, Ranger mentioned that he forgot to retrieve our ice from the McCool's freezer. That's why I called you so we could stop by and get it."

Nico nodded. "Then if the freezer was empty on Saturday night, what happened to all of the meat?"

"That is exactly what I want to know."

"McCool could have given it to a neighbor to free up some freezer space for his party," Nico suggested.

"I agree. But now we know that Doctor McCool met with someone between the time I saw him on Friday afternoon and when we arrived on Saturday afternoon. Whoever it was might have information that will help us."

Nico grinned. "Help *us*?"

Terza chuckled. "Yes, help us. You said I have good logic."

"You do. And yes, I agree it is important to find out who has this missing meat. If you promise to stop placing yourself in danger, I promise to keep you somewhat informed."

"What does *somewhat informed* mean?" Terza asked.

"Well, I can't be expected to call you with every aspect of our case, but I will let you know if we have a suspect."

"Okay, I promise to stop placing myself in danger," Terza said. *I'm sure your definition of danger is far different than mine.*

"Good. Now let's get back to your mention of bocce ball. Do you play?"

"I'm Italian," Terza stated. "What do you think?"

"Well, I'm Italian, too. Yes, I play, and yes, I am good."

Terza's eyes sparkled. "Really? How good are you?"

"I am very good. Some might say I am excellent, almost professional."

"Then you are definitely coming to a Sunday dinner at my parent's house, Detective Garza."

Nico grinned. "And why is that?"

"Because after our family dinner we all walk over to the bocce ball courts for a Tiepolo tournament. With you on my team I am bound to beat my brother!"

"That sounds like a plan. After this case is over you can count me in."

Terza clapped her hands together. "Winning is going to be such fun!"

"Well *this* has been fun, but I need to get back to work." Nico stood and held out a hand to Terza.

"Thank you," she said, accepting his hand. She also stood and walked toward the front door. "Thank you for the gelato."

"It was my pleasure. We'll have to do it again."

"Yes, we will." *Soon, I hope.*

Nico escorted Terza to Macaroni on Wheels before saying goodbye. "Ciao."

"Ciao, ciao," she responded while unlocking the door.

After watching the detective walk away, Terza entered her office and closed the door. She leaned against the wood, deep in thought. She felt comfortable with Nico like they had been friends for years. Her stomach churned with something that definitely was not indigestion. *Could I be falling in love?*

The soon-to-be-setting sun shot rays of bright sunlight through her partially opened blinds. Terza stood motionless as she observed the thousands of dust particles dance through the light beams. Even after the gelato she was hungry for dinner. Terza finally moved from her spot and closed the blinds. She double-checked the kitchen, making sure everything was in order and left through her back door.

While walking the short distance to her condominium,

Terza's mind returned to Doctor McCool's murder. She felt pulled to think about Nicolas Garza but changed her focus to the case. Now that she had shared the missing meat information with Nico, Rose McCool was the last of her suspects to investigate.

When Terza reached her building, she used her key fob to open the front lobby door automatically. After entering, she stepped into the elevator and selected the fourth floor. Another eighty steps brought Terza to the front door of her condo.

She thrived on the enthusiastic activity of Little Italy, and yet she adored coming home to her sanctuary. While living with her parents, their street-front location brought many visitors all hours of the day and night. Her condominium project required any guests to telephone before gaining access. Whenever Terza arrived home, she felt like a drawbridge had lifted, allowing her to be alone in her condominium castle.

Although small, Terza's one-bedroom condominium met all her needs. She had a comfortable living room with a powder room perfect for guests. Her master bedroom suite was spacious, and the master bathroom was more than she ever expected. The builders made up for the single bedroom size by creating a spa-like bathroom. She had a soaking bathtub and a separate rain shower. Many nights after work, Terza made herself a cup of London Fog tea, lit candles, and relaxed in a warm bubble bath to read a good book. "I don't need a man to make me happy," she would often say aloud to her cat Olive.

Tonight would not be one for relaxing, as Terza had a plan. First, she turned on her oven to preheat and placed her leftover risotto into a glass casserole dish. While waiting, she filled Olive's bowl and topped it with two spoons of wet food. As usual, Olive purred with delight. Terza then dialed Conner's number.

"Hey there," he answered.

"What are you doing on Saturday night?"

"I have no plans, so I'll be at home just waiting for an

amazing dinner on Sunday."

"How would you like an amazing dinner on Saturday?"

"Do you mean instead of Sunday?"

"No, including Sunday," Terza told him. "Ranger and Moheenie are coming over on Saturday night, and I thought you might like to join us."

"Oh no, what do you need?"

Terza crinkled her nose. "Forget it, Conner," she snapped.

"I'm sorry, Terza. Yes, I would like to come over. Thank you very much."

"You're welcome," she spoke softly. "I'm sorry too. I didn't mean to snap at you. Can you come to Macaroni on Wheels at six?"

"That sounds great. Are we staying there or going to your place?"

"We're staying at *MOW*. Have you ever heard of a Sartù Di Riso?"

"No, I can't say that I have. Is it a car?"

Terza laughed. "No, silly, Sartù Di Riso is an Italian dish. Moheenie and I have to make two of them for a catering job on Friday evening. Since we're going to all the trouble, we decided to make three and enjoy one together on Saturday night."

"I really appreciate the invitation, Terza. Wow, I feel special. I get to see you two days in a row."

Terza instantly grew worried. Conner was so sweet and very nice. She hated to give him the wrong impression. "You *are* special, Conner," she said. "Plus, you and Ranger are such good friends. I thought it would be fun."

"That does sound like fun." Conner paused. "Now, how can I help?"

"I didn't say I needed any help."

"I know, but if you do, I am offering."

"I can always walk down to the county administration office to look up any addresses I might need," Terza spoke with confidence.

"I know you can."

"On the other hand, maybe you could save me the time. It would be nice to have the address tonight."

"Why would you need an address tonight? You aren't planning to go somewhere, are you?"

"Of course not," she lied. "I'm just getting my facts together."

Conner laughed. "I'm surprised you don't have a murder board set up."

His comment sent Terza's mind spinning with ideas. *A murder board? What a great idea! I know just the place!*

"Are you still there?"

"Yes, yes, so will you help me?"

"I'm already on the site and waiting for a name."

"Rose McCool."

"Isn't that the wife of the murder victim?"

"Yes, it is."

"Okay, hang on." Terza heard him typing. She stood at her counter waiting, pen in hand. "I've got it," Conner said. "Are you ready?"

"Go ahead."

Conner recited a La Jolla address to Terza. "What can I bring on Saturday?"

"Hmm. How about a bottle of Chianti?"

"That sounds perfect. And what can I bring to family dinner on Sunday?"

"That one is easy. Bring flowers, as my mother can never get enough. But please do not spend very much. She loves sunflowers, so just pick up a bunch at the local store."

"That sounds perfect, too. Sunflowers it is."

"Well, I better get going. Thanks for your help, Conner."

"You're welcome. And thanks for the dinner invite. I'll see you at six on Saturday."

"See you on Saturday. Ciao."

After disconnecting, Terza placed her risotto in the oven and set the timer. Then she sent a text to Moheenie:

Where is Ranger?

Five minutes later, Moheenie responded:

At CrossFit.

Terza read the text and called Moheenie.

"Yes," Moheenie answered.

"How long will he be there?"

"At least two hours, maybe more. Ranger just left, and he has to drive there, so probably three total. Ranger usually showers at the gym, so he doesn't have to drive home all sweaty."

"Good," Terza said. "Can you go out?"

"Sure, where are we going?"

"We haven't looked into Rose McCool at all. I think we should take a drive over to her house."

"Would we go in?"

"No, not unless we can think of a good reason. I just thought we could take a look around."

"Oh, like a stakeout?"

"Well, kind of."

"Cool! Then let's wear all black." Moheenie sounded excited.

"That's not a bad idea, actually. If we do decide to look around, it will help with the camouflage. Wear something with a hood, too," Terza instructed.

"Got it. When are we going?"

"Let's see." Terza looked at the green clock numbers on her microwave. "It's almost six-thirty, and I am just warming some risotto. If you don't mind driving, you could pick me up at seven-thirty. It should be dark by then."

"Seven-thirty works for me. I'll send Ranger a text and tell him not to hurry."

"What will you tell him?"

"Nothing until I get home. Then the truth, I guess."

"Oh, man, he's going to give us such a bad time."

"I know, but we can take it. See you soon," Moheenie said.

"Okay. Just park out front. I'll wait for you in the lobby, so you don't have to get out."

"Perfect."

"Oh, and remember to bring your binoculars."

"Will do."

"And remind me to tell you about Nico," Terza said.

"Oh, now it's Nico, huh? Did you talk to him?"

"I talked with him and saw him. We had gelato!"

"What!" Moheenie squealed. "Tell me, Tee!"

"No, I've got to go. We'll talk in the car."

Terza ended her call with Moheenie and immediately went to change. She selected black yoga pants, a black T-shirt, and a black hoody. Fortunately, she also had black high-top tennis shoes.

She then removed the risotto from the oven and spooned it onto a dinner plate. Terza decided to enjoy her meal out on the balcony. It was a beautiful night, one perfect for a stakeout.

CHAPTER NINE: LADIES IN BLACK

By 7:25 p.m. Terza stood waiting in her lobby. The streets were busy, and Terza scrutinized every car passing by. Less than five minutes later, Moheenie drove up and parked her black Jeep Rubicon directly in front of Terza's building. She honked.

"You look perfect," Moheenie said after Terza opened the car door and climbed into the front bucket seat.

Terza surveyed Moheenie's outfit. "You do too. I see that we both selected yoga pants."

"None better. Maybe we can share a new slogan! These yoga pants are as perfect for the gym as they are for a stakeout." Moheenie grinned. "Where are we going?"

"La Jolla, so get on Interstate Five North," Terza said.

"Got it. Do you have the address?"

"It's in my phone. Once we are closer, I'll bring up the navigation."

"Great. Now tell me about *Nico*." Moheenie emphasized the detective's nickname.

Terza watched Moheenie turn the corner and drive toward the freeway on-ramp. "I called to tell him about Henry Follett because I wanted to avoid a situation. I figured it would be best to tell him before Mr. Follett complained."

Moheenie glanced at Terza. "Good plan. I agree."

"But when I called, he suggested we speak in person."

"Wow. Did he sound interested?"

"Maybe a little, but maybe not. I'm just not sure. He did sound flirty though."

"So, he came over, and then what happened?"

"First I showed him around the kitchen. Then when we were talking, I mentioned that his shirt was the color of lemon gelato."

Moheenie lifted her chin. "What kind of shirt?"

"It was just a golf shirt."

"Was it baggy or tight?"

"It was medium, and yes, you could tell he has a nice build."

Moheenie grinned widely.

"After I mentioned the lemon gelato, we got into a conversation about the best flavors. Of course I mentioned that lemon gelato was my favorite. So, he invited me to go for an impromptu taste."

"Now that's what I call a *smooth move*."

"Do you really think so?" Terza glanced at Mo. "Was Nico making a move?"

"Of course he was! Why else would he ask you out?"

"To taste gelato," Terza answered.

"Oh please, Tee! That was just an excuse. You made it easy for him."

Terza smiled. "I guess I did." She lifted her phone and activated the GPS. "Okay, the directions are ready to go."

The automated voice instructed them to remain on Interstate Five North for another four miles.

"Oh, by the way, I invited Conner to join us on Saturday night," Terza said.

"That will be nice. Especially for Ranger, but aren't you worried about leading him on?"

"Yes, but I needed more information, and I didn't want him to think I was just using him."

"Ha! I think he thinks that already," Moheenie said.

"I know he does. But, I can't help the fact he has access to everything!"

"You're right about that. Did he give you Rose McCool's address?"

"Yes, that's why I called him. I could have gone to the county administration building tomorrow, but I didn't want to waste another day. If Rose did kill her husband, she has already had three days to destroy any evidence."

"I really don't know what you expect us to find." Moheenie peeked at Terza. "But, who cares? I wouldn't miss this for the world!"

"I don't know either, Mo. But Conner gave me a great idea without realizing it."

"What kind of idea?"

"A murder board," Terza said. "You know the ones we read about in our mystery book club? I thought we could use the back of our whiteboard. When we are working on the case, we can take the board down and use the back."

"That's a great idea, but while we're working on the back, won't we mess up the writing on the front?"

Terza nodded. "May-be," she stretched out the word while thinking.

"Why don't we have two whiteboards?" Moheenie suggested. "That way we can hang whichever one we need."

"That's a great idea, but where will we keep the murder board when we are not using it? I don't want anyone else to see it."

"We can slide it between the two refrigerators. I think there might be room."

"You're right. It can slide right in, and nobody will notice it." Terza stopped talking so she could listen to the directions. "Did you hear that?"

"Yes, I'm taking the next exit."

"Veer left until you reach Via La Jolla. Then turn right," Terza said.

"Will do."

After exiting the freeway, Moheenie followed the directions to a residential area in the hills of La Jolla. She slowed at the address of Rose McCool's home. "Where should I park?"

"Let's park across the street just beyond the house. That way it will look like we are guests of someone else."

Moheenie turned her Jeep around, drove by Rose's house, and pulled toward the opposite curb.

Terza then pointed to a long curb situated between two large estate-style homes. "What do you think of that area? We will be parked right between the two houses. I really don't think our car can be seen because of all the trees."

"Good point." Moheenie drove slowly forward along the curb and stopped halfway.

"Perfect. Did you bring your binoculars?"

"Yes, they are in the back. How about if I hop over the seat? That way we both will have a window?"

"Great idea." Terza retrieved her own binoculars, while Moheenie climbed into the back. They simultaneously raised them and focused on Rose McCool's home.

"Her curtains are closed," Moheenie said.

"Yes, but look to the right. Is that a kitchen window?"

"I believe it is. It looks like she has only a valance along the top of the window. I think I see the microwave."

"Me too." Terza pressed her nose against the glass. "What about that vehicle in the driveway? Do you think it is her car?"

"I don't know." Moheenie hesitated. "Would a woman drive such a large SUV?"

"It could have been Doctor McCool's vehicle," Terza suggested.

"Maybe she got it in the divorce. But I would expect Rose to park in the garage."

"Maybe, maybe not," Terza said. She pointed her binoculars toward the garage and focused on a small window. "Check out the garage door," she told Moheenie. "Do you see the window?"

"I do. Shall we go take a look?"

"Yes, but in a minute. I'd like to see if there is movement in the house."

Terza and Moheenie sat quietly, watching for any activity. Before long, they noticed people in the kitchen.

"Somebody is definitely home," Terza stated. "Can you make out any features?"

"I can tell one person is a woman by the hair," Moheenie said. "But I cannot make out the other person."

"This angle is horrible." Terza groaned. "Let's get out."

They each fumbled to exit the Jeep using the side away from the McCool's house.

"Good thing we're petite." Terza crouched and slid out. "Your Jeep is not the perfect spy vehicle!"

"That's for sure." Moheenie softly closed the car door. "But I love it!"

"Me too."

They crept in crouched positions along the curb. When they stood directly opposite Rose's home, they used another parked vehicle as cover. Terza and Moheenie raised their binoculars for another look.

"Oh my goodness!" Terza whispered. "It's Henry Follett! Henry Follett is in the kitchen with Rose McCool!"

"Are you sure?"

"Yes, I'm positive. I just saw him yesterday. Wow! Maybe they were both in on it."

"Or maybe they are just friends," Moheenie said. "He might be there for support."

"I doubt it."

"Now what do we do?"

"I have no idea." Terza shrugged. "I just wish we could somehow talk to Rose. At least then we might get a feeling of whether she is in mourning."

"Shall we take a look inside Follett's SUV?"

"Sure, why not? Let's go," Terza said.

Terza and Moheenie tiptoed across the street and immediately took cover behind Henry's vehicle.

"Keep an eye on them," Terza instructed Moheenie. "I'll look through the car windows."

Moheenie nodded and moved closer to the kitchen window.

Terza activated the flashlight on her phone and directed the light beam toward the front seat. Nothing. She guided her light to the back seat. It too, was clear. Terza then turned off the light. "Come on," she whispered to Moheenie.

Moheenie tiptoed back to Terza. "Did you find anything?"

"No, nothing. His car is spotless, almost as if he just detailed it."

"Maybe he did," Moheenie suggested.

"Well, this was a bust," Terza said as they walked toward Moheenie's car. She suddenly froze. "Or maybe not!"

"What do you mean?"

"It's Tuesday, and tomorrow is trash pick-up," Terza announced. "We know the coast is clear at Henry Follett's house. Let's go take a look in his trash bins."

"What are we looking for exactly?"

"I don't know. There might just be something to give us another lead."

Moheenie shrugged. "Why not? It can't hurt. Let's go!"

After driving to the murder street, as they now called it, Terza suggested they park down the block in one of the grocery store lots. They got out, walked into the store's front door, and then out the side door. Fortunately, the parking lot guard was too busy to notice their lack of shopping.

"Wow, it's dark back here," Terza remarked as they entered the alley.

"It sure is, but at least there are a few streetlights."

"Dim ones." Terza groaned. "How about if I check the bins and you keep watch?"

"Good idea. I'll yell out something if I see someone."

"Okay, but don't use my name."

"Of course I won't."

"Hey look." Terza pointed to the alley behind the Mann's home. "Alan and Caroline have already brought out their trash bins, too."

"Now you can look through both. Be quiet though," Moheenie warned.

"I will."

"And be careful," Moheenie whispered. She quickly walked by the Mann home and crouched alongside the fence.

Terza quietly opened Henry's trash bin and looked inside. She lifted one of the three white plastic trash bags and placed it upon the asphalt. Terza then used both hands to rip open one of the other bags still resting inside the bin. She pushed through fast-food wrappers, frozen dinner cartons, and wet tissues. *Yuck.* She shuddered.

After ripping through the second bag, Terza found a similar assortment. She then returned the third bag to the trash bin and ripped through the plastic. On top, Terza saw the familiar white wrapper of butcher paper. Carefully, she began opening the crumpled paper. While doing so, Terza thought she noticed a porch light turn on, but she kept working.

"Hi, Dalton, it's nice to see you!" Moheenie called loudly.

Terza instantly lowered the trash bin lid and hid behind the side.

"Alan, who is it?" Caroline Mann called.

"I don't see anyone. It sounded like some friends just talking in the alley." Terza heard Alan Mann less than twenty-five feet away! She kept very still and tried not to breathe. Moments later, she heard a door close.

Seconds after that Moheenie tiptoed next to her. "It's all clear. Did you find anything?"

"I might have," Terza whispered. "But I really need another look. Plus, I haven't checked the Mann's trash bin yet."

"No, it's too dangerous." Moheenie widened her eyes. "Let's get out of here."

"Okay." Terza sighed. "You're probably right. Let's go."

The two friends walked and talked on their way back to the grocery store. "I think Henry Follett might have the missing meat," Terza announced.

"But you only saw one packet, right?"

"Yes, but there could easily have been more. I only saw the one on top. Plus, maybe he only ate one of the steaks."

"He also may have purchased just one steak from the butcher," Moheenie added.

"Or..." Terza raised her voice. "What if Rose McCool took the meat and shared it with him?"

"This has to go on our murder board," Moheenie said.

"I agree!"

When they returned to Moheenie's Jeep, she commented, "It's still early. I might just beat Ranger home."

"That's a good point. Now you won't have to tell him where we were."

"Exactly right, and he won't be able to tease us!"

After Moheenie dropped Terza off in the front of her building, Terza felt grateful to be home. It was time for a long, relaxing hot bath. She needed to turn off her mind and get a good night's sleep.

CHAPTER TEN: ALIBI OR NOT

Wednesday

Terza awoke refreshed and energized. The time neared 6:30 a.m., and Terza calculated she had finally slept for more than eight hours. Now, she had plenty of time to make coffee at home. After brewing a dark roast and filling her mug with the aromatic liquid, she opened her balcony door and stepped outside. Olive quickly followed.

"It's brisk out here, isn't it Olive?" Terza placed her mug on the patio table. Olive rubbed against Terza's bare leg. "That beautiful fur is keeping you warm."

She went inside for both a sweatshirt and her Bible, and then returned to the balcony. Olive followed her every move and seemed grateful when Terza finally sat. Olive leaped high, landing perfectly in the chair opposite Terza. Her four paws moved around until Olive located the ideal sleeping position. "I just got up, and now you're going to sleep?" Terza asked. Olive opened one eye as if to say, "Don't bother me."

Terza shook her head and laughed. She opened her Bible and rested it on the table before reaching for her mug. Her first sip of the delicious coffee brought a smile to her face. The hot liquid warmed her throat as the mug warmed her hands. Today was already shaping up to be a good day.

At quarter past seven, Terza went inside to call her mother. The telephone rang only once before Benedette answered.

"*Buon giorno*, my love. How are you this morning?"

"*Buon giorno*, Mom. I feel wonderful! Can you believe I actually got over eight hours of sleep?"

"Finally! You work too hard."

"Not nearly as hard as you and Papa. At least you are off today. What do you have planned?"

"I am taking a class at the nursery," Benedette said.

"How fun. What type of class?" Terza asked.

"How to grow herbs in Southern California."

Terza chuckled. "Are you certain you're not *teaching* that class? Have they seen your garden?"

"There is always room for improvement, my love. Now, I've been thinking. How are you going to call me every morning when you are married and have children to feed?"

"First off, that is a long way away," Terza told her. "And second, I will probably need your advice."

"Terza, your father means well, and I adore our morning conversations. I just don't ever want you to feel like you have to call me."

"Mom, how long do we usually talk?"

"I don't know. Two to three minutes I suppose."

"And how many minutes are there in a day?"

Benedette laughed. "I definitely do not know that one!"

"Well, I do. There are one thousand, four hundred and forty."

"That is a lot," Benedette commented.

"I know. So, I truly think I can take just two or three of those one thousand, four hundred and forty minutes to call my mom."

"Do you know how much I love you?"

"Not nearly as much as I love you! Now tell me, what are you having for dinner on Saturday evening?"

"I have no idea, but you know we typically eat light on Saturdays."

"Would you like to have Sartù Di Riso?" Terza asked.

"Of course I would. Your father and I adore Sartù Di Riso! But I am certainly not preparing a meal with that many steps on the night before our family dinner."

"You don't have to because I'm already making it. Since I needed to make two pans for a catering job, I figured one more would be just as easy. If we are going to the trouble of preparing this very special dish, we might as well enjoy it too."

"But I don't want to take yours," Benedette said.

"Don't worry, you're not. Ranger, Moheenie, and Conner are coming over Saturday night for a small dinner party. I plan on baking the Sartù Di Riso around six. Once it is finished, I'll have the boys run your portion over."

"If I remember correctly, each pan serves eight, right?"

"Yes, so there will definitely be plenty," Terza replied. "We're having a salad and garlic bread as well, plus, I plan on making a dessert too."

"Then I will do the same, except for the dessert of course. Your father does not need any extra calories."

"Poor Papa." Terza chuckled.

"Don't feel sorry for your father. He gets plenty of sweets. This is also going to be a real treat for him. Sartù Di Riso is one of his favorites."

"Then you should make it for him another time," Terza teased.

Benedette laughed. "No, I think I will let you have the honor."

"That sounds like a plan. Well, I have to get moving. Have a great day, Mom. Ciao!"

"Arrivederci."

Terza's fingers hovered over the phone after she ended the call. She knew her sister was probably busy getting ready for work but took the chance and pressed her number.

"Hey, you!" Angeline answered. "Good morning."

"Hi, Ange. Good morning."

"What's up?"

"Nothing. I just got off the phone with Mom and wanted to say hi to my favorite sister."

"You sound like Papa! You know I am your *only* sister."

"Ahh, but you are still my favorite. Are you off to work?"

"Yes, very soon. I have a meeting this morning."

"Make sure you keep that law firm in line," Terza said. "I am going to be in your area this afternoon."

"What's going on?"

"We are catering an afternoon board meeting down on Sixth."

"That's just two streets over. Did you say that you're catering a board meeting?"

"Yes, it's an executive board meeting. Why?"

"Wow, that must be nice," Angeline commented. "We're lucky to get coffee at our meetings."

"Well, I better let you go. Love you, sis."

"Love you too!"

Terza realized she had better hurry. She rapidly showered and dressed in casual shorts and a T-shirt. Before heading to their catering job, she and Moheenie would be changing into their Macaroni on Wheels uniforms.

A few minutes before eight in the morning, Terza unlocked the front door of her business. She went into the kitchen and immediately reached for her apron. As she tied the strings, Moheenie entered.

"Good morning."

"Good morning, Mo. Thanks for coming in early."

"No problem at all." Moheenie put on her apron. "What shall we start on first?" she asked while securing the strings.

"I think the two lasagnas for tomorrow. We need to be downtown today, and completely set up by three-thirty. That means we should leave here no later than two-thirty."

"Do you think we need an entire hour?"

Terza shrugged. "I don't know. It is a bit much, but I would rather be early than late. I just hate to feel rushed."

"You're right. Two thirty it is. That means we had better begin preparing our trays an hour before."

"Exactly. Let's work until one-thirty and then switch to the trays. We have to remember to change though."

"We can take turns changing right before it's time to go," Moheenie suggested.

"Perfect," Terza said. "Let's do this."

Terza and Moheenie worked in syncopated cadence as they methodically prepared the two lasagna dishes. Moheenie took the lead on the meat sauce, while Terza focused on the chicken. They ate yogurts for lunch and only stopped for potty breaks.

By 2:20 p.m., everything for the board meeting was prepared, and they had changed into their uniforms. At 2:30 p.m., the van was loaded, and they were pulling out of the driveway. By quarter past three, the catering duo stood in the boardroom waiting for their guests. They were back in their van before the clock turned four.

Terza sat at the wheel and looked over to Moheenie. "Wow! What a day."

"You're telling me. At least we got a lot done."

"Do you want to run by the craft store?" Terza asked.

Moheenie's smile grew brighter. "So we can buy our murder board?"

Terza returned the smile. "Of course. Plus, I have a fifty percent off coupon." She started the engine. "Let's go!"

"We better be careful and not tell anyone. I don't think they would understand."

"I agree. It's the mystery we enjoy, not the fact that poor Doctor McCool is dead."

The craft store was located beyond Little Italy, closer to the airport. The end-of-day rush hour traffic slowly began to build, with less than an hour until it boiled. Terza pulled into the parking lot, selected a space, and turned off the engine. They exited the van and headed straight for the store.

Inside, Moheenie made her way directly to the whiteboards.

"What happened? Did you study the floor plan last night?" Terza teased.

"Don't be silly. I was in here the other day and just remembered seeing them."

"Why were you here?" Terza narrowed her eyes.

"Why not? I had a coupon, too."

"Uh-huh." Terza faked suspicion. "And what did you buy?"

Moheenie moved her face just inches from Terza. "Ribbon, if you must know." Moheenie picked up one of the boards. "What do you think? Is it big enough?"

Terza studied the size. "Is it three by five?"

"I think so," Moheenie answered while looking for the size. "I don't see any markings."

"Don't you think twenty-two dollars is a bit high?"

"Yes and no. Whiteboards are expensive. Plus, it is really only eleven with the coupon. I say we get it."

"You're right." Terza looked through the stack of boards and selected the best one. She handed it to Moheenie.

While they made their way to the register Moheenie passed the board back to Terza and reached into her purse. "Here's my half," she said, handing Terza seven dollars. "This should also cover the tax."

"Thank you, but put that away, Mo. This is a business expense."

"It's a murder board, Tee."

"Yes, but once we figure out who did it, this will be a great backup for our menu board."

"Are you sure?"

"Yes, I'm positive."

With the new whiteboard bought and paid for, Terza handed Moheenie the keys to unlock the van's side door. She slid it onto the seat just as her phone rang.

"It's Nico!"

"What are you waiting for? Answer it!"

She swiped the green light to the right. "Hello."

"I thought you answered, 'Macaroni on Wheels'?"

"Not when I see who is calling."

"You knew it was me?"

"Of course, detective. I programmed your number in case I lost your card."

"I see. Is that an honor to be in your phone?"

"Am I in yours?"

Nico laughed loudly. "It's a possibility."

"Now what can I do for you?"

"It's what I can do for you. I promised to keep you in the loop if you stayed out of trouble. Have you bothered any more suspects?"

"Have I bothered any more suspects?" Terza repeated his question for Moheenie's benefit. "Of course not. I have been much too busy at work." She struggled to keep a straight face as she watched Moheenie shake with laughter.

"Alright then, I can tell you that Rose McCool has an alibi."

"What kind of alibi?"

"She was at the gym. And yes, before you ask, we checked with the gym, and she scanned her card."

Terza narrowed her eyes with suspicion. "What's the name of the gym?"

"I believe it's called The Seaside Gym," Nico said.

"The Seaside Gym?" Terza looked at Moheenie. They both realized it was the same gym where Moheenie's sister-in-law, Sage, worked. Now anxious to end her call, Terza rushed to ask, "Did you ask her about the missing meat?

"No, I haven't spoken to Rose McCool personally yet. I just finished talking with the detective who interviewed her."

"Well, okay then," Terza hoped to sound disappointed.

"You don't have to say it. I will talk to her."

"Soon?"

"Yes, soon. I want to solve this case more than you do," Nico told her.

"It doesn't seem like it."

"Hey! Be nice, or I'm going to stop sharing with you."

"I'm sorry, Nico. Truly, I am sorry." She winked at Moheenie.

"Well, you should be."

"I've got to run, but thanks for calling me."

"Ciao," Nico said.

"Ciao."

Terza looked at her phone to make certain she had successfully ended her call. Then, to be safe, she placed the phone in her purse.

"What are you doing?"

"Making certain Nico cannot hear us. We have *got* to call Sage!"

Moheenie held her phone up as she scrolled through her contacts. "I'm already dialing." She pressed the speaker button and held the phone between them.

"Hi, Mo!" Sage answered.

"Hey, honey. I'm here with Terza. You're on speaker."

"Hi, Terza. How are you?"

"I'm doing great. Thank you. How are you, Sage?"

"Just fine. Thanks! So what's up?"

Terza looked around at the busy parking lot and realized they might be overheard. "Hang on a second, Sage. I think we'll have more privacy in the van." She walked around to the driver's side and climbed in. By this time, Moheenie was also seated with her door closed. Moheenie's phone rested in the center console.

"Thanks for waiting, Sage. We're back," Moheenie said.

"This all sounds like cloak-and-dagger. What's going on?" Sage asked.

"Do you still work at The Seaside Gym?" Terza asked.

"Yes, I'm here now and just ready to begin my shift."

"That's great!" Terza responded. "So let me ask you something. Do you have surveillance cameras?"

"Yes, definitely," Sage said.

"Are the cameras also at the front?"

"Terza, we have cameras everywhere except the locker rooms. Why do you ask?"

"I'll let Moheenie fill you in on everything later, but right now we need to know if you can check something for us. Do you have access to the recordings?"

"I don't, but I know who does. It's Barney, and he'll definitely help me out. Just tell me what time, what day, and who."

"The day is last Saturday. As far as the time, I'm not sure. Supposedly, a woman by the name of Rose McCool went to the gym that day," Terza said.

"Rose McCool? I know Rose."

"Sage, that's great! Are you certain it is the same Rose McCool?" Moheenie asked.

"We only have one member named Rose McCool," Sage told her. "She's very nice and recently divorced."

Terza and Moheenie both nodded. "That's her," Terza said.

"I feel kind of sorry for her. From the first day she started coming, Rose has been trying to lose the same fifteen pounds. Instead of being happy with her progress, she always seems to blame her weight on any problem that comes her way."

"How do you know so much about her?" Moheenie asked.

"What can I say? She likes me and always comes up to talk. Did you want me to look and see what time she scanned her membership card?"

"Yes, please," Terza answered. "But if you can, we would like you to track her movements. We want to make certain she didn't just scan her card and then leave shortly thereafter."

"Why would she do that?" Sage asked.

"To kill her husband," Moheenie said.

"Doctor McCool is dead?" Sage seemed surprised.

"Yes, he died on Saturday," Moheenie told her.

"Holy smokes! Okay, let me get to work, and I will talk with Barney just as soon as I can. I'll give you a call the moment I have an answer."

"Thank you, Sage. You're a doll," Moheenie said.

"Yes, thank you Sage," Terza echoed. "We're really grateful."

"No problem at all. I've got to go."

"Bye!" Terza and Moheenie both said before Moheenie ended the call. She looked to Terza. "Wow! We might have some progress."

"I know! Let's get going so we can begin working on our board."

Back in the Macaroni on Wheels Kitchen, Terza placed their new whiteboard on the counter while Moheenie secured a black marker. "You can do the honors," she said, handing the marker to Terza.

"Let's see, our first subject is Alan Mann." Terza printed his name.

"And also Caroline Mann," Moheenie spoke while Terza made a column for the second name.

On top of the third column she printed Henry Follett's name, then looked to Moheenie. "We are listing Rose McCool, aren't we?"

"Of course we are!"

Terza printed Rose McCool's name. "Okay, we have four suspects, so now let's talk about motive. What is Alan Mann's?"

"He lost his job," Moheenie told her. "Losing a job means losing money, and money is always a motive."

"I agree," Terza said as she continued printing. "Caroline Mann actually has the same motive as her husband. When he lost money, so did she. Plus, we can add love to the equation. The love she has for her husband could have caused her to want revenge."

"You're right about that, Tee. Love could also be the motive for Henry Follett. He loved Rose McCool and could not stand to see her so upset," Moheenie said.

"Yes, but I think he also has another motive. What if Henry Follett wanted to get Doctor McCool out of the picture? That way, she would be free to marry him."

"But Rose McCool was already free to marry Henry Follett," Moheenie reminded. "Wasn't their divorce final?"

"Yes, she was free on paper, but I mean free emotionally," Terza explained. "Henry probably knew that Rose was still in love with her husband."

"Good point. Write that down."

Terza printed motive phrases under Henry Follett's name. First she wrote the phrase, *in love with Rose*, followed by the phrase, *he wanted Dr. McCool out of the way*. She looked up at Moheenie. "Remember, he also might have the missing meat."

"Yes, write that down too."

Terza then wrote, *may have missing meat*.

"What about the motives for Rose?" Moheenie asked. "Are we listing love as her motive?"

"Most definitely, one of her motives is love, but we should also add jealousy. I actually think jealousy is a stronger motive," Terza said.

She wrote while Moheenie spoke. "You're right. If we are correct in assuming Rose was jealous of Doctor McCool's new life, then that jealousy coupled with her love for him might make her our number one suspect."

"She also could have taken the missing meat," Terza said. She added it to the column under Rose McCool's name. "We still need to find out about the gym. Hopefully, Sage will call us soon."

"I can't wait any longer," Moheenie said while reaching for her phone. "Let's call her."

Terza watched Moheenie listen and then disconnect the call.

"It went straight to voicemail." Moments later Moheenie's phone rang. "It's Sage!" she told Terza then answered. "Hi Sage, do you have any news?" Moheenie nodded and said, "Okay, thank you. I will let Terza know."

Terza tapped her tennis shoe on their tiled kitchen floor as she waited for Moheenie to end the second call. "What did she say?"

"Barney is not in today, and she doesn't dare ask the other security guard."

"Darn!" Terza moaned. "Will he be in tomorrow?"

"Yes, and Sage is working too. She said we should know something tomorrow before the end of the day."

"Okay, I guess we have no choice but to wait." She looked up at their kitchen cat clock. "It's just before six. Do you want to call it a night?"

"Yes, I better get home." Moheenie walked toward the white catering board hanging on the wall. After reading it, she said, "We are almost ready for tomorrow's bridal shower, so that should be easy."

"I agree. Friday is going to be the hardest day."

"Speaking of whiteboards..." Moheenie tapped the side of the board. "You better hide our new one."

"I'm on it!" Terza lifted the white murder board and carefully slid it between the two refrigerators. She then wrapped an arm tenderly around Moheenie's shoulders. "Thanks for a great day. Have a good night."

"You too, Tee. Goodbye."

"Ciao."

Terza remained in the kitchen while Moheenie left through the front office door. It was too early to head home, and she was not quite ready for dinner. She almost felt lost, not knowing what to do next.

"That does it," Terza spoke aloud. "I'm going to see my mom."

She locked both the front and back doors and then used the adjoining door to enter the Tiepolo Mercato.

"Hi, Papa!" Terza greeted her father with a wave.

"*Buona sera*, my little gnocchi," Ezio called from behind the meat counter. "What are your plans for this fine evening?"

"I'm just cutting through," Terza told him with a laugh.

"Cutting through? That must mean you are on the way to visit your mother. Am I right?"

"You are right, Papa," Terza told him. "Will you be home soon?"

"I will be home very soon. I am leaving in thirty minutes."

"Great! I'll see you then."

CHAPTER ELEVEN: MOTHER-DAUGHTER BONDING

Terza walked out the front glass door of the Tiepolo Mercato, crossed the sidewalk, and then carefully dodged traffic to cross over Little Italy's main street to her parent's home.

Using her keys, she first unlocked the front gate and then the house. "Hi, Mom, it's me!" No answer. Terza moved through her childhood home, checking each room as she continued to call out. "Mom, are you home?" After searching the entire house, she scolded herself for not checking the backyard first. Terza went through the kitchen and out the back door. When she stepped onto the rear concrete patio, Terza saw her mom crouched over a bed of herbs. "Hello there."

Benedette turned. "Hello, my love."

Terza joined her mother in front of the herb garden. "I don't know why I looked for you in the house. I should have checked out here first," she said, giving her mother a quick hug. "So how was your class? Did you teach them everything you know?" Terza asked with a chuckle.

Benedette laughed while she straightened and slapped the soil from her pink gardening gloves. "Quite the opposite. Believe it or not, I learned a great deal today."

"That's good news, but I do find it hard to believe." Terza took a step back, placing both hands on her hips. "Only you, Mom, can look adorable while gardening."

"Adorable? You do realize I am wearing overalls, don't you?"

"I can see that," Terza said. She surveyed her mother's gardening attire. "You are wearing denim overalls and a red T-shirt, and just like I said, you look adorable."

Benedette smiled. "I do not agree, but thank you, sweet daughter. Now, to what do I owe the pleasure of this unexpected visit?"

Terza shrugged. "We finished our afternoon catering job, and my prep work is all caught up."

"Does that mean you are staying for dinner?"

"That depends. What are you having?" Terza muttered. They both knew she would say yes no matter what Benedette answered.

"Didn't you see the large bunch of fresh basil in the kitchen?"

"I did not, but let me guess. Are you making pesto?"

Benedette nodded. "Doesn't it sound perfect for a summer day?"

"Yum-o! No wonder I didn't smell anything cooking. Of course I'm staying for dinner."

"I had a feeling you might." Benedette smiled warmly at her daughter, then paused for a moment. "Tell me what is bothering you, my love?"

"Bothering me? Nothing is bothering me," Terza said, biting her lip. "Why do you ask?"

"Because I see the joy in your face, but I can sense the sadness in your heart."

Terza lowered her eyes and waited to respond. She blinked in a futile attempt to stop the tears. Instead, they pooled behind her eyelids.

Benedette drew her close. "Tell me, my love. What is it?"

Terza pushed away to wipe her eyes. "This is so silly," she said between a combination of laughter and tears. "Deep down, I knew it was bothering me, but I can't believe you could possibly tell."

"I'm your mother," Benedette told her. "I know things."

"You seem to know things about me that I don't even know. Mom, it's just..." She stopped talking and exhaled loudly. "Moheenie leaves work and goes home to Ranger. You and Papa leave work and are together every night. I leave work and go home to an empty house."

"You have Olive," Benedette reminded her.

"I know, and don't get me wrong. I love Olive. But it's not the same."

"Of course it's not," Benedette said. "I'm just trying to cheer you up."

"I want to be married, Mom," Terza spoke suddenly. "I want to fall in love again, and I desperately want to be married."

"I thought you were determined never to fall in love again?"

"Well, I lied.... mostly to myself. Did you really think I planned to stay single all of my life?"

"No, but I knew only you would know when the time is right. You were hurt and needed time to heal." Benedette took Terza's hand and pulled her toward the covered patio. "Come, let's sit."

Terza dragged an orange wrought iron chair out from under the matching table while her mother did the same. They both sat on the orange-and-white striped, sailcloth chair pillows.

"I don't think you want to get married just for the sake of marrying," her mother said.

Terza rested her elbows on the glass tabletop. "You're right. I don't. I just feel like such a loser at times."

Benedette laughed aggressively. "You have got to be kidding! How can you possibly feel like a loser when you have accomplished so much at such a young age? You are barely twenty-three years old, and you own a successful business!"

"I know, Mom, and I don't mean to complain. I wonder if I am just frustrated with how pathetically I am acting right now?"

"What do you mean?"

Terza clasped her hands together. "Every time I meet a somewhat interesting guy, I tend to overanalyze whether he could be the one. It's pitiful, Mom!"

"It's not pitiful if you are the only one who knows." Benedette tilted her head. "Why do you think you overanalyze the situation?"

"Because I know that deep down inside, I want to be married. It's just stupid."

"I don't think you should be in a rush, honey. When you find the right man, you will know it."

"So that means Nico can't possibly be the right man because I don't know how I feel?"

"Hang on a second. Who is Nico?"

"Nico is the detective working on the murder of my client, Doctor McCool."

"And you like this Nico?" Benedette pressed.

"That's my point, Mom. I don't know how I feel, but yes, I am acting pathetic once again. When I see him, I can't help but wonder if he could be the one. Why can't I just live my life one day at a time?"

"Honey, I am not talking about love at first sight. Nico might be the one, and he might not. When and if he is, you will know it. I was friends with your father before we fell in love. If you remember my stories, I dated your father's best friend."

Terza finally cracked a smile. "Yes, I do remember."

"Besides, I thought Conner was joining us for family dinner."

"He is, and that is another problem. Conner is so sweet it's ridiculous, and I think he likes me enough to have a serious relationship. So what do I do?" Terza flipped her hands into the air. "Every time I see him, I wonder if I should give it a try."

"Absolutely you should not." Benedette sounded firm. "You will know when it is right, Terza. You have to stop trying to plan the future of your love life and allow it to simply happen."

"What love life? I don't have one!"

"Exactly," Benedette told her. "You do not have one right now, so just let it be. Enjoy your time with Conner, and then enjoy your time with Nico. You will know when and if either one of these young men is right for you. If not, you will find someone else."

"But when will that be?" Terza pressed.

"I don't know, my love. But here is what I do know. You have a wonderful life, a great family, and a fantastic job. You have your health, for which you should be extremely grateful, especially when so many others are suffering. You must thank God for your many blessings, Terza."

"I know, Mom," Terza said, her shoulders slumping. "Now I feel like crap for complaining."

"Who is complaining about what?" Ezio asked as he stepped out onto the patio.

Benedette stood. "We are complaining." She kissed her husband on each cheek. "About you," she teased.

"Me?" Ezio looked surprised.

"Yes, about you taking your sweet time. We're starving!" Benedette turned her head to wink at her daughter.

Ezio checked his watch. "I'm not late. Besides, it doesn't smell like we are having dinner."

"Then that means more pesto for me," Terza joked.

Ezio's eyes widened. "We're having pesto? I love your pesto."

"I know you do," Benedette told her husband. "Terza, if you would please put a pot of water on the stove, I will run and change."

"What should I do?" Ezio looked between them.

"Wash up and set the table for three."

Ezio smiled at Terza. "Three it is! What a treat, having dinner with my little gnocchi on a weeknight. No hot date?"

Terza shook her head. "No hot date. Ha! I don't even have a not-so-hot date. In fact, I have no date at all!"

Ezio wrapped his arm around Terza's waist. "Just the way I like it."

"Papa, if you had your way, I would never get married."

"That's not true," he argued.

"Isn't it?"

Ezio lowered his eyes. "Well, maybe a little. I am fine if both of my girls remain single."

"Ange might not be ready to get married, but I am really starting to think about it," Terza told him.

"And who is the lucky man?"

"That's the problem," she said. "I don't know."

CHAPTER TWELVE: WAITING GAME

Thursday

Moheenie parked her Jeep just as Terza was unlocking the back door at Macaroni on Wheels.

"Good morning," she said while getting out.

"Good morning, Mo. Did you sleep well?"

"Like a baby." Moheenie wrinkled her nose. "Why do people say that?"

Terza shrugged. "I don't know, but maybe because babies sleep a lot."

"But do they really?" Moheenie asked. "All of the babies I know are up for a feeding every few hours."

"You're right. So how did you sleep?" Terza snickered.

Moheenie looked to the sky for her answer. "I slept like a bear in hibernation."

"Well, I'm glad you woke up! Come on, girlfriend." Terza wrapped an arm around the back of Moheenie's neck. "Let's get this party started."

Moheenie hung her bag onto a large hook in the kitchen and then retrieved her apron. She tied the knots while reviewing the whiteboard of recipes. "Do you think the lasagna will stay nice and hot in our warming bag?"

"I do, but I also had an idea to run by you." Terza put on her apron and reached for the long strings. "Since the office building is just down the street, why don't we put the lasagna in the oven right before we leave? It will take us under ten minutes to get there and say another fifteen minutes to unload. I can come back for the lasagna. It should be a perfect temperature by the time we serve it."

"That sounds like a great plan. Good idea, Tee."

"Thanks, Mo."

The ladies worked nonstop until 11:00 a.m. Before leaving for the luncheon, they took a quick break and enjoyed peanut butter and jelly sandwiches. Terza finished chewing and sipped her milk. "Do you think we should call Sage when we return?"

"Yes definitely. I don't know why she hasn't called yet." Moheenie nodded toward the oven. "What time are you going to start the lasagna?"

"Right at eleven-thirty. I had better preheat the oven." Terza walked over and turned the knob to 350 degrees. "Okay, it's time to start loading."

"The shower begins at one, is that correct?"

"Yes, and they want to eat first, before opening the presents. I think they purposefully planned lunch a bit later than normal. The office manager knew she would have a hard time getting everyone back to work after the shower."

"Are they having alcohol?"

Terza laughed. "I'm not sure, but you know how office parties can get."

"Do I ever!" Moheenie joined in the laughter. "Do you remember that luncheon we catered last year?"

"The one when all of the executives returned from golfing?"

"That's the one. I don't know why they even bothered coming back to work," Moheenie said.

"I think just to eat!" Terza added.

"I think it was just the next stop on a long night ahead."

Terza nodded. "You are probably right. It's a good thing we didn't supply all of that alcohol."

"It's a very good thing."

After loading the catering van, Terza drove them to the downtown office building less than ten blocks away. She parked the van in the delivery zone, then walked over to the attendant's booth.

"Good afternoon," she said to the elderly man.

"Good afternoon, young lady. You cannot leave your van there," he warned.

"I know," Terza said with a smile. "I will be moving it the moment we unload. That is what I came to tell you."

"That was very nice of you." The man snorted. "Most people just park and run."

Terza crossed her heart. "Never, ever would I do that to you."

By the time Terza returned to the van, Moheenie had unloaded their collapsible rolling cart and was busy loading the plastic food bins. "Is it okay to park here?"

"Just while we unload," Terza said. "I'll park in the garage when I return." She looked at the contents on the cart and completed a mental inventory. "It looks like we are good to go. Let's get this party started!"

"Let's do this," Moheenie said while taking the silver cart handle. Terza grabbed hold of the other side, and together they rolled the cart through the front lobby door.

Once upstairs, they located the suite and greeted their contact. Terza left Moheenie to set up while she returned to retrieve the waiting lasagna. She arrived at their kitchen with ten minutes left on the oven timer.

"Hmm," Terza murmured aloud. On a specific mission, she opened a storage cabinet and removed a package of small, brown unmade boxes. She withdrew one from the stack, formed it into a box, and tucked in the tabs. Terza then went to the refrigerator and selected a chocolate cannoli. She wrapped the dessert in parchment paper and carefully lowered it into the box. After closing the lid, Terza placed a Macaroni on Wheels sticker on the top and tied it with red twine. She smiled to herself as the oven timer chimed.

A short while later, Terza rolled the van into the same parking spot as before. She left the lasagna in the back and walked toward the guard booth.

"You still cannot park there," he warned.

"I wouldn't think of it." Terza laughed. She held out the dessert box. "I hope you like chocolate cannoli."

"Did you say cannoli?" His eyes widened. "Did you say chocolate cannoli?"

Terza thought the man might faint. "Yes, it's homemade." She pushed the box closer. "Take it."

He accepted the box and stood there speechless.

"Do you like cannoli?" Terza asked, feeling a bit concerned.

The man finally blinked. "My mama used to make cannoli every Sunday, and chocolate cannoli is my favorite. How did you know?"

"Well, I didn't know, but I am thrilled it's your favorite. I have to run, but please enjoy." She turned and walked toward the van.

"Miss!" the man called out to her.

Terza looked over her shoulder. "Yes?"

"There is no need to move the van. You can park there, and I'll watch it for you."

"Why thank you!" Terza said. "Thank you very much!" She unloaded the lasagna trays onto a second rolling cart while smiling brightly. *Mama was right. It pays to be polite.*

Minutes later, she joined Moheenie in the small kitchen area of the office suite. "How are we doing?" Terza asked.

"Everything is going perfectly so far," Moheenie said. "I just served the antipasto salads and left the two trays on the table."

"I think that was the best idea. At least you hand served them, but now each person can select extra of their favorite items."

Moheenie nodded. "Shall we begin plating the lasagna?"

"Yes, it should be at a perfect temperature for slicing. Let's go slowly and take two of each type into the conference room. After we pass them out we can come back for more. That way, people do not feel rushed if they are still enjoying their antipasto salad."

Moheenie and Terza each lifted a tray of lasagna from the cart and began slicing it into generous-sized portions. "What about the garlic bread?" Terza asked.

"It's already in a basket on the table." Moheenie suddenly laughed. "I barely had time to set the basket of bread down before the first person dug in."

"Isn't that always the case with garlic bread? It's the least expensive item on our menu and the most popular."

"Oh, by the way," Moheenie said. "Barney is sick."

"Who's Barney?"

"You know, he's the security guard at Sage's gym."

"That's right," Terza remembered. "Oh no, he's sick?"

"Yes, and Sage is not certain how long he will be out."

"Darn!"

"Double darn!" Moheenie added.

Armed with one chicken and one meat lasagna each, the ladies entered the conference room and began offering lasagna.

"Wow!" one of the male guests exclaimed after taking a bite. "This is the best lasagna I have ever eaten."

"Why thank you," Terza said.

"Did you make it from scratch?" he asked.

Terza laughed. "Of course we did. Moheenie and I make everything from scratch."

Moheenie smiled. "It's Terza's recipe. I just help out."

"Well, it is fantastic," he said.

"Thank you again." Terza grinned. "We will be right back with more."

After they left the room, Moheenie commented, "That was nice."

"It sure was. All in all, today has been a good day."

"A good day, with the exception of Barney," Moheenie added.

"Yes, except for Barney."

CHAPTER THIRTEEN: DINNER PARTY

Friday

With coordinated movements, Moheenie and Terza chopped, cooked, mixed, and pressed the Sartù di Riso ingredients into the three separate Bundt pans. "How can you remember all of the steps?" Moheenie asked Terza. "You haven't looked at a single recipe since we started."

Terza shrugged. "I don't know. It just all makes sense to me."

"You are amazing, Tee."

"No, you are amazing for learning so quickly. We are going to make a professional chef out of you yet!"

"Are we baking the dishes here or at the catering job?"

"We need to bake them at the home of our client." Terza wiped her hands down the front of her apron and then reached for the computer tablet at the far end of the kitchen counter. She scrolled through, searching for the catering page for this evening. Reading, she said, "The guests will begin arriving at six. Our hostess would like cocktail hour without the appetizers from six until six-thirty. At six-thirty, she would like us to pass the bruschetta."

"When are we making that?" Moheenie asked.

"We will have everything ready and then just assemble the bruschetta right as the guests arrive."

Moheenie nodded her head. "That should work perfectly."

"By the way," Terza added, "our client's name is Gretchen Sinclair. I already asked, and she prefers that we call her Gretchen."

"Then Gretchen it is."

"Okay, back to the schedule." Terza looked at her tablet screen. "The guests are to be seated at seven, and we will serve the petite salad wedges. We can add the dressing and candied nuts as they are enjoying the bruschetta."

"What time should we put the Sartù Di Riso in the oven?"

"I need to calculate this backwards. The earliest we will serve the main dish is seven-twenty, and the Sartù Di Riso needs to rest for at least thirty minutes."

"So it needs to come out of the oven at ten minutes before seven," Moheenie said. "How long does it take to cook?"

"Fifty minutes," Terza told her. "That means we need to place the Sartù Di Riso into the oven at exactly six o'clock, right?"

Moheenie laughed. "My brain must be fried because this is simple math, and I still have to think about it! Yes, six it is."

"Great. Will you please set an alarm on your phone for six?"

Moheenie wiped her hands then reached for her phone. "You got it." She set the alarm. "What about the Tiramisu?"

"We are working on that next."

Moheenie glanced at the kitchen wall clock. "Our cat clock says it's twelve-thirty so we better hustle."

"Ranger is still coming at three-thirty, right?"

"Yes, and what time are we leaving?"

"I would like to be out the door by four. Gretchen lives in Point Loma, and it could take us up to twenty-five minutes with Friday night traffic. We need at least an hour and a half to set up."

"That sounds good to me." When Moheenie's phone rang, her sister-in-law's name flashed across the screen. "It's Sage!" she blurted out.

Before Moheenie answered, Terza's phone also rang. "I

can't believe it. It's Nico." Terza lifted her phone. "You talk to Sage, and I'll talk to Nico in the office."

"Hi, Nico."

"Hi, Terza. Are you busy?"

"I am crazy busy. We are catering a dinner party tonight."

"Oh that's right. You are making that special rice dish."

"Sartù Di Riso," Terza said.

"I won't keep you," Nico told her, "but I might have found your missing meat."

"You did? Who took it?"

"We're not positive, but maybe the wife, Rose McCool."

"What makes you say that she *maybe* took it?"

"Well, I haven't asked her directly, but we know she was cooking beef stew," Nico said.

"She was making beef stew? When and how do you know that?"

"Another detective interviewed Rose on the day after the murder," Nico explained. "When we were talking about the case just a few moments ago, I happened to mention the missing meat. That's when he told me Rose might have it, as she was making beef stew."

Terza's mind raced. "Who makes beef stew in the summer?"

"Don't ask me. You're the chef."

"I can tell you that most people do not make stew in the summer. The house would heat up because it takes time to simmer the ingredients properly, and stew typically calls for root vegetables. They are at their peak in the winter."

Nico chuckled. "Good to know!"

"So when are you going to see her?" Terza asked.

"Maybe tomorrow, but I'm not sure."

"Will you let me know?"

"Of course I will. Have a fun party," Nico said.

"We're not going to the party. We are working the party," Terza explained.

"You can still have fun."

"I guess you're right. Thanks for calling."

"Ciao."

"Ciao."

Terza returned to the kitchen as Moheenie was ending her call. "Rose McCool left," Moheenie announced.

"What do you mean she left?"

"She left the gym!" Moheenie shrieked. "You have got to call Nico. Rose scanned her card, went into the locker room, and then immediately came out! She was at the gym for less than five minutes, Terza! She does not have an alibi, Tee."

"She was also making beef stew."

"Beef stew? What are you talking about?"

"Nico just told me that Rose was making beef stew on the day after the murder. He hasn't checked yet, but Nico thinks she might have taken the missing meat."

"Doctor McCool probably gave it to her," Moheenie suggested.

"Maybe, but what if it happened another way?"

"What do you mean?"

Terza narrowed her eyes. "What if Doctor McCool asked Rose to take the meat, and she got mad?"

"Why would she get mad?"

"She might get mad because she knew he was trying to make room in his freezer for the party."

"You're right." Moheenie nodded. "When Nico questions her about the meat he should also ask her about the gym."

"I'm not going to tell him yet," Terza spoke matter-of-factly.

Moheenie's eyes ballooned.

"Don't give me that look, Mo! We are the ones who found out about Rose leaving the gym. I am not ready to give up our leads just yet. I need to think about this, and right now, I don't have the time to think."

Moheenie raised her right hand. "Don't worry, I won't tell."

Terza laughed. "Good, now let's get busy on this Tiramisu."

The back door opened, and Ranger walked in just after 3:00 p.m. "Hello you two beautiful ladies," he said.

"Hi, honey." Moheenie walked toward her husband.

"Hi, Ranger," Terza said. "You are nice and early."

Moheenie kissed him. "You *are* early."

"I came early hoping for food. I need to eat before we leave."

"Look in the left refrigerator on the top shelf," Terza told him. "There is a sub with your name on it."

"You made him a sandwich?" Moheenie asked. "That was sweet!"

"Thank you, but I didn't. My pop made it for Ranger. He brought it over this morning before we even opened."

Ranger placed the wrapped sandwich on the kitchen counter. "I'll be right back."

"Don't stay and talk to him too long," Terza called as Ranger walked through the adjoining door to the Tiepolo Mercato.

"Your dad is very special, Tee," Moheenie said.

"Thanks, Mo. I know he is."

Moments later, Ranger returned, unwrapped his sandwich, and took a gigantic bite. "Yum, this is delicious," he said with a full mouth.

"My dad has always made a great sandwich," Terza said. She then turned to Moheenie. "We had better change."

"I take it we are wearing our dress uniforms?" Moheenie asked.

"Yes, they are laundered and in the bathroom closet. Why don't you get ready, and I'll be right there?"

Moheenie touched her head. "How should I wear my hair?"

"I think we should both go with low ponytails," Terza suggested.

"How should I wear my hair?" Ranger grinned.

Moheenie rubbed her hand over his shaved crew cut. "You are one funny guy, Ranger Brickman."

"Right back at you, Lakalaka."

After dressing, Moheenie returned wearing a crisp white shirt tucked into a black pencil skirt. The cute Macaroni on Wheels logo, a noodle with racing wheels and wearing a chef's hat, was embroidered on the shirt's left pocket. She also wore black ballet flats, and a black velvet ribbon secured her ponytail.

"You look cute," Ranger commented.

Moheenie half curtsied. "Thank you, honey. Okay, Terza, it's your turn."

"I'm going to load the van before I change," Ranger told them.

"I can show you where everything is," Moheenie offered.

"Are you sure I don't need anything for the bar?" he asked.

"Positive," Moheenie said. "We are in charge of bringing only the food tonight. Our hostess will be providing everything you will need for the bar."

"But what about the ice?" he teased. "Will she have enough ice?"

"I don't know." Terza chuckled. "But if not, that's her problem."

"Mark this day down in history," Ranger announced loudly. "Terza Tiepolo is not concerned with the amount of ice we have."

Terza shook her head and smiled as she left the room. She changed, pulled back her hair, and did a quick refresh of her makeup. While Ranger got ready, Terza and Moheenie checked and double-checked their supplies. As planned, they left by 4:00 p.m. and made it to the Sinclair home within a half-hour.

Terza first greeted her hostess and then introduced Gretchen to Moheenie and Ranger. As they were busy setting up for the dinner party, Gretchen pulled Terza aside.

"I am very sorry about Doctor McCool," she whispered.

"Did you know Mitchell McCool?"

"Not personally, but indirectly. One of my dinner party guests used to work with his neighbor," Gretchen told her.

Terza's mind instantly raced. "Do you know the neighbor's name?"

"No, he never said."

I bet it's Alan Mann.

"It was such a coincidence," Gretchen continued. "When you and I last spoke, you mentioned the unfortunate event. Since I did not know those involved I never brought it up. That is until I spoke with Faulkner, one of my guests. When he asked what he could bring to my party, I told him it was being catered, and his presence was all that mattered."

"That was a sweet reply," Terza said.

Gretchen smiled warmly. "Thank you, but on with the story. When I mentioned catering, Faulkner said that a caterer had just found a client dead."

"He knew about me?"

"Well, he knew about a caterer, but not specifically about you. Of course, I asked what he meant. Faulkner explained that his friend lived next door to a Doctor McCool who had been found dead by the caterer of his party."

"What a small world," Terza remarked.

"It definitely is. Of course I did not tell Faulkner that you were the same caterer, and hopefully it will not come up. We want to have a fun dinner party, and death is not a fun subject."

Terza nodded. "I will be certain not to mention a word."

"Thank you, Terza, but knowing Faulkner, he just might make a catering comment. That is why I wanted to give you a heads up."

"I understand. Please do not worry. I will be able to handle it."

"I knew you would," Gretchen said.

"Thank you." Terza clapped her hands together. "Now, I better get moving." She joined Moheenie in the kitchen and looked back to where Gretchen had stood. Through the window Terza could see that Gretchen was now outside.

"You are never going to believe this!" she whisper-shouted to Moheenie.

"Believe what?"

"One of the guests tonight knows Doctor McCool's neighbor. They used to work together."

"Which one?"

"His name is Faulkner, but I don't know if that is his first or last name," Terza said.

"Not which guest." Moheenie laughed. "Which neighbor?"

"Oh, I don't know, but we have got to find out."

"We have to be careful though," Moheenie warned.

"Of course we do! I would never act inappropriately, and we simply cannot jeopardize *MOW's* good name. But somehow, some way, we have got to find out which neighbor. It may give us another clue."

"I will keep my ears open," Moheenie said.

"Ears open for what?" Ranger asked from behind.

Terza and Moheenie both turned in surprise.

"Quit sneaking up on us!" Moheenie said. She looked around cautiously. "Where is Gretchen?"

"Outside picking flowers, so don't worry. Whatever you two are conniving is safe with me."

"We aren't conniving anything," Moheenie said.

Ranger laughed. "I don't know what it is, but I can guarantee you that it is something."

"Is your bar ready?" Terza asked, trying to sound firm.

"Yes, and quit trying to get rid of me."

Right at 6:00 p.m., the guests began arriving. Ranger served cocktails while Moheenie and Terza took coats and jackets.

They both listened for names, waiting not so patiently for Faulkner to arrive. Several men entered alone, and Terza had yet to hear all of their names.

Thirty minutes later Terza and Moheenie met in the kitchen to retrieve the bruschetta.

"Any luck?" Terza asked.

"Nothing yet, but look at the man who just walked in. He looks like a Faulkner," Moheenie said.

Terza looked up and saw an elegant-looking man shaking hands with another guest. The new arrival wore beige linen pants and a white linen shirt. His long sleeves were rolled to just below his elbows.

Terza chuckled. "He is dressed nicely, but why does he look like a Faulkner?"

"I don't know, Tee. He just looks kind of artistic, and the name Faulkner sounds artistic."

Terza tilted her head in thought. "I guess you're right." Armed with trays of bruschetta, Terza said, "Let's go find out." She walked slowly by the guests, offering each an appetizer, with the new arrival her specific destination. Terza stood face to face with him. "Would you like a bruschetta?" She extended the silver tray.

"Ah, a caterer," he said. "I was just going to ask if—"

Gretchen stepped next to the man and slid an arm around his. "Hello, Faulkner," she said, cutting his sentence short. "Welcome to my get-together. Please tell me you are not bothering the staff?"

"Of course I am not," he said with a wink while accepting the bruschetta.

Terza shot Gretchen a knowing smile and then moved to another guest. *Good job of guessing, Moheenie. We have our man!*

When all of the bruschetta appetizers were consumed, Terza and Moheenie returned to the kitchen. "You were right," Terza told Moheenie. "The new guest is Faulkner."

"Faulkner Baine," Moheenie announced.

"Faulkner Baine? So Faulkner is his first name. What a great job, Moheenie! How did you find out his last name is Baine?"

"I heard a male guest introduce him as Faulkner Baine to his wife."

"Did you hear anything else?"

"Not yet," Moheenie said. "But I'm on a roll, so watch out!"

They returned to the party area as Gretchen directed her guests to their seats. Terza and Moheenie made certain that each guest had a beverage, and then refilled water glasses as necessary. When they met again in the kitchen to retrieve the salad wedges, Moheenie's excitement finally burst.

"It's Alan Mann!" she proudly announced.

"How do you know that?" Terza asked. "We were almost side by side, and I didn't hear anything."

"I was directly behind Faulkner as he was walking to the table. It sounded like he was finishing up a conversation with another man. I heard him say something about golfing with Alan. He then ended by saying, 'Mann wasn't too happy about the funding. I wouldn't put it past him,' or something close to that."

"Do you think he was talking about the murder of Doctor McCool?"

"I can't be certain," Moheenie said. "But I think so. What else could it be?"

Terza and Moheenie each lifted a tray of salad wedges. "Let's go," Terza said. "Maybe we will hear something more."

The salad course led to the main course, followed by dessert. Terza and Moheenie busied themselves with the initial cleanup while Ranger continued making specialty coffee drinks.

"Ranger is such a cute barista, isn't he?" Terza asked.

"I think so," Moheenie looked to her husband. "But then, I am biased."

"Of course you are!" Terza leaned in to whisper, "We have to add this new information to our murder board."

"That's for sure! Now even Faulkner thinks Alan has a motive," Moheenie said.

"I still cannot stop thinking about Rose McCool though."

"We definitely have suspects," Moheenie commented.

"Good thing we have a place to write them." Terza grinned.

Moheenie raised her eyebrows and smiled. "Yes it is!"

The trio of caterers waited until the final guest left before packing up. The time neared 11:30 p.m., and they were all exhausted. Ranger drove them back to Macaroni on Wheels, where they had to unload and clean up even more. The clock struck 1:00 a.m. when Terza finally pressed the elevator button in her lobby. *Home.* She sighed.

After a quick shower and a little loving for Olive, Terza struggled to fall asleep. The gears of her mind continued to grind. Alan Mann was a definite suspect and even more so after hearing Faulkner's comments. But not once did Terza stop thinking about Rose McCool making beef stew. The thought had nagged her throughout the party and continued to nag her as she tossed and turned beneath the covers. Terza willed the morning to hurry and the Tiepolo Mercato to open. She needed to talk to a butcher, and fortunately there was one in the family.

CHAPTER FOURTEEN: BOVINE BONE

Saturday

Two more hours until the Tiepolo Mercato opened! Terza knew her father would come in early if she asked, which is why she didn't. Waiting gave her time to enjoy her morning coffee, read her Bible out on the balcony, and play with Olive. She telephoned her mother, took a shower, and was out the door by 8:30 a.m. Although the Tiepolo Mercato opened at 9:00 a.m., Terza's father typically arrived at least fifteen minutes before.

She walked from her condominium to the store, planning to wait outside the front door. Her wait proved almost nonexistent as Terza could see her father already leaving his house. He arrived within minutes.

"*Buon giorno*, my little gnocchi! Why didn't you wait inside?"

"I'm avoiding my office," she said, kissing his right cheek and then his left. Her father returned her kisses and then placed another kiss firmly on Terza's forehead.

"Why are you avoiding your office?" He unlocked the front door.

"Because I already have too much to think about, and right now, I need a butcher."

Ezio smiled. "I am a butcher," he announced proudly.

"There is none better. That's why I am here."

"Then don't stand outside. Come on in." Ezio held the door for her. "It's not nine so I won't open yet."

Terza walked inside so he could relock the door. "Don't you have any help today?"

"Of course I have help. Simon should be here any moment. Now, I know that you talked with your mother this morning, but did you read your Bible?"

"Yes, Papa, I did."

"Then you, Terza Tiepolo, are my favorite daughter," he told her while walking behind the butcher case. "Now, what can I do for you?"

Terza blew out a loud breath. "Papa, tell me something. Why would someone have a huge bone in their freezer?"

"Because they have a huge dog?" He laughed. "Is this supposed to be a riddle?"

Terza tsked twice. "No. I really need to know," she said while joining him behind the case. With palms facing in Terza spread her hands to an approximate shoulder's width. "The bone was about this big."

Ezio briefly studied the gap between Terza's hands and turned toward the wall opposite his glass meat case. A row of five chrome doors provided access to the built-in refrigerators behind.

Terza watched as her father placed his calloused fingers upon the shiny latch of the second cabinet. He pulled slightly, quickly changed his mind, and then opened the third door instead. After his torso disappeared behind the silver door, Terza could hear her father rummaging inside. Moments later, Ezio's head popped into view. And with a broad smile highlighting his pudgy face, he removed his surprise package.

"Was it like this?" Ezio held up a substantial-sized bone.

Terza's eyes widened. "Yes, it was exactly like that!" She reached for the caveman-style bone and closely examined the knobby ends. "This would make some weapon," she commented.

Her father's graying brow furrowed in mock concern. "Is there something I should know?"

"Ha! Papa, tell me." She handed him the bone. "Why would someone have a bone this size in their freezer?"

Ezio rested the bone on its wrapper to free his hands. He then grabbed his thigh to explain. "This particular bone is a femur, taken from the hindquarter of a cow. Now, I can't say for sure, but someone with a bone like this probably purchased a hindquarter of beef."

Terza's head bobbed in agreement. "That would make sense. Besides the bone, there were a bunch of white packages all wrapped inside plastic bags."

"Then that's what they did," Ezio confirmed. "I have a few, not many, but still a few customers that prefer to purchase the entire hindquarter."

Terza rubbed her forehead. "Why?"

Ezio directed her attention to a butcher's chart on the wall above the refrigerators. "It's simple." He pointed to the diagram. "Purchasing this section provides the customer with an assortment of steaks, such as porterhouses, filets, and T-bones. They end up with a variety of roasts and can request each selection cut specifically. And of course, there's always sirloin available for grinding."

"That's certainly a lot of meat!" Terza grimaced.

Ezio chuckled. "What's with the sour face? Customers do not eat it all at once," he explained. "It's for freezing."

"I would rather have fresh," she announced.

"Not everyone has the ability to simply walk next door and select the steak of his or her choice." Ezio gently squeezed his daughter's shoulder. "I think my little gnocchi is spoiled."

Terza lovingly placed her hand on top of his. "I am spoiled, and I think a certain butcher is to blame."

"Is it my fault that I have such a beautiful daughter?"

"You're too kind, Papa. And yes, as a matter of fact everything about me is your fault! It's your fault and Mom's fault, but I wouldn't have it any other way. I have the best parents on earth."

"Of course you do." Ezio winked.

Terza once again reached for the femur bone. "Tell me more about this bone. When someone orders a hindquarter, do you just automatically throw in this caveman artifact?"

"I have to admit that most customers ask me to saw the femur bone into several pieces because, of course, it is great for stew. Perhaps your friends really do have a dog," Ezio suggested. "An extremely large dog, or maybe even a lion!"

"I'm not sure about that, the dog part, but I don't think so." She held the bone high to visually measure its length. "I don't think this will fit into one of those large stock pots, do you?"

Ezio shook his head. "I don't think it will. That is why I am typically asked to saw the bones."

Ezio wrapped his arms around Terza as she leaned into his chest. She then lifted her face to kiss each of his cheeks. "Thanks, Papa," she said. "I've got to go."

Terza was halfway to the front door when her father called out. "You're taking my bone?"

"It's all right, isn't it?"

"Well, I don't know. You can take it only if you fill me in on this big mystery of yours."

"Papa," she pleaded while marching in place. "I really have to go. May I please, please tell you later?"

Terza closely watched his expression as he pretended to sound firm. "Are you still making us the Sartù Di Riso tonight, or are you too busy?" Although his smile was barely visible, the sparkle in her father's eyes exposed his humor.

"It's already made." Terza stood frozen in a *getaway* stance.

"Then you may take my bone," he said. "Let me unlock the door for you."

Terza waited while Ezio unlocked and opened the door. She then rushed out while saying, "I love you, Papa! And thanks!"

"Arrivederci," he called.

"Ciao, ciao!"

Terza looked down at her jean skirt and flip-flopped feet and instantly realized that a change of clothes was first on her list. She attempted to run home to her condo, but a fast walk was all that her tight, denim skirt would allow. And with her mind focused on a plan, Terza failed to recognize the entertainment value of her six-block walk home.

As Terza speed walked with flip-flops slapping wildly, she noticed more than one person stop to watch with amusement. Thinking that they were laughing at her bone, Terza lowered it to her side in a less conspicuous place.

"Hey, Pebbles!" Terza heard someone call. "Hey, Terza!" he called again.

Terza turned to see Romano, her favorite barista, standing on the opposite corner.

"Hi, Romano," she automatically used her bone to wave and then quickly lowered it.

"You look like Pebbles Flintstone," he called.

She wrinkled her nose. "Who?"

"You know, Pebbles Flintstone from *The Flintstones* cartoon. Don't you watch old cartoons?"

"Sometimes, but I like *The Jetsons*."

"Me too, but you better check out *The Flintstones*. You look just like Pebbles with your hair in that high ponytail and that huge bone."

"Is that why everyone is laughing at me?"

"Probably, because you are kind of a sight to see right now. Besides, what are you doing with that bone?"

"It's a long story, Romano. I'll have to catch you up another day at the coffee lounge."

"Okay, but come in soon. I have a feeling it's a story worth hearing."

"I will. Have a great day!"

"You too. Bye!" Romano called out.

"Ciao!"

In under a half-hour later, Terza stood in her bedroom and surveyed her image in the full-length mirror. She wore her one and only power suit, a black wool gabardine, over a crisp white shirt. "It looks like I am going to an interview," she said with a sigh.

Terza smoothed the sides of her hair and then turned to glance over her shoulder and check the back. Her ponytail was secured closely to her nape in a professional style. "This is it," Terza said. She exhaled loudly and lifted her soft-sided briefcase from the bedroom chair. Fortunately, when everything else had been removed, Terza was able to just fit the femur bone inside. Only the top peaked out.

She grabbed her keys, took the elevator down to the garage, and headed for her next stop, the medical examiner's office. Before changing, Terza had researched online and knew the address. She did not know the hours, if the office was open on Saturday, or even how to get in. Terza considered calling Nico but decided against it. She would reach out to him later if necessary. Now, she just had to give her idea a try.

After an approximate fifteen-minute drive, she parked in front of the three-story green stucco building and walked toward the door. Not knowing what to expect, Terza pushed through the single glass door and entered a dining-room sized reception area. She was instantly greeted by a robust-looking female who reminded Terza of a prison warden.

"May I help you?" the receptionist asked simultaneous to a ringing telephone. But before she could answer, the receptionist motioned with her hand for Terza to wait.

Terza did so, grateful for the time to quickly assess her options. There appeared to be only one door leading from the reception area, and she had no way of knowing if the door was unlocked.

"I'm sorry." Terza heard the receptionist say to her. "Now, how may I help you?"

"No, I'm sorry," Terza said as a plan of attack popped into her head. "Silly me, I left my identification in the car. I'll be right back."

The receptionist nodded while she answered another call.

Terza walked to her car and unlocked the trunk. Inside the zippered pouch of her lime green workout bag, Terza withdrew her gym membership card and clipped it to the bottom right side of her suit jacket. Then, to obscure a clear view, she blocked it with her briefcase. When Terza returned to the building, she stood off to the side of the glass door and waited. From the reflection in the glass, she was able to watch the warden.

After a few minutes, the receptionist answered several calls in a row and appeared to be busy. Terza made her move by rushing through the door as if late for an appointment. Once again, the receptionist motioned for her to wait.

"That's okay," Terza said. She flashed her badge from behind her briefcase while moving toward the lone door. "You're busy, and I know the way."

Terza turned the knob, pushed the door open, and passed through without making eye contact. As she quickly closed the door, Terza heard the receptionist call her back.

"Not a chance," Terza whispered under her breath. She hoped that the ringing telephones would prevent the receptionist from tracking her down.

As Terza hurried along the isolated corridor, the heels of her black pumps ricocheted upon the tile floor. Her priority was to walk as if she owned the place, but Terza could not help noticing the strange color combination of the square floor tiles. Alternating hues of light peach and grass green created a retro look. It seemed odd for a government office.

Once beyond the first corridor, Terza planned to catch her breath and formulate her next move. But after she made the turn, her mission was spelled out in bold letters on the double doors she faced. Without hesitating, Terza fearlessly pushed her way through to the medical examiner's office and instantly collided with a blast of putrid air.

"Who are you?" a man asked.

Terza heard the man's question but could not bring herself to answer. Instead, she stumbled forward and grabbed hold of the nearest chair.

"Breathe from your mouth." His voice was void of any sympathy.

When Terza did as he instructed, she could feel her head clear slightly.

"How did you get in here?" The man stood at an arm's length from her.

Terza parted her lips to explain when a sudden tug on her jacket pulled her toward him.

"What is this?" he yelled. "This is not proper identification. Who let you in with this fitness club badge?"

"I ... I," she stammered. Terza then rapidly decided to stand her ground. "Hey! Are you always this mean?"

A look of shock registered on the Medical Examiner's face. "You think I am mean?"

For the first time, Terza actually looked at the white-coated medical examiner. She guessed him to be pushing sixty, about five years older than her father, as his once-chiseled features had softened with age.

"You don't look mean." She noted the disheveled appearance of his white hair. "In fact, you look like a scientist."

He raised his chin proudly. "My wife thinks I look like a mad scientist."

"Well..." Terza chuckled. "You kind of do."

The mad scientist withdrew a small tin from the pocket of his lab coat, twisted off the top, and offered it to Terza. "Put some under your nose," he instructed. "It will help."

She gratefully accepted the tin, captured the balm with her finger, and dabbed it under her nostrils. Relief came instantly as Terza could now only smell the menthol. Feeling better, she watched as the medical examiner removed a pair of smudged reading glasses from his head and place them loosely upon the bridge of his nose. He bent at the waist to read her badge.

"Terza Tiepolo. What kind of name is Terza?"

"The kind my parents gave me."

"You, I like." His clipped words hinted at an accent. "You have spunk. What I don't like is strangers coming in here, especially when they are unannounced."

Terza noticed the warmness in his sea-green eyes contradicted the tight scowl on his face. "But I'm no longer a stranger," she said sweetly. Terza extended her palm. "It's nice to meet you, Mister..." She paused, waiting for his name.

He looked at her palm as if wondering why it was extended.

"Jacob," he said, pronouncing the *j* with a *y* sound. "It's a strong Biblical name," he added.

"I agree." She pushed her hand closer while spreading her fingers.

Jacob's warm hand finally intercepted hers. "Doctor Jacob Radovan."

"It is very nice to meet you, Doctor Radovan. And now, we are no longer strangers."

"However," he said, withdrawing his hand, "you do remain unannounced."

"I am very sorry. I do apologize. I was worried if I went through the proper channels, it might be too late."

"Go on then. Explain your logic to me."

Terza removed the bone from her bag.

"Nice femur bone," Radovan said. He took it and held it at eye level. "Bovine, I presume?"

She nodded. "Yes, a cow to be exact." Terza watched as Radovan visually examined the bone. "I am hoping this bone can help solve a murder," she said softly.

"How so?"

"You see, I am the one who found Doctor Mitchell McCool's body."

"I'm listening."

"Of course, I don't know how he died, but I do know a bone like this was in Doctor McCool's freezer the day before." She talked briefly about the hindquarter of beef in his freezer and ended her story by saying, "So you see, Doctor Radovan, when Detective Garza told me that Rose McCool was making stew, it finally hit me. I just couldn't get it out of my head that she was purposefully attempting to destroy the murder weapon."

Terza finished and waited for Radovan to respond. But instead of speaking, he closely analyzed the larger, knobbier end of the femur bone. He slowly rotated it while taking turns looking through and then above his glasses. "I think you've got something," he finally said. "You *do* have something! Wait here."

A jingling sound came from his pocket as Radovan rushed to the far end of the expansive room. The clinking stopped when he paused in front of a rolling metal table. Even from across the room Terza easily recognized the shape of a body beneath the green sheet. Still holding the bone in one hand, Radovan grabbed the sheet with the other. He looked up at Terza. "I think you should remain over there."

She cringed as he uncovered the head. "I think so, too."

Radovan brought himself eye level to closely reexamine the cranial contusions. Then, he used just the tips of his fingers to gently follow the outline of the femur joint. "I told them to look for a rounded weapon," he spoke softly to himself.

Terza saw the medical examiner suddenly lift the femur bone and then strike the air with a blow. He turned toward her, with the bone lifted like a torch. "Do you see this knobby end?"

Terza nodded. "I see it." She also saw his eyes darting wildly and decided to take another step backward. The space between them now exceeded twenty feet.

"It has the exact same rounded curves as the murder weapon." Radovan took another practice swing.

"What do you think?"

"I'll show you. Come, come." Radovan urged Terza with a wave as he scurried toward a collection of microscopes. His voice competed with the jingle of keys and a pocket obviously filled with loose change. "Come and see this."

Terza caught up to Doctor Radovan and then watched him confirm the label of a specific slide. He placed it under the scope and peered into the lens. With a complete change of subject, he said, "Your name, Terza. It's like third in Italian, as in the number three."

"Yes. I have two siblings, a brother and a sister."

"Do you have parents?"

Terza chuckled at his directness. "Yes, they are both alive and well and happily married."

With his head still facing down, Terza watched his lips curve into a slight smile. He looked up. "Let's see. You are the baby of the family, and I think perhaps you're spoiled."

Terza felt her face instantly flush. "You're very perceptive."

"That's my job." Radovan stepped aside. "Go ahead," he said, pointing to the microscope. "Take a look."

Terza could have been looking at anything. "All I see are some squiggly lines. What do you see?"

"I see something that just might prove your theory. Tell me. Was the bone you saw in the freezer wrapped in anything?"

Terza pulled away from the microscope to think. Then, after several long seconds, she said, "Why, yes, I remember that it was covered in plastic wrap."

"I haven't had time to complete my analysis, but I am quite certain that slide contains a piece of kitchen cling wrap. I discovered a microscopic piece in the victim's wound."

Terza's eyes widened. "You did? So what do we do now?"

"*We* do not do anything. You, Number Three, need to go."

"I need to go?"

"Yes, go." He pushed her gently toward the door. "I have a great deal of work, and time is of the absolute essence."

"But shouldn't we call Detective Garza?"

"Again, *we* should not, but I plan to telephone him right away."

"Please, please, please may I stay?" she begged, her hands in the prayer position.

Terza watched as Radovan stared blindly ahead. His prolonged stillness made her wonder if he had fallen asleep while standing. She thought about touching him, or calling his name but elected to simply wait out the silence. Finally, he spoke. "Thirty minutes."

"Thirty minutes what?"

"I will give you thirty minutes." Radovan moved toward the black telephone on his desk. When he lifted the receiver, he spoke before dialing. "I'll call Detective Garza. If he is here within thirty minutes, you can see him. One minute longer and you go."

"But what if he is on another case?"

"That is not my problem. Do you agree or do you not?"

Terza lowered her chin. "I agree. Thank you." She waited in quiet submission while Radovan dialed Nico's number.

"Good morning, Detective Garza. This is Jacob. I have a sweet young lady here in my lab. She has brought me something very interesting. It is about the McCool case, so I think you better come right away." Radovan looked directly at Terza. "Who is the young lady, you ask? I would say she is about five feet." Radovan hesitated.

Terza held up three fingers.

"She is five feet three inches tall," he said with authority, "and has dark brown hair and dark brown eyes." Radovan winked at Terza as he listened. "Is her hair long?" Radovan had obviously repeated Nico's question.

Terza turned to show him her ponytail.

"Yes. Her hair is long and filled with curls." He smiled. "Why don't you just ask me the young lady's name?" Radovan listened to the answer and laughed aloud. Still laughing, he said, "I will see you soon." He lowered the receiver to its cradle.

"What did he say?" Terza asked.

"Detective Garza told me he did not wish to hear the name Terza."

Terza placed both hands upon her hips. "Well, how rude!"

"Don't worry, Number Three. He was laughing, too. I think Detective Garza might have a little crush on you."

Terza's heart raced. "What makes you say that?"

"When he questioned if your hair was long, our detective made a point of asking if you had beautiful long hair."

She fingered her ponytail. "He thinks my hair is beautiful?"

Radovan smiled. "Yes, and I think the crush might go both ways."

"I didn't say that," Terza argued.

"Don't forget, young lady. I read people for a living."

Terza chuckled. "Only dead people."

"You are a funny one, aren't you? Come now." Radovan motioned for Terza to follow him. "I want to get a closer look at that bone."

Terza followed Radovan to an area in front of the microscopes. He placed the bone on top of a table and switched on the light. Terza was surprised to see light coming from the bottom of the tabletop surface. She then watched the medical examiner position a large magnifying glass over the knobby joint end of the bone. As he looked through the glass Terza could hear him humming.

"This is a nice piece of equipment," she commented.

Radovan smiled. "It is, isn't it?"

As he continued to analyze the bone, Terza impatiently waited for Nico to arrive. Before long she heard the receptionist's voice over the loudspeaker. "Doctor Radovan, Detective Nicolas Garza is here to see you."

"Thank you. Please send him back." Radovan looked up at Terza. "Did you hear that?"

Terza hesitated, not understanding. "Yes, I did. Why do you ask?"

"I ask because that, Number Three, is a proper announcement. You did not wait for an invitation. You barged in without asking."

"Are we going to start this all over again? I told you I am truly sorry."

"And I am not upset. I just want to prepare you for the next time."

"Ah-ha! You think I will be seeing you again."

"I do. And next time, please just check in with the receptionist. When she announces that Terza Tiepolo is here to see me, I will allow you to pass."

Terza laughed. "You will, will you? Wow, it is great to know I have complete access to the medical examiner's office."

"Do not go overboard, Number Three. I said you could pass. I said nothing about complete access."

"But you know I speak the truth," Terza said with a wink.

Radovan rolled his eyes just as Nico pushed open the doors. Before he spoke a word, Terza watched him rub menthol around his nostrils. "I don't believe it. You carry your own?"

Nico held up a small round tin before dropping it into his T-shirt pocket. "Only when I come to see the good doc." Nico walked toward the duo and extended his hand to Radovan. "It's nice to see you, Doctor." He looked at Terza. "It's nice to see you too, Miss Tiepolo." He flashed a crooked smile.

"Thank you, Mr. Garza," she spoke with a hint of sarcasm.

Nico leaned over the light table and scrutinized the bone. "So, what do we have here?"

"Number Three brought us a present," Radovan spoke.

Nico looked at Radovan and then at Terza. She could see the question in his eyes.

"That's me," she told him. "You get it? Terza, third born, Number Three."

"Wow. I'm supposed to be the detective, and the thought never crossed my mind," Nico told them.

"You must have been blinded by my beauty," she teased.

Nico's eyes captured hers and held them longer than expected. "I must have," he said, then quickly moved to look through the magnifying glass. "Tell me things," he said to Radovan.

"I can tell you our victim was hit with an object exactly like this. The curvature of the wound is a perfect match to this bone. Without Number Three here, I might never have figured out the murder weapon."

Nico shot Terza a quick glance. Unfortunately, his expression was noncommittal.

Radovan continued, "I also found a small piece of plastic."

"Wouldn't the plastic have led you to the murder weapon?" Nico asked.

Radovan shook his head. "Not in the least."

"Why? Weren't there any particulates?"

"Of course, there were plenty," Radovan answered the detective. "But every single one was from our victim. We had blood, epithelia, and hair. They all belonged to Doctor McCool."

"And none of the bone transferred to the plastic?" Nico pressed.

"None, nada, zero."

Nico stood up straight and looked directly at Terza. "Then I owe you my gratitude, Number Three." He cracked a smile. "Thank you."

Terza returned his smile. "You're welcome."

Nico rubbed his chin. "Tell me, Terza. What's your theory on Rose McCool?"

"I think she just lost it when she went over to retrieve the meat. Maybe she had the bone in her hand and then just whacked Doctor McCool out of rage."

"Do you think it was jealous rage?" Nico asked.

Terza nodded. "Yes, I do. I think she was jealous that he was getting on with his life without her. Rose probably had no idea her ex-husband didn't even want the party and that he was just trying to appease his friends."

"So you think she whacked him and went home to make stew?" Nico asked. "Aren't you forgetting her alibi?"

Terza looked down at the tile flooring.

"What are you not telling me, Terza?"

"Rose McCool's alibi didn't check out."

"Her alibi did not check out? And how might you know that?"

"Do not be angry with me." Terza rushed to explain. "Moheenie and I didn't do anything wrong."

"Somehow I knew Moheenie must have been involved with this," Nico said. "What did you two do?"

"Basically, we did your job." When Terza immediately noticed Nico's scowl, she quickly added, "I'm sorry I said that."

"Just go on," Nico snapped.

Terza now felt bad, and she hoped her news would make up for her comment. "When you told me that Rose McCool went to the Seaside Gym, Moheenie and I called her sister-in-law, Sage. She works at the Seaside Gym, and we also found out she knows Rose."

"So now you are placing someone else at risk?"

"It's not like that, Nico," Terza explained. "Sage never said a word to Rose. We had the feeling that Rose might not have stayed at the gym, so we called Sage and asked if there were security cameras. Of course, as in most public places, there are many cameras. Sage has a friend named Barney, who is one of the security guards."

"Of course she does." Sarcasm laced Nico's tone.

"What does that mean?"

"Behave children, behave," Radovan joked.

"Terza, please finish your story," Nico pressed.

"The bottom line is Barney checked the videos. Rose McCool scanned her card, went into the women's locker room, and then left a few minutes later."

Nico crossed his arms. "So you think she drove to her former beach house intending to kill her ex-husband?"

"No, like I said, I think it was a jealous rage. This murder was definitely not premeditated." She played with the bracelet on her right wrist while thinking. Terza also noticed that Radovan seemed glued to her story. "I believe she must have become numb when she realized what had happened. If that's true, she would have methodically collected the frozen meat, the bone, and all of her belongings, then drove home in a daze." Terza paused for a breath. "Later, when she returned home, it probably hit her."

"Just like she *hit* him." Radovan attempted to make a joke. He looked around. "Do you get it?"

Terza and Nico both rolled their eyes. "We get it," Terza said.

Nico lowered his arms. His lips curled into a sardonic smile. "Yes, we get it." He turned his attention back to Terza. "Please go on. What do you think happened when she got home?"

"Rose probably realized she was in big trouble," Terza said. "I can imagine her looking at the bone and wondering how to dispose of the murder weapon."

"Okay, let's say she decided to make stew. You're the chef, so tell me what happens to the bone. It doesn't dissolve, does it?" Nico asked.

"Of course it doesn't. The bone won't even change its shape. Maybe she was trying to destroy the evidence."

"That is kind of gross," Radovan spoke up. "You think she boiled the bone to remove any blood?"

Terza chuckled. "Ha! How can you possibly think that is gross when you work on dead bodies all day?"

"I don't eat them," Radovan protested. "I examine them."

"Still," Terza said. "How do we know she even noticed the missing piece of plastic? I think Rose wanted to alter the evidence rather than destroy it. She couldn't have simply tossed the bone into the garbage bin. But if she made stew, it would make sense to throw out the bone after cooking it with the sauce."

Nico touched his temple. "I wonder what she did with the plastic wrap?"

Radovan nodded. "Good point. That certainly wouldn't go in the soup."

"I doubt she just tossed it." Nico looked to Terza.

"I agree. She could have pressed it into a ball and flushed it down the toilet."

Nico exhaled. "That plastic wrap is our only concrete evidence. If Rose McCool did destroy it, we might have nothing."

"How can you say that?" Terza strived to organize her scattered thoughts. "We have the bone. It may be in the landfill by now, but the shape of Doctor McCool's wound will match."

"Yes, but how do we prove the bone we might find was ever in Rose McCool's possession?" Nico asked.

Radovan joined the conversation. "How do we know the bone is not in Rose McCool's garbage bin right now?"

"We don't," Nico answered. "But it has been a week, so I'm certain that bone is long gone."

"So what are you going to do next?" Terza asked him.

"Your theory sounds like a great one," Nico said. "I plan on paying Rose a visit and hopefully get her to confess."

"Are you going there right now?" Terza asked.

"No, I have another appointment, and no, you are not going with me," Nico announced.

Terza opened her mouth in feigned shock. "I wouldn't

dream of going with you. Besides, I do have a life of my own, and today, I am very busy."

"I am busy, too," Radovan said. "I thank you very much, Number Three, but it is time for both of you to leave. I need to do my job." He herded them toward the door, pushed it open, and stood waiting for them to pass.

Nico reached his hand out. "It was nice to see you again, Doc. Please keep me posted."

Holding the door open with his back, Radovan shook hands with Nico. "I always do, Detective." He then winked at Terza. "Number Three, you are quite a young lady."

"Is that a good thing or a bad thing?" Terza lifted her eyebrows.

"Ask Detective Garza," he responded with a chuckle.

While they walked side by side along the corridor, Terza looked sideways at Nico. But when she opened her mouth to speak, he quickly said, "Don't ask."

Terza shook her head. "Men," she mumbled under her breath.

"Can't live with them and can't live without them," Nico remarked.

"I can easily live without them," she stated firmly.

He laughed. "We'll see."

"What is that supposed to mean?"

"Questions, questions," Nico said.

Standing a few yards from her car, Terza pressed her key fob and watched the lights flash.

"You're smiling," Nico said.

Terza giggled. "He winked."

"Who winked?"

"Cab winked," she told him. "When I press my key fob, the lights flash, and it looks like my car is winking."

"But you said Cab?" Nico sounded confused.

"Yes, Cab as in Cabernet. I named my car Cab."

"You named your car?"

"Of course I did. I name all my cars. Doesn't everyone?"

"Not everyone I know," Nico responded.

She opened the driver's side door, placed her briefcase onto the passenger's seat, and paused to capture Nico's attention. "You are grateful, aren't you?"

Nico removed a wisp of hair from the soft skin next to her eye. His touch ignited her female hormones.

"Number Three, I am very grateful," he spoke tenderly.

"My name is Terza." Her voice softened as she appraised the kindness in her eyes.

Nico smiled. "I know, Terza. I'm just teasing. Seriously, you did a good job today. I owe you one."

"Thank you. I appreciate you saying that."

"Drive safely," Nico said before closing her car door.

Terza started her car and drove away. She wanted to ask Nico the specifics on how and when he planned to interrogate Rose McCool. Terza also knew she had a busy day ahead of her, but when she tried to focus on her next task, a brilliant idea flashed through her mind. *Should I call Nico and tell him first? Not a chance.* She looked at the digital clock in her car. 11:21. She could do it. There was time. Terza could be at Rose's house in less than thirty minutes.

CHAPTER FIFTEEN: IF THE BONE FITS

Terza parked her car next to the curb of Rose McCool's La Jolla home, turned off the engine, and slowly got out. She rehearsed her opening speech while purposefully walking at a snail's pace along the concrete pathway leading up to the door. *The rest just has to come naturally.*

Terza rang the bell then waited. Fortunately, Rose was home. After opening her wooden front door, Rose greeted Terza through the screen.

"May I help you?"

"Mrs. McCool, my name is Terza Tiepolo. I own the Macaroni on Wheels catering company."

"I'm not planning on having any parties, but thank you anyway." Rose began closing her front door.

"That is not why I am here," Terza spoke quickly. "I found your husband dead."

"Then what do you want with me?" Rose demanded.

"It's not like that." Terza looked toward the ground then slowly lifted her eyes. "I am very sorry for your loss, Mrs. McCool. I came to share something with you."

"What can you possibly share?"

"Before your husband died—"

"Ex-husband," Rose McCool interrupted, sounding terse.

"Excuse me," Terza spoke softly. "Before your ex-husband died, he told me how much he loved you."

Rose stared at Terza without responding. In a trance-like manner, she opened the screen door, allowing Terza to enter. Terza watched the blood drain from Rose's face.

"Are you alright?"

Rose nodded methodically.

Terza processed a series of conflicted emotions both on Rose's face and in her demeanor. Terza felt genuine sorrow for the doctor's wife while also feeling a sense of horror. She could be standing face-to-face with someone who had committed murder. A definite first!

"I truly loved him," Rose mumbled.

Terza reached for Rose's hand when she seemed ready to fall. Taking the role of hostess, Terza asked, "Shall we sit?"

Rose blinked rapidly as if trying to clear her vision. "Yes, please follow me." She led the way to the open kitchen and dining room area and offered Terza a seat at the table.

"Thank you, Mrs. McCool."

"I'm sorry. What is your name again?"

"It's Terza."

Without offering to shake her hand, Rose sat adjacent to Terza. "It is nice to meet you, Terza. You may call me Rose."

"It is nice to meet you as well, Rose," Terza replied. They shared a brief smile and then returned to the somber mood.

"Please tell me about my husband." Rose lowered her eyes.

Terza instantly noticed how she had now referred to Doctor McCool as her husband, and not her ex-husband. "I was at Doctor McCool's home on the Friday when you came over."

"Oh," Rose said, obviously feeling embarrassed by her previous outburst. Her shoulders slumped. "I'm very sorry. I should not have acted the way I did."

For Terza's plan to work she needed Rose as her ally. "Please," she responded quickly. "There is no need to apologize. You were probably just caught off guard. I completely understand."

"You are so right. I *was* caught off guard. I had no idea Mitchell was planning a party."

"It wasn't his idea, Rose," Terza spoke sympathetically. "Doctor McCool didn't want to have a party."

Rose's face grimaced in pain. "I don't understand. Whatever do you mean?"

"Doctor McCool told me that he was only having the party to appease his friends. From what he said, his friends were giving him a hard time about getting on with his life."

Rose lowered her eyes. "His friends wanted Mitchell to get on with his life? That means they wanted him to get away from me," Rose whispered.

"Excuse me if I am out of line, but Doctor McCool said it was you who asked for the divorce."

Rose looked up. "I did, and how could I be so stupid?" She shook her head. "I had been feeling so unloved and very unattractive. When I asked Mitchell for a divorce, I only did so hoping he would beg me to stay."

"But he didn't beg you?"

"No, not like I wanted. But now when I look back on it all, I think Mitchell really did ask me to stay. He just didn't grovel like I expected." Rose buried her face within the palms of both hands.

"I know he still loved you," Terza said. "Doctor McCool told me he did."

Rose peeked through her fingers. "Did you know my husband well?"

Terza shook her head. "No, in fact we only spoke on the telephone. Friday was the first day we met."

"Then why would he tell you something so personal about loving me?"

"It sounds odd, but it really wasn't," Terza explained. "After you left the beach house, Doctor McCool talked to me about the party and why he was having one. Then he explained how he was originally shocked when you asked for the divorce. It was at that point he mentioned how much he still loved you but knew he needed to get on with his life."

"What have I done?" Rose asked softly.

"What do you mean?" Terza asked, semi hoping for a confession.

"I should never have asked for the divorce. It was so stupid of me."

Killing your husband was even more stupid. "At least you can take comfort knowing that Doctor McCool never stopped loving you."

"Yes, I do. Thank you for telling me. It really means a lot." Rose abruptly turned to look into the kitchen. "Where are my manners? Would you like something to drink?"

"Oh, no, thank you. I really must be going." Terza said a silent prayer that Rose would take the bait. "I am off in search of a pot that might not exist."

"A pot? What kind of pot?"

Bingo! Bait taken. "I need a quality cooking pot, a very large one. As you know, I am a caterer. When I prepare sauces, such as marinara, it is typically for a crowd."

"Have you been to the restaurant supply store downtown?"

"Of course. I frequently shop there."

"Well, I don't cater, but I love to cook, and that restaurant supply store is a real treat," Rose said. "I am positive I saw large pots the last time I was in there."

"I already have several, but those restaurant-style pots are just not the same. Do you ever cook with cast iron or enamel?"

"Oh yes, they are wonderful pots. Is that what you need?" Rose asked.

"That is what I am hoping to find. The pots at the restaurant supply do the job, but they just don't seem to conduct the heat as well as my quality cookware. I am hoping to find an enamel-coated cast-iron pot in an extra-large size."

"Honey, I don't think you are going to find what you are looking for. I do a great deal of cooking and have an entire set of several different brands. My largest pot is probably smaller than you need for your business."

"May I see it?"

"Of course you may." Rose instantly stood and walked into the kitchen. She moved behind the kitchen island and ducked below sight. Terza heard the sound of what she assumed to be cooking pots being moved around. Moments later, Rose appeared and placed a large red pot onto the granite counter.

Terza walked over to inspect the pot. "What size is this?"

"I'm not certain how many quarts, but I am sure it is the largest they make."

"Are you positive?"

"I am. I've been known to prepare a mean marinara myself," Rose said. "You see, Mitchell and I used to entertain frequently."

Terza glanced up as she heard Rose's voice soften.

"Unfortunately," Rose added. "I haven't cooked for a long time."

What about the beef stew you made last week? "So, you make a mean marinara?" Terza asked to lighten the mood.

Rose's slight smile barely curved her lips. "I'm sure mine is not half as good as yours."

"You are too kind. I bet your marinara is delicious." Terza exhaled loudly. "Well, I do thank you. At least you saved me a trip to the mall."

"I wouldn't give up," Rose said. "Maybe one of the high-end brands carries larger pots online."

"That's a great idea. If I find something larger would you like me to let you know?"

"I would love it," Rose said, her smile finally reaching her eyes. She jotted something on a kitchen notepad, tore off the top sheet, and handed it to Terza. "Here is my phone number."

"Thank you. I will let you know what I find."

Rose escorted Terza to the front door, where they said their goodbyes. It then took all of Terza's willpower not to jump for joy as she walked to her car. She settled in, drove around the corner, and parked. Terza then pumped both fists into the air and let out a loud squeal. *I may have just solved the murder!*

Grabbing her phone, Terza called her father. "Do you have another bone like the one you gave me this morning?" she asked the moment he answered the phone.

"Would you like to say hello first?"

"Hello, Papa. Now do you or don't you?"

"Hold on, let me look."

Terza impatiently waited several minutes.

"No, my little gnocchi, I am fresh out."

"Okay, thank you." Terza disconnected the call before her father could ask any questions. She would make it up to him later. *Back to see Radovan.*

She returned to the medical examiner's building, parked her car, and entered the same door as earlier in the morning. This time Terza approached the reception desk and waited for the receptionist to finish a telephone call.

"May I help you?"

"Yes, thank you. I'm Terza Tiepolo here to see Doctor Radovan."

"Do you have an appointment?"

"No, I do not."

After shooting her a *shame on you look*, the receptionist lifted the telephone receiver, pressed three buttons, and said, "Doctor Radovan, a Terza Tiepolo is here to see you, and she does *not* have an appointment." Terza watched as the receptionist's snotty expression turned to one of surprise. The receptionist slowly lowered the receiver and then glared at Terza. "You may go in," she said with a fake smile.

"Thank you," Terza replied with a genuine smile. *What is her problem?* She retraced her morning steps, stopping just short of the double doors. Before entering the medical examiner's office, Terza took a deep breath, and then held it.

After walking in, she instantly grabbed the jar of menthol and saturated her nose with the pungent gel.

"Welcome back, Number Three!" Radovan greeted her.

"Hello again, Doctor Radovan," Terza said. "May I please borrow the bone?"

"First you throw me a bone, and now you want to take it back?"

Terza could not figure out if his statement was a joke. "I only wish to borrow it. I will return the bone in less than two hours."

He narrowed his eyes. "And why do you wish to borrow the bone?"

"I, uh..." Terza hesitated. "I am working on a theory."

"Working on a theory, are you? Does Detective Garza know about this theory?"

"No he does not." She paused. "You aren't going to tell him, are you?"

She sensed a smile on the doctor's face. Using the palm of his hand, Terza watched Radovan cover both eyes with one hand and pretend to zip his mouth closed with the other. "I see nothing. I hear nothing."

Terza moved closer, lifted onto her tiptoes, and kissed him on the cheek. "You are an angel. Thank you."

"Last time you said I was mean."

Terza smiled warmly. "Last time I was wrong." She looked around the lab. "Now, where's my bone?"

Radovan walked to the microscope area and pulled the bone from a top cabinet. While handing it out to her, he said, "It's *my* bone now, and yes you can borrow it." Terza grabbed hold of one end, and Radovan held tightly to the other. "Did you know a human thigh bone is stronger than concrete?" he quizzed her.

"I did not know that," Terza responded. "Is this bone stronger than concrete, too?"

"I'm not sure. I have not studied bovine bones, but I just might have to do my research." Radovan continued to hold firmly. "Two hours, max."

"Two hours max. Thank you," she said when Radovan finally released his end.

"Goodbye, Number Three."

"Goodbye, Number One!" she countered.

Terza left the lab, exited the building, and rushed to her car. She was quickly running out of time. She wanted to be dressed and ready to go by 5:00 p.m. The gang was coming over at 6:00 p.m., and Terza still needed to make a salad and garlic bread. Without wasting another moment she started the engine and drove to the specialty chef store in the Mission Valley area.

As typical for a Saturday, the parking lot appeared crowded. Terza selected the first spot at the far end of the lot. She could run faster than drive at this point.

When Terza entered the store with bone in hand, a female store clerk greeted her. "Nice bone!" She laughed.

Terza joined in the laughter. "Thanks! I am looking for your enamel pots."

"Right this way," the clerk said, walking toward the back of the store. "Although I don't think we have a pot large enough for that bone."

"I just need to check." When they reached the enamel cookware section, Terza instantly located an exact replica of Rose McCool's largest pot. She lifted the lid, handed it to the clerk, and attempted to place the bone inside.

"It doesn't fit," the clerk offered.

"No it doesn't."

"You should just ask a butcher to saw it in half," the clerk suggested.

Terza flashed a knowing smile. "You are exactly right. Thank you." She walked away carrying her bone.

Before returning to the medical examiner's office for a third time, she dialed Nico's number.

He answered after several rings. "Hello again."

"Nico, when are you going to see Rose McCool?"

"I'm not sure," Nico said. "It might not be until tomorrow."

"Tomorrow?" Terza groaned. "Why aren't you going today?"

"Because I am waiting for a warrant," Nico told her. "We want to search her entire house and garage."

"I understand. But be sure and check any saws she might have in her garage."

"Terza," he spoke firmly. "What did you do?" She remained quiet, he persisted. "Tell me, Terza."

"I will tell you only if you promise not to be mad."

"No, I'm not going to promise anything," Nico insisted. "Now quit stalling and tell me."

Terza did tell him, everything, beginning with her visit with Rose and ending with the confirmation of her theory at the chef store. "You see, there is no way the bone would fit in Rose's largest pot," Terza explained. "If Rose was in fact making beef stew like the detective told you, and if she used the bone in her stew, she had to cut it first."

"How do you cut a bone like that?"

"Typically you would ask the butcher to cut it, but Rose could not do that. She would have used some type of saw, and I'm positive she did not think to clean it."

"You're telling me that Rose McCool sawed the murder weapon in half and then cooked stew with it?"

"That is exactly what I am telling you," Terza said.

"And if we search her garage, we will find a saw with trace evidence of a cow bone?"

"I am confident that is exactly what you are going to find."

"Confident enough for a wager?"

"Yes, I am," Terza said.

"What shall we bet on?"

"Shall we bet a lemon gelato?"

Nico chuckled. "Make it pistachio, and you have a deal."

"How about the winner gets to select their own flavor?" Terza suggested.

"That sounds like a plan." Nico paused before saying, "You know I should be mad at you."

"But you're not, right?"

"I am a little. You are just too feisty for your own good."

"I'm sorry," she said.

"No, you're not. Now hang up before I really start thinking about how mad I should be."

Terza wasted no time. "Ciao."

"Ciao."

Twenty minutes later she walked into the medical examiner's front office and smiled at the same receptionist. "Hello again."

"Is he expecting you this time?"

"Yes, he is."

"May I please have your name once more?"

"Terza Tiepolo."

The receptionist lifted the receiver to announce Terza's name. Then after placing it to rest, she looked up. "You may go in."

Terza smiled. "Thank you very much," she said and proceeded through the door.

When Terza reached the medical examiner's office she decided to forgo the menthol and opted to remain outside at the double doors. She pushed one door open. "Doctor Radovan, I am returning the bone."

"Thank you," Radovan called out. "Please just leave it on my desk. My hands are full right now."

Terza took a deep breath, held it, and rushed in with the bone. She rapidly placed the bone on the doctor's desk and sprinted for the door. "Thank you and goodbye!" she said while exiting.

"Goodbye, Number Three," she heard the doctor say.

CHAPTER SIXTEEN: AN EVENING OFF

What a day! Comfortably dressed in a black linen sundress and matching woven platform slides, Terza strolled casually from her condominium to the Macaroni on Wheels office. While walking she pressed the favorite button on her phone to dial her mother.

"*Buona sera*, my love," Benedette answered.

"*Buona sera*, Mom. What are *you* doing?"

"I just finished picking some fresh vegetables for the salad. What are you doing?"

"Like mother, like daughter, I am on my way to work, also to begin making the salad."

"Would you like me to bring you some fresh greens?"

"No, Mom, but thank you very much. I still have some from my visit the other evening. The reason I called is to give you a quick update on our dinner tonight."

"Tell me."

Terza opened her mouth to speak and then froze. Shock rippled through her system as she stood face to face with Henry Follett. "Mr. Follett," she stammered.

"Is everything alright, Terza?" her mother asked.

"Yes, Mom. I will call you right back."

"No you will not!" Benedette demanded. "I don't like the tone of your voice. Stay on the line so I can make certain you are safe."

"Okay, I got it," Terza spoke to her mother and turned her attention to Henry Follett.

"Stay away from Rose McCool," he spoke firmly.

"Excuse me?"

"You heard me," he said.

"You had better stay away from me, or I will call the police."

"I will be the one calling the police if you don't stay away from Rose." Follett turned and walked away.

Terza breathed deeply. "I'm back, Mom."

"And I am already out the door," Benedette said. "Who was that man?"

"No, Mom! Go back inside. He is already gone."

"Are you positive?"

"Yes, I am positive," Terza said. "I can see him driving away."

"Who is he?"

"He's the man who lives next door to Doctor McCool, my client who was murdered."

"What does he want with you?"

Terza thought about explaining it to her mother and then quickly decided against it. She knew her mother would only worry more. "I'm not sure, Mom. Moheenie and I have been asking around. Perhaps he is just extra concerned about his privacy."

"What do you mean about asking around?" Benedette pressed. "Terza Tiepolo, you are not a detective! Besides, that man could be the murderer."

That he could. "Actually, I think it might be someone else," she responded casually.

"It *might* be someone else? Terza Tiepolo, answer me yes or no. Could that man have murdered Doctor McCool?"

Terza hesitated. "Well—"

"Yes or no," Benedette pressed.

"Yes, I guess he could. But right now I am just not certain."

"Good grief! Terza, where are you right this moment?"

"I am near my office. Mom, he is gone, and I'm safe."

"That's not good enough. Catch me up on dinner tonight. I am staying on the line until you are safely inside."

"Okay." Terza sighed. "My friends are expected at six, and I think the Sartù Di Riso should go into the oven right when they arrive."

"I forgot, how long does it take to cook?"

"Fifty minutes, and it needs to rest for twenty to thirty minutes. Enjoy your salad and plan to receive the Sartù Di Riso right about a quarter past seven."

"That sounds perfect. Shall I send your father over at seven?"

"No, let him relax. I will slice your portions of the Sartù Di Riso first, and then send the boys over to deliver it. By the time they return, their plates will be ready."

"Well, thank you, my love. This is such a nice treat," Benedette told her.

"Just make certain Papa does not talk Conner and Ranger to death. I don't want their meals to get cold, and I don't want yours to get cold either."

"Don't worry, I will personally wait outside with him. They won't even have to cross through the gate."

"Perfect. Enjoy your dinner, and I will see you tomorrow."

"Don't you dare hang up yet. Are you safely inside?"

"Almost." Terza unlocked the door, entered, and locked it behind her. "I'm in!"

"Good. See you tomorrow. Enjoy your evening."

"Thanks, Mom. Ciao."

"Arrivederci," Benedette said. "I love you."

"I love you, too. Now hang up," Terza told her mother.

"You are inside, aren't you?"

"Yes, Mom."

"Is the door locked?"

"Yes, again. Ciao!"

Terza shook her head in disbelief at the audacity of Henry Follett. She immediately retrieved their murder board and placed it upon the island counter. "Let's see," she spoke out loud. Terza withdrew a black dry erase marker from the drawer and wrote, *could be guilty – threatened me*, under Henry Follett's name. Under Alan Mann's name she wrote, *Faulkner thinks Alan had a motive*. Then without thinking, and almost instinctively, she wrote four words under the name of Rose McCool. *Had to cut bone.*

Finally, Terza tried to put the events of the day out of her mind by returning the murder board to its hiding place alongside one of their refrigerators. She needed to focus and prepare for her evening. Knowing they were eating at the large kitchen island, Terza placed a red-and-white checkered tablecloth on one end. She then added an Italian-style straw Chianti bottle with a candle in the bottle's neck. Terza set the table with two plates on one side of the counter and two plates on the opposite side. She added matching cloth napkins, knives, forks, water glasses, and wine balloon glasses. An extra napkin served as a cover for the breadbasket, which Terza placed next to the wine bottle candle.

Preparing the salad came next. When finished tossing the greens, Terza mixed the roasted garlic with butter for her garlic bread. She sliced the baguette lengthwise and heavily smeared it with the garlic butter mixture. For the finishing touch, Terza minced freshly picked Italian parsley and set it aside. *Thanks, Mom.* The parsley was just one of the herbs from her mother's garden. After toasting the bread, she would brighten the flavor by sprinkling on the fresh parsley.

Moheenie and Ranger arrived first. Entering through the back door, Moheenie called, "We're here! It's just us." She handed Terza a colorful bouquet of flowers. "For the hostess," she said with a huge smile.

"Wow, Moheenie, thanks! You cooked too, so you didn't have to bring me flowers."

Still smiling, Moheenie looked at her husband. "It was Ranger's idea. Isn't he sweet?"

"He certainly is." Terza hugged Ranger first, then hugged Moheenie. "Thank you both. Now, come in."

"Terza, I love the way you used the island for a table!" Moheenie said. "It looks great."

"Thanks, Mo. The tablecloth just made it seem cozier."

"I agree," Ranger added.

"Thank you. Conner is bringing the wine, but we can also open a bottle now," Terza suggested.

"No, let's wait," Ranger said. "Shall I unlock the front door? He might not know to come through the back."

"Yes please."

The doorbell chimed right as Ranger left. Moments later he returned to the kitchen with Conner bringing up the rear.

"Moheenie, so nice to see you," Conner said. "Give me a hug. My hands are full."

She wrapped an arm around his waist. "Hey, Conner. It has been way too long. Good to see you, too. I notice you still have those gorgeous baby blues!"

Conner's smile brightened the room. "You are too kind, Mo."

"You brought two bottles?" Terza approached Conner. "Thank you very much." Terza accepted the two identical bottles and read one of the labels. "Chianti, *Denominazione di Origine Controllata e Garantita*," she spoke in perfect Italian.

Conner grinned. "That sounded fantastic, but what does it mean?"

Terza placed the bottles next to the sink. "The short answer is that you spent way too much on this wine." She wrapped both arms around his neck.

When Conner placed his hands on the small of her back Terza felt a twinge. Of what, she was not sure, but it felt tantalizing.

"Nothing is too good for you, Terza." Conner pulled back and looked into her eyes. "Now what's the long answer?"

Terza reached for one of the Chianti bottles and pointed to the label. "The abbreviation for *Denominazione di Origine Controllata e Garantita* is DOCG, and it is basically the status given to an Italian wine based upon Italy's wine laws. Think of it like an award."

Conner took the bottle from Terza and studied the label. "How would you translate this in English?"

Terza shook her head. "Roughly it means *controlled designation of origin and guaranteed*, but it would never be printed in English as this is an Italian wine. Every country has its own wine laws. You are very sweet, Conner. Thank you."

He placed the bottle on the counter and held Terza's hand. "You're welcome. Besides, your father gave me the family discount."

Terza laughed. "You bought the wine from my pop?"

"Of course I did. I knew your father would have a good selection, and I also thought it would be nice to say hello."

"I forgot, you *do* know my father."

"Saturday morning subs," Ranger said, giving Conner a high five.

"No one makes them better than Ezio Tiepolo," Conner added. "Terza, your dad is famous among the surf crowd."

Terza smiled. "That's so nice to hear."

"Do you also know Terza's mom, Benedette?" Moheenie asked Conner.

"I only met her once because we typically go on Saturday." Conner turned to Terza. "Your mom takes Saturday off, right?"

"Yes, and I am glad. Both of my parents work too hard."

"By the way, Terza," Conner said, "your mom is gorgeous. She kind of reminds me of that beautiful Italian actress. You know the one from the fifties."

"I think I do, but I can't remember her name," Terza said.

"She does, doesn't she?" Moheenie added. "What is her name?"

"We'll all remember when we are not trying to think of it," Terza said. She turned to Ranger. "Would you care to open the wine?"

"Certainly. Shall I use the decanter?"

"I think you should. This is such a great wine so let's treat it with tender loving care."

While Ranger opened and decanted the wine, Terza placed the Sartù Di Riso in the oven and set the timer. Moheenie laughed at Conner analyzing Ranger's every move.

"What are you doing?" Conner asked Ranger.

"Decanting the wine," Ranger told him. "How much do you know about wine?"

"Not much," Conner answered. "You know me. I'm more of a beer kind of guy. I thought you were too."

"What can I say? My tastes are improving." Ranger finished pouring the wine from the bottle into the decanter before explaining. "Quality wine tastes better when it is aerated, meaning that oxygen is added. It is often referred to as opening up the wine."

"Opening the bottle?" Conner asked.

"No, opening the wine or adding air to it. Have you seen people swirl wine in their glasses?"

"I have," Conner said. "I've also heard the term *open the bottle so it can breathe.*"

"Exactly." Ranger rinsed out the empty bottle. "The bottle of wine you bought should taste fantastic once it has been aerated. Adding oxygen softens the taste. But since we want to drink it now, just removing the cork will not allow enough air to penetrate the wine. The bottle's neck is too narrow."

"So that's why you decant it," Conner added.

"You've got it."

"Ranger is our best bartender," Terza told them.

Ranger laughed. "Aren't I your only bartender?" He finished buffing one of the wine glasses.

Terza handed Ranger a second glass. "No, remember my brother helps out occasionally when you are busy."

"I can help," Conner offered, grinning. "Especially now I know so much about wine."

"Well, thank you, Conner," Terza said. "I will keep your offer in mind."

"That would be a hoot." Moheenie helped Ranger buff the final two glasses. "DEA agent by day and bartender by night."

"Do you think your clients would mind?" Conner asked.

"I don't know, but maybe a little," Terza answered. "You know how people get around any kind of law enforcement."

Conner moved toward the sheet pan filled with garlic bread. "This bread smells amazing, Terza. Is the garlic fresh?"

"Of course it is," she told him, slapping his hand away from the pan. "Are you hungry?"

"No, I'm starving." Conner raised his eyebrows. "Did you make snacks?"

Terza chuckled. "I made appetizers, but just a few. I don't want you boys filling up before dinner."

"Yum. What did you make?" Conner asked as Terza removed the plastic wrap covering from a pig-shaped wooden board.

"A small Salumi E Formaggi board."

"It looks like meat and cheese," Conner told her.

It was Moheenie's turn to laugh. "You're funny Conner! Salumi E Formaggi is meat and cheese in Italian."

"How am I supposed to know? I don't speak Italian."

"But you spend enough time in the Tiepolo Mercato," Moheenie told him. "Don't you ever read the signs?"

"I guess not. I just walk in, place my order, and find an outside table."

"Don't worry, Conner," Ranger said. "I had no idea what these lovely ladies were saying until I started working with them. Heck, now I feel half Italian. And don't get me started about Lakalaka here. Moheenie is the first Italian Hawaiian I have ever met."

Moheenie slid an arm around Ranger's waist. "And you love it, don't you?"

"Of course I do. After a great Italian meal I get to watch you hula."

Moheenie slapped at his bicep. "When do I ever hula dance in the house?"

Ranger shrugged. "I don't know. It sounded good."

"Come now, dig in," Terza told them.

Conner selected a slice of meat and placed a piece of cheese on top. "You don't have to ask me twice." He popped the selection in his mouth, smiled while chewing, and then said, "This is delicious! Somehow it tastes better with the Italian name."

Terza laughed. "It must be mind over matter."

"So tell us about your last case," Moheenie spoke to Conner. "Ranger said you went down to Mexico, right?"

"Yes, I've been back less than two weeks."

"Is there anything you can share?" Moheenie asked.

"I don't know, Mo. Let me think." Conner was quiet for several minutes before saying, "I can tell you that I was working with Mando. Do you remember Armando De la Cruz?"

"I'm not sure," Moheenie said.

"Yes, you do," Ranger spoke. "Remember, Mo, we met Mando when he came with Conner to the lifeguard games. He's Latino with dark hair and dark eyes."

"Oh, yes. Now I remember."

"Where was I?" Terza asked.

"I'm not sure," Ranger answered.

"Was I invited?" Terza pressed.

"Of course you were invited," Moheenie told her. "If I remember correctly, you had afternoon tickets to the theater."

"That's right. My mom and I went to the opera."

"Okay, back to Mando." Moheenie directed Conner to finish his story.

"He and I rented a condo in Cancun so we could set up surveillance—"

"And?" Moheenie pushed. "Why did you stop? Tell us."

"I just figured out that I probably shouldn't say anymore."

"Who were you monitoring?" Moheenie asked.

"Just a woman," Conner replied.

"A woman, huh?" Terza folded her arms. "Was she the bad guy?"

"No, she is related to the bad guy," Conner said.

"So, the bad guy is actually a guy, like as in a man?" Moheenie pressed.

"Yes, and that is all I am going to say. Somehow I feel as if I am being interrogated."

"It's their murder mystery book club," Ranger commented. "Once a month these two amateur sleuths get together with a group of other murder mystery readers."

Conner tented his fingers. "That sounds like work."

"That's only because you are a detective." Terza planted her palms on the kitchen island. "Solving mysteries is fun for us."

"Catching the bad guy is fun for me, too."

"You just can't tell us about it, Conner," Moheenie whined.

"Remind me later. I might be able to tell you more then."

"Do you mean later tonight?" Terza asked with a wink.

"No, silly, later in life. Perhaps a few months from now."

Terza flashed Conner a smile before turning to look at the oven timer. Their dinner had ten minutes to go.

"Would you like me to dress the salad, Terza?" Moheenie asked.

"Thank you, but let's wait. We still have twenty to thirty minutes while the Sartù di Riso rests."

"I have no idea what we are eating, but it smells heavenly." Conner rubbed his stomach.

"This is a new one for me, too," Ranger added. "Terza served it the other night, but I still am not sure what it is."

"It is an Italian meat and rice dish," Terza told them. "You will know soon enough."

When the oven timer chimed, Terza reached for two towels and attempted to open the oven door. She laughed as both Ranger and Conner pressed in to look through the glass. "If you two don't move our dinner is going to burn."

They instantly stepped back.

Terza opened the oven door and carefully withdrew the Bundt pan. She placed it onto a cookie sheet before carrying it to the counter.

Conner leaned over the pan. "That looks amazing, Terza."

"Thank you, Conner. In about twenty-five minutes, I hope it tastes amazing, too. Are you both up for taking two slices to my parents?"

"Of course," Ranger said.

"Shall we go now?" Conner asked.

"No, not yet. It still needs to rest. Ranger, the wine should be perfect for serving, and Moheenie you may now dress the salad."

"What about the garlic bread?" Moheenie asked.

"I'll begin toasting it just before we sit."

"Terza, you sound like a caterer," Conner said.

"Is that a good thing or a bad thing?"

Conner laughed. "It's a good thing, especially when it comes to food entering my mouth."

Ranger handed a glass of wine to Terza and then one to Moheenie. He poured the third for Conner and held on to the fourth. "Who is going to do the honors?"

"I will." Conner held out his glass to Terza. "First to the head chef. I thank you for the invitation." Their glasses clinked. "To my surf buddy," he said, toasting Ranger. "Now that I'm back from Mexico we'll have to go more often."

Ranger nodded. "Here, here."

Conner stood face to face with Moheenie. "And to Ranger's beautiful wife and my good friend."

Moheenie touched her glass to his. "Why thank you, Conner. Here's to good friends all around." The four leaned in for a final toast.

"This wine is remarkable, Conner," Terza said. "Thank you."

"It was my pleasure."

When it was time, Terza carefully sliced two pieces of Sartù di Riso and placed each into a hard cardboard to-go container. She closed the lids and handed one box to Conner and one to Ranger. "Okay, here is your mission if you choose to accept it." She looked at the clock. "It is seven-fifteen so my parents should be waiting out front. Please carefully deliver these two boxes and do not stay and talk."

"We can't just hand them out and leave," Ranger said. "That would be rude."

"Yes, you can," Terza said. "Besides, your food will be ready in five minutes, so you better hurry."

"Five minutes?" Conner asked. "It will take us five minutes to walk there."

"You can make it there and back in less than five minutes. Now get going!" Terza ordered.

"Yes, ma'am," they spoke in harmony.

As the men walked out the backdoor, Conner whispered, "She's one tough cookie."

"Conner, I heard that!" Terza stifled a laugh. "So Mo, do you think they will hurry?"

"I am sure of it. All you had to do was mention food. Now tell me, is there anything new on the case?"

"Rose McCool did it, I am positive," Terza told her, "Well. kind of."

"What makes you certain?"

"I don't have time to get into it now, but I went to see her today."

Moheenie's eyes bulged open. "You did? Tell me, hurry!"

"There's no time. Call me when you get home."

"Yes, but what if Ranger is a nosey butt?"

"He'll never know what I am saying," Terza explained.

"Okay, but I can't take not knowing," Moheenie whined.

"Oh, and I ran into Henry Follett," Terza added.

"What?"

"And I updated our murder board," Terza said. She looked up in thought. "Come to think of it, I am still not certain. It could be Henry, Alan or Rose."

"Let me look at the board," Moheenie said. "It helps to see all of the names at once."

"Moheenie, no, we don't have time. I promise to tell you everything later."

"Do I have a choice?"

"Nope." Terza turned the oven knob to broil and uncovered the garlic bread while Moheenie finished tossing the salad and filling the glasses with water.

"It looks like we are all set," Moheenie said.

"It sure does." Terza sliced the rest of the Sartù di Riso. "Let's get this party started!"

Moheenie flashed Terza a bright smile. "I knew you'd say that."

Terza giggled while placing portions on each of their plates. She then carried them to the impromptu table.

"We're back!" Conner said.

"How long did we take?" Ranger asked.

Moheenie checked the time. "You made it in just over five minutes. Good job, guys!"

"Terza, I feel a little sorry for your dad," Conner said. "You could tell he wanted us to stay and talk."

Terza grunted. "My mom stopped him, didn't she, Conner?"

"She sure did. Your mom practically dragged him into the house."

"Well, don't feel sorry for him. Besides, you can talk to my father all you want at tomorrow's dinner."

"Wow! I get to have a home-cooked meal two nights in a row," Conner commented. "And it's Italian, my favorite."

"I am sorry to disappoint you, but we are not having an Italian dinner tomorrow night." Terza paused for effect. "We are having spaghetti and meatballs."

Conner angled his head. "I don't get the joke."

"Spaghetti and meatballs are American, not Italian."

His eyes ballooned open. "Are you sure?"

"I'm positive. My mom makes it once a month just for the kiddos, and tomorrow is the night."

"Oh man, Conner, you are one lucky guy," Ranger said. "Wait until you taste Mrs. Tiepolo's meatballs!"

"Are they really good?"

"Do you like spaghetti and meatballs?" Ranger quizzed Conner.

"Of course I do."

"Well, Mrs. Tiepolo's meatballs are a work of art. If you are extra nice, she might wrap up a few for a sandwich."

Terza watched Ranger practically drool.

"Be sure and ask for sauce, too," Ranger told him.

Conner smiled at Terza. "Don't worry, I am not going to ask for a doggy bag. I'm just happy to be invited in the first place!"

"You won't have to ask. My mother always makes sure everyone goes home with a little something. I just know she is going to take good care of you. Now, everyone, please begin eating. I just have to bring the garlic bread."

"I think I'm in Heaven," Conner said.

"Are you still thinking of my mom's meatballs?"

"No, I just took a bite. This is the best dish I have ever tasted!"

Terza placed the bread basket in the center of their dining table and leaned in to kiss Conner on the cheek. "What a sweet thing to say. Thank you, Conner. Moheenie made it, too."

"Thank *you* for making it, and thank you, Mo. It is delicious."

"You're welcome," Moheenie said with a smile.

"Hey, Conner, haven't you ever tasted the meatball submarine at Tiepolo Mercato?" Ranger asked.

"Yes, that sandwich is amazing."

"Who do you think makes the meatballs, goof?" Terza teased.

Conner rubbed his chin. "I am guessing your mom?"

"Of course my mom makes them. My pop is a great butcher, but just an okay cook."

"Now I am even more excited about tomorrow night."

"You better be even extra excited about beating my brother in bocce ball," Terza told him. "Especially if you want to be invited back."

"Oh, I will beat him. Nothing motivates me more than food."

"Speaking of games," Moheenie chimed in. "What are we playing tonight?"

"What about Monopoly?" Ranger asked.

"That takes too long," Terza and Moheenie spoke simultaneously, looked at each other, and laughed.

"It is now obvious how much time you two spend together," Ranger commented.

"I'll say," Conner agreed.

The foursome decided on Scrabble, which they played while enjoying some amaretto chocolate dip. Each time an Italian cookie was dipped into the decadent chocolate Terza could not help but smile at the ongoing groans of elation.

"It certainly doesn't take much to make all of you happy, does it?"

Moheenie moaned. "Terza, this chocolate is to die for."

"I'm glad you like it."

"It's still warm." Conner licked his lips. "I barely noticed you making it."

"It was nothing. I already did the prep work, and everything was ready to just pop in the saucepan. Basically, all I had to do was stir it while you and Ranger were busy with the espresso machine making our coffee. By the way." She lifted her cup. "This latte is pretty spectacular."

"Why thank you," Conner said. "Ranger did all the work while I watched."

"Thank you, Ranger."

"I'm learning."

"Yes you are, honey." Moheenie patted his shoulder. "You are becoming quite the expert behind that bar."

Three Scrabble games later, and the foursome finally decided to end their wonderful evening.

"Conner, I cannot believe you won all three games," Terza told him.

"I might have cheated," he confessed.

"How did you cheat?" Moheenie asked, laughing. "I didn't see you smuggle in a dictionary."

"I've been on a lot of stakeouts lately, and it does get boring," Conner told them.

Terza brushed her palms. "So you play Scrabble?"

"I just play on my phone."

Moheenie grunted. "Aren't you supposed to be watching for the bad guy?"

"It's not always like that. On the last case we were just waiting for someone to come home."

"Waiting for someone?" Moheenie asked. "Was this someone a guy or a girl?"

Conner laughed. "I can't tell you that."

"Come on, Lakalaka." Ranger took Moheenie's hand. "It's after ten. I'm ready to hit the sack."

"Okay, just a minute. I need to make certain we haven't left any mess for Terza to clean."

"We're done, Mo," Terza said. "Taking turns while we played worked out perfectly."

"Okay then, Mr. Brickman, let's go home."

Ranger and Moheenie said their goodbyes, leaving Conner and Terza alone. For a moment, Terza felt a twinge of excited anticipation. She wondered if Conner would try and kiss her good night.

Conner turned to face Terza. "You are amazing," he said. "Thank you for all of the incredible food and even better company."

"I'm really glad you came. And just think, we get to do it all over again tomorrow night."

He smiled. "I know. Maybe you will start to enjoy having me around on a regular basis."

"Oh, Conner, you know I always like having you around," Terza said.

"You walked over, right?"

"Yes I did. Are you planning to drive me home?"

"I can either drive you or escort you home and then walk back to my car."

"Did you drive the Cherry Bomb?" Terza referred to his candy-apple red classic Mustang.

"I sure did. But we probably should walk. I parked between your condo and here. We will most likely pass my car on the way back to your home."

"Why didn't you park behind Macaroni on Wheels?"

"I wasn't sure if there would be room."

"Make sure you park here tomorrow. I'll be walking to my parent's house so the spot will be free."

"Do you want to walk over together?"

"Definitely. I'll meet you here at four. Does that work for you?"

"It's perfect." He grinned. "Plus that means I can walk you home tomorrow, too."

Terza smiled. "I really appreciate it, Conner, especially today."

His eyes narrowed. "Why, what happened today?"

She thought about her brief confrontation with Henry Follett, considered sharing it with Conner, but quickly dismissed the thought. "Nothing special happened. I just like to feel safe and secure with a DEA agent on my arm."

Conner tapped the side of his waist. "Especially when I am carrying."

"Carrying what?"

"Carrying my gun, silly. I always have it with me."

Terza raised her eyebrows. "How did I not know that?"

"Because you don't spend enough time with me," he replied. While standing at Terza's front office door, Conner looked around. "Did you lock up the back?"

"Yes, I'm locked up and ready to go." Terza opened the door, waited for Conner to pass through, and then secured the deadbolt. She slid her hand around his bicep. "Lead the way."

As they walked along the urban neighborhood, Terza thought about how comfortable she felt with Conner. *He's cute. He has a fantastic job, and he is probably the kindest man she had ever met. Except for my father of course.*

"So let's talk about tomorrow," Conner said. "I really would like to bring something more than just sunflowers. I can bring another bottle of wine."

"Wine is my father's job, and you definitely cannot steal his thunder. He goes to great lengths to select the perfect wine for whatever my mother is serving. Trust me, Conner, when I tell you that sunflowers will make my mom smile."

"Then sunflowers it is."

When they reached the lobby to her building Terza punched in the code to open the glass double doors. Conner held the door for Terza and then flopped down into the cushiony sofa. "This is nice, Terza. Your lobby looks like a home."

"I agree. It is a great place for guests to wait. Are we saying goodbye here or at my front door?"

"Are you planning to invite me in?" His tone sounded suggestive.

Terza smiled. "Absolutely not. It is time for you to go home, my friend, and I need my beauty sleep. Do you remember that I attend first service?"

"I do indeed. It starts at eight, correct?"

"You are right about that, and I fully expect to see you there," Terza said.

"Ha! I'll make it to church but not at eight."

When the elevator door opened Terza stepped inside, followed by Conner. "Don't worry. I am only walking you to your front door."

Four floors later they exited the elevator, and Conner walked Terza directly to her front door. "Thank you again," he said while placing his palm on the small of her back. He drew her near. "I had a wonderful time, Miss Tiepolo."

She allowed herself to nestle within his arms. "Did you now, Mr. Reeves?"

"Yes, I did," he said right before locking his lips onto hers.

Terza could not believe how soft his lips felt. She closed her eyes and enjoyed every moment. Terza forced herself to pull away when she felt herself growing weak in the knees.

"Not yet," he moaned.

"You have to go, Conner," she whispered

"Do I have to?"

"Yes, you do."

Conner finally released his grasp and stood motionless, just staring into her eyes.

"Are you alright?"

"No, you are making me leave," he whined.

"We are seeing each other tomorrow," she reminded him.

His smile grew. "That we are." Conner leaned in to kiss

Terza on the forehead. "Lock up right away. I'll be dreaming about you."

"Ciao," she said before closing the door. Terza then leaned against the door and relived her kiss with Conner. She remembered kissing him before but not like this. Something about his kiss seemed to awaken her passion for him. *Conner? Nico? They are both in law enforcement. Maybe that is the attraction? Or maybe... Conner is enhancing the feelings I might have for Nico.* "Men!" she finally said aloud.

Terza placed her tote on the kitchen counter stool and then reached for her phone. Moheenie had yet to call. She sent a text:

I'm home. Can you talk?

Moheenie responded:

Not now.

Terza replied:

Conner kissed me.

Her phone instantly rang.

"I thought you couldn't talk."

"I can't, but oh my!" Moheenie squealed. "Was it short or long?"

"Long and lovely. Why can't you talk?"

"Ranger's not sleepy," Moheenie spoke with implication.

"Oh. I got it. Say no more. We can catch up tomorrow."

CHAPTER SEVENTEEN: THE SUSPECT LIST GROWS

Sunday

Church service lifted Terza's spirits, and now a much-needed Grande Americano would boost her energy. Romano waved vigorously after she entered the coffee lounge. "Terza, the chocolate cannoli was amazing. Thank you!"

"I'm glad they saved you one, Romano. You weren't here when I dropped them off, so I was a bit worried."

He smiled. "They saved me two in fact." Romano held up two fingers. "Everyone knows I'm your favorite barista."

"That you are." Terza returned his smile.

"Take a seat. Chocolate cannoli deserves personal service."

"Thanks, Romano. I won't argue with that."

Terza selected an out-of-the-way outside table. She had phone calls to make, and the first belonged to Nico. But before she had time to dial, Terza's phone rang. Moheenie's smiling face filled the screen.

Terza answered. "Good morning."

"Finally, I can talk. Ranger went out for a run. Now please, please catch me up on our murder suspects."

Terza first explained the entire bone sequence. She told Moheenie about Jacob Radovan, the medical examiner, and ended with her visit to see Rose McCool.

"I cannot believe you went to see Rose without me!" Moheenie whined.

"I'm sorry, Mo, but that just wouldn't have looked right. I went to tell her about my conversation with her husband."

"I understand. So you are confident that she is the killer?"

Terza hesitated. "I was, but once again I have my doubts."

"Is it because of Henry Follett?"

"Hang on a second," Terza said when Romano approached. He placed a large mug of steaming coffee in front of her, along with a plate filled with an assortment of petite scones.

"On the house," Romano said with a huge smile.

"Why thank you," Terza replied. "You are too kind." She waited until Romano walked away. "I'm back. Romano just brought me coffee and scones."

"I am guessing they liked the cannoli?" Moheenie asked.

"That would be a yes." Terza sipped her coffee. "You might be right about Henry Follett being a suspect. Yesterday, when I was walking from my condo to the office, I ran right into him."

"Was it a coincidence?"

"Oh no! You could tell he was looking for me. Basically, he told me to stay away from Rose McCool."

"So he has a temper," Moheenie suggested.

"Exactly. Plus, we already know that he had a meat packet in his trash bin. Perhaps Rose and Doctor McCool got into some sort of argument, and Henry Follett lashed out to protect her."

"Maybe Follett killed Doctor McCool, and Rose knows about it," Moheenie offered. "She could have taken the murder weapon with plans to destroy it, and protect Henry."

"That is a possibility. Do you think I should tell Nico? I was just planning to call him."

"Yes, I do. But, before you go..." Moheenie chuckled. "Tell me about this kiss with Conner."

Terza smiled. "Well, I must say it was quite yummy."

"Maybe you really do have feelings for him, Tee."

Terza shrugged. "I don't know. Do I have feelings for him, or am I just looking for love?" She sipped her piping hot coffee.

"We both know you are looking for love, but you're the one who kissed him," Moheenie said. "Only you can know how you feel about him."

"I did feel something, that's for certain."

"Then maybe Conner is more than just a friend."

"Maybe." Terza looked up to the sky. She observed how white and fluffy the clouds looked against the blue sky. "It certainly is a beautiful day."

"Good grief!" Moheenie laughed. "You must be in love!"

"Have you even been outside?"

"Not yet," Moheenie answered dryly.

"Then when you get off of your lazy butt and finally make it outside, you too, will notice the day."

Moheenie continued laughing. "Not as much as you."

"Whatever. I'm going to hang up now and call Nico."

"Okay. Be sure and call me back."

"I will, sweet friend. Ciao!"

"Bye!"

Terza savored a bite of each scone before dialing the detective.

"*Buon giorno*, Miss Tiepolo."

"*Buon giorno*."

"To what do I owe the pleasure? Are you calling to ask me about Rose McCool again?" Nico asked.

"Not really," Terza responded.

"Good, because we may have another suspect."

"Really," Terza said while sitting up straight. "Who is it?"

"I will probably regret telling you this, but we are still investigating Alan Mann. We've interviewed several people involved with the clinical trials. It seems that Mann was holding a grudge against Mitchell McCool."

Terza thought about her previous conversation with Conner. She remembered hearing how Alan Mann had to be escorted from the building. "Do you have any evidence that he might have committed the murder?"

"We are presently following up on a lead," Nico told her. "Are you aware there are cameras throughout the boardwalk?"

"Yes, I believe so."

"The cameras are located closer to the business sections and not in front of the homes. However, we were fortunate enough to locate a camera in the back alley."

Terza instantly recalled her trash bin diving episode and wondered if the event was caught on camera. She shuddered at the thought.

Nico continued, "On the afternoon of the McCool party the camera picked up an image of Alan Mann entering the McCool's garage."

"If Alan Mann was in the garage, then he would have had access to the house."

"Exactly."

"What did he say, Nico?"

"We haven't spoken with him yet. It is always best to be prepared before an interrogation. That way you can catch someone in a lie."

"There are no cameras in the front, right?"

"That is correct."

"So you would not be able to see Rose McCool enter from that angle, correct?"

"You are right again."

"But now we have a problem. There is no parking at the front of the houses. They all face the bay," Terza said.

"How is that a problem?" Nico asked.

"I still think Rose did it. But"—Terza paused for a split second—"if she did, you should be able to see her car when she parked in the alley behind their beach house."

"We ran the tapes, and there is nothing," Nico said.

"But how did Alan Mann get into the garage? Are you positive he actually went inside?"

"That's the problem. It looks like Mann went into the garage, but from the angle it is not clear. Henry Follett's garage is set back. Mann could have gone around the corner without us knowing."

"Speaking of Henry Follett, that is why I called. First off, if you check the cameras for Tuesday night you just might see me dumpster diving."

"Dumpster diving?"

Terza chuckled. "Well, bin diving is more like it. On Tuesday night Moheenie and I went to check the trash bins."

"Didn't I see you on Tuesday night?"

"That would be a yes but more like Tuesday evening," Terza corrected him.

"You went back to the crime scene after we had gelato?"

"You sound upset. Is it because I went out after gelato?"

"Of course that is not what bothers me." Nico spoke firmly. "I just can't believe you went out investigating after we talked about you leaving it up to me."

"All we did was spy on Rose McCool. She didn't even see us," Terza told him.

"Rose McCool? I thought you searched Follett's trash can?"

Terza sighed loudly. "When we covertly watched Rose McCool's home—"

"Covertly watched?" Nico interrupted.

"Yes, covertly. Now stop teasing me!"

"I'm not teasing you," Nico said.

"Yes you are, and we both know it. Moheenie and I watched Rose's home and discovered that Henry Follett was there visiting her. So of course, that meant he was not at his own house."

"That gave you and your partner in crime the green light to spy some more?"

"Not exactly," Terza answered. "Since Henry wasn't home, and typically people put their trash bins out on Tuesday evening—"

"I put mine out Wednesday morning," Nico interrupted again.

"Not everyone wants to get up that early."

"It's a security issue. I don't like people going through my garbage."

"You are changing the subject."

Terza thought she heard a slight chuckle.

"Go on," he said.

"Moheenie and I thought it might be a good idea to check the trash bins."

"Looking for what exactly? Were you planning to find a murder weapon?"

"Maybe," Terza said. "When I looked in Henry's bin I found a white meat wrapper like the butcher uses."

"That settles it." Nico laughed loudly. "Henry Follett is the murderer because he eats steak!"

"Will you stop it?"

"What did you find in Alan Mann's trash?"

"I didn't. He came out so we left," Terza said.

"Did he see you?"

"I can't believe you actually sound concerned."

"I am always concerned," Nico said. "You just seem to crack me up, Terza."

"No, we were not seen. But yesterday, when I was walking from my condo to *MOW*, I ran headfirst into Henry Follett. He was obviously looking for me."

"Did he hurt you?"

"No, he didn't touch me. All he said was to leave Rose McCool alone. But he definitely has a temper. You should have seen the look in his eyes. They were seething!"

"He is also very protective over her," Nico said.

"And don't laugh, but he could have the missing meat. I think you should investigate him, as well."

"Maybe I should place *you* under surveillance as a way of keeping you safe," Nico told her.

"Who would be in charge of the stakeout?"

"I would, of course."

"Would I be able to bring you food?" Terza laughed.

"Only if it's homemade Italian food." He joined in her laughter.

"Oh it would be. I have connections."

"Well, my little Italian friend, I have lots of work to do."

"It's Sunday," Terza said.

"Yes, and my murder is a week old. Talk later. Ciao."

"Ciao, Nico."

She was finally able to do more than just sip her coffee, as it was the perfect temperature for drinking. Terza preferred her coffee hot, but not so that it burnt her tongue. She also thoroughly enjoyed the selection of petite scones and could not pick a favorite. As Terza relaxed she reflected on her kiss with Conner, and she also thought about Nico. They were both very different, and she found special things about each man. *I am so confused!*

Terza once again looked up to admire the sky. The day could not be more perfect, and she had plenty of time to enjoy it. With her mind made up, Terza rushed home to change into her swimsuit, board shorts, and T-shirt. She then raced back to her company van, drove the few blocks to her parents' home, and hurried inside.

"It's me," she spoke to the empty house. Terza reached for the notepad by the kitchen telephone and wrote a note. It read:

Buon giorno! I took my board out of the garage. The day is too beautiful to stay indoors. Conner is meeting me at MOW at 4:00. See you right after. I trust you had a wonderful time at church. Love you! T. (Your Favorite Daughter!)

P.S. Yes, Papa. Ask Mom and she will tell you that we spoke this morning. I also read my Bible!

After securing her stand-up paddleboard in the company van, she started the engine and drove straight to the bay. Summer traffic would be heavy, and parking would be limited. But Terza was a local and possessed a secret. Right after the first bridge, but before the main bridge leading to Mission Bay Park, a right-hand turn led to a hidden parking lot directly in front of the bay. Before 11:00 a.m., Terza was standing on her board with paddle in hand. She felt wonderful. Terza even thought about spending another evening with Conner Reeves. She planned to kiss him if he didn't kiss her first. Terza's heart raced at the thought of Conner's soft lips. *Yum!*

The only problem with stand-up paddleboarding before family dinner involved Terza's thick, long hair. She had no choice but to wash it, and that event took a minimum of one hour. After her shampoo, Terza separated her hair into sections and carefully dried each portion. It did not hurt remembering how much Conner liked her hair down loose. When he picked her up at Macaroni on Wheels her hair was the first thing Conner mentioned.

"Your hair looks amazing, Terza."

"Thank you, Conner. I went SUP boarding today and had to wash it."

"How was the water?"

"It was so warm," Terza told him. "I think maybe up to seventy-five degrees."

"Well, you look gorgeous, and I really like your dress."

Terza smoothed the fabric of her striped black dress. "Thanks, Conner. Guess how much?"

"Guess how much what?"

"How much I paid for this dress."

Conner took a step back. "I'm not sure. Turn around."

Terza slowly turned.

"Again, please," he directed.

First she obeyed and then stopped. Terza pivoted to face him. "Are you looking at my dress or checking me out?"

Conner laughed. "Both, of course. Where did you buy it?"

"You have to guess the price first."

"Seventy-five dollars."

"Nine!"

"I don't believe it. You paid nine dollars?"

"Isn't that great? I have this one and a navy-blue polka-dotted one," Terza announced proudly.

"It fits you perfectly, Terza. But aren't you supposed to keep the price a secret?"

"Not from you, silly."

"I don't know whether to take that as a compliment or an insult," Conner replied.

Terza reached for his hand. "It's a compliment. Now let's go."

Conner and Terza walked hand in hand the short distance to the Tiepolo home. When they reached the front gate Terza slid her key into the lock and pushed it open. Seconds later she looked up to see Charley rushing to meet her.

"Auntie Tee," Charley called while sprinting into Terza's arms. "Oh, I love your hair."

"You are such a goofball, Charley. Last week you wanted nice and straight hair just like Moheenie."

Charley's small hand held onto one of Terza's long curls. "Now I like yours better. It's so shiny." Charlie leaned in to smell Terza's hair. "Your hair smells pretty too."

"Why thank you," Terza said.

"Charley," Rain called.

Terza looked up to see Charley's mother, Rain, standing in the opened doorway. "Tell your auntie Tee when you last allowed me to wash your hair."

Charley made a face.

"You don't like to have your hair washed?" Terza asked.

The six-year-old shook her head vigorously.

"That is an understatement," Rain added. She stepped

down from the front porch and extended her palm to Conner. "Hi, I'm Rain, Terza's sister-in-law."

Conner shook her hand. "It is nice to meet you. Damiano is your husband, right?"

"Yes, and this is our daughter Charley. I'm surprised Caleb hasn't rushed outside yet. He cannot wait to meet a real policeman."

Conner seemed to hesitate. "Does he know I'm not an actual police officer?"

Terza chortled. "He's four years old, Conner. Do you catch bad guys?"

"Well yes," Conner answered.

"Then you are a policeman," Terza told him.

The moment they entered the Tiepolo home Caleb ran to meet Conner. "Do you have a badge?"

Rain instantly intervened. "Mind your manners, young man. Please say hello to Mr. Reeves and introduce yourself."

"Is it okay if he calls me Conner?"

"Of course." Rain told Caleb, "You may introduce yourself to Conner."

"Hi, Conner." Caleb stabbed his arm straight forward. "My name is Caleb."

Conner smiled widely, lowered himself, and shook the young boy's hand. "It is very nice to meet you, Caleb."

"Do you have a badge?" Caleb asked a second time.

"May I please see your badge?" Rain corrected him.

"May I please see your badge," Caleb repeated.

Conner reached through the neck of his aqua golf shirt and withdrew his DEA badge. It was attached to a leather holder around his neck. He pulled the badge over his head and handed it to Caleb.

"Wow!" Caleb's eyes opened with excitement.

"You can wear it if you like," Conner told him.

Caleb looked to his mother. "Can I, Mommy?"

"Of course you may. Thank you for asking."

Caleb's chest visibly puffed when he placed the badge around his neck. "Look at me, Daddy!"

Damiano joined them at the front door. "That is pretty impressive, little man! Where did you get it?"

Caleb pointed sideways at Conner. "Conner gave it to me," he answered proudly.

"I'm very sure that Conner is just letting you wear his badge for a little while," Damiano said. He reached over Caleb and offered his hand. "Hi, Conner. I'm Damiano, Terza's brother."

"It's nice to meet you, Damiano."

Damiano slid to the side and placed an arm around Terza. "Hey, sis, is he any good?"

"Time will tell, big brother. Take note, Conner is on my team."

Conner laughed. "From what I can tell, this family certainly takes bocce ball seriously."

"That it does," Damiano answered. "Now come on in and meet our parents."

"Conner already knows Papa," Terza said.

"In this town, who doesn't?" Damiano chuckled. "Let me guess, you know him from the deli?"

"None better," Conner answered.

After Damiano finished the introductions and Conner won their mom's heart with the sunflowers he brought, everyone selected their seats for dinner. Caleb had to sit by Conner, and Charley insisted on sitting by both of them. That meant Conner was left sitting between the two children instead of next to Terza.

"Do you mind?" she asked him.

"Of course I don't mind," Conner told her, earning extra points.

Terza first looked at Conner while thinking how naturally he fit in with the family. Her mother then looked at her with a slight smile, obviously thinking the same thing.

Ezio asked the family to hold hands as he offered the prayer and blessed their time together. Things seemed almost too good to be true.

At the end of the evening Conner walked Terza back to Macaroni on Wheels and his Mustang. He opened the rear door and placed his meal sack on the back seat. "Your mom is amazing, Terza. Your family is very special." He turned and pulled her close.

Terza caught her breath as Conner ran his fingers through her hair.

"*You* are amazing," he said before pressing his lips to hers.

Terza inhaled his delicious scent while savoring his tender touch. She moaned with pleasure before pulling away.

"Let's go to your place," he whispered.

"Oh no, we can't."

"Why can't we?"

"Because I have zero willpower around you, Conner Reeves."

"Then that's a good thing."

"Seriously, we better call it a night."

Conner smiled his acceptance, kissed her on the forehead, and asked, "Do you want me to drive you home, or shall we walk?"

"Let's drive. I haven't been in the Cherry Bomb for a while."

"Then drive it is." He opened the passenger's door and helped her inside.

When they reached Terza's building, Conner pulled up to the curb and walked around to open her door. He then escorted her to the lobby and waited for her to punch in the code.

Terza stood in the opened doorway. "Conner, you are such a gentleman."

"It's my pleasure. Thank you for an amazing two days."

"It has been fun, hasn't it?"

"Yes, and it's not going to stop. I plan to call you."

"Then I will plan to answer," she told him before saying goodbye.

Terza watched Conner wait until she was safely inside the elevator. She then waved to him as the door rolled closed.

After she entered her condominium, Terza looked at the clock on her microwave. At a few minutes before nine she knew it was still early enough to call Moheenie. But first she waited for Olive to appear.

"Olive! Mommy's home and all alone." It was too late for more food so Terza searched the living room for Olive's favorite toy. The hard plastic ball made a knocking sound as she shook it vigorously. Several minutes later Terza saw Olive's face peek around the bedroom door.

"There you are, sweet baby girl. I bet you were hiding under my bed," Terza spoke gently to her Siamese cat. "Come out and play."

Olive boldly left the safety of the bedroom and walked confidently toward Terza. Her purring increased as she closed the gap between them.

"Look at you, my beauty." Terza reached down and brought Olive to her chest. As she stroked Olive's head, her cat stretched out a paw as if yawning. "You were sleeping, weren't you? I know your style. Sleep all day and play all night." Terza laughed.

She lowered Olive to the plush area rug and dropped the orange ball. Olive instantly batted it with her right paw. It rolled into the dining room and under the table. As an added treat Terza went into her kitchen to retrieve a brown paper grocery bag. She opened it wide and placed it under the dining room table next to the ball.

"Now you have two play toys. I bet you select the bag." Terza watched Olive look from the orange ball to the brown bag. "Pick one, silly girl!" Terza shook her head, laughing as Olive obviously could not decide.

She sent Moheenie a text:

Can you talk?

Terza's cell phone rang. "I'm so confused," she told Moheenie.

"I take it you had a nice time?"

"Oh, Mo, we had a wonderful time." Terza flopped onto her cushiony sofa.

"More important, did you win?"

"Ha! Yes, we won. Conner must have practiced bocce ball with Ranger."

"I think he did. How did Conner fit in with your family?"

"Like it was meant to be," Terza told her. "But I bet Nico will fit in just as well."

"He probably will, Tee. Whatever are you going to do?"

"First off, I really do not have a choice. Nico hasn't asked me out. Right now, my only decision is to see Conner."

"How does that feel to you?"

"You sound like a therapist."

"Just call me Doctor Mo." Moheenie giggled. "What is that noise?"

Terza watched Olive race in and out of the bag. "It's Olive. I gave her a paper bag. She loves rushing in headfirst, turning around while still inside the bag, and then racing out."

"Olive is so cute."

"Yes, she is." Terza burst into laughter.

"What happened?"

"You should see Olive! One of the bag handles got caught on her ear. She is running around like a crazy cat."

"Go help her."

"She's good now."

"Doesn't Olive also like your shoes?"

"She adores sitting on my shoes, and I can't figure out why. How can that be comfortable? Plus, have you ever seen Olive push her bowl?"

"I don't think so," Moheenie said. "What does she do?"

Terza chuckled. "If her bowl is empty, Olive will walk up to it and slide her bowl to one side with her paw. She then uses the other paw to slide it back, all the while hoping I will notice and give her more food."

Moheenie laughed. "And do you give in?"

"Of course not," Terza said. "Olive would be an overweight kitty if I gave in every time she tried to con me into giving her more food. Back to my problem. I just don't know what to do. I have fun with Conner, but my mind keeps returning to Nico. I really think something might be there."

"Just take it one day at a time."

"That's easier said than done."

"What other choice do you have?"

"None, I guess," Terza said. "You're right. From now on that's what I plan to do. I am taking it one day at a time."

"Good girl."

"Thanks, Mo. Good night."

"Good night, Tee."

Terza ended the call and sat watching Olive inch back toward the empty bag. Terza then went into her bathroom, secured her hair beneath an extra-wide terrycloth headband, and took a quick shower. After dressing for bed Terza went to check on Olive. Her cat was fast asleep deep inside the bag. "Good night, Olive. I'm going to bed."

Terza took her remote with her as she settled under the covers. She waited a few minutes until 10:00 p.m. and then surfed through all the local news channels. Terza hoped to hear of an arrest. When nothing appeared, she used her remote to check for any recorded shows. She selected a true crime mystery and watched half of it before falling asleep.

CHAPTER EIGHTEEN: BONE APPETITO

Monday

When Terza woke she felt like camping under the covers all day. At first she felt guilty, but she quickly changed her mind and decided to remain in bed.

"Everyone deserves a day off," she announced to her bedroom walls. Olive instantly ran and jumped up before Terza even had a chance to pat the bed.

"Good morning, Olive. Did you get in any trouble last night?"

Olive responded by curling up next to Terza's warm body.

Terza massaged Olive's neck area with one hand and reached for the television remote with the other. Once again she stopped on the local morning news. An arrest for the McCool murder was yet to be announced. She decided to watch the end of her crime show while Olive slept peacefully. When her show finished, Terza called her mother and headed into the kitchen to make coffee.

Olive continued to sleep while Terza enjoyed her coffee and read her Bible for more than an hour. At 9:30 a.m., she showered and dressed casually in shorts and a T-shirt. She kicked Olive out of her bed so she could make it before leaving, and checked her phone. Terza had two missed calls and a text.

Moheenie wrote:

Can you believe it? Ranger took the day off! We are going to breakfast and a movie. If you need me—too bad! LOL!

Terza responded:

Have fun.

She punched the button for her voice mail and heard Conner's message. He first thanked her for a great weekend and then told her about his unexpected trip. Without expanding on the details, Conner explained that he had to return to Mexico for a case.

Terza's father rounded out the final message. He was making breakfast sandwiches and wanted to know if Terza would like to join him.

She quickly dialed his number.

"Tiepolo Mercato," Ezio answered.

"*Buon giorno*, Papa. Before you ask, yes I called Mom this morning, and yes I read my Bible. And since I am now your favorite daughter, I would love a breakfast sandwich!"

"*Buon giorno*, my little gnocchi. When are you leaving?"

"How about right now? I am starving!"

"Your sandwich will be waiting."

"Did you know that you are my favorite father?"

"I am your only father."

"Ah-ha! Two can play this game! See you in five minutes!"

"Ciao." Ezio chuckled.

"Ciao, ciao."

Terza jogged to the Tiepolo Mercato and raced through the front door. She waved to her mother, who was busy helping a customer and then walked straight to the butcher's counter. Her father smiled and handed her a wrapped sandwich. "That was fast," he commented.

"I ran," she said, accepting the sandwich. It was still warm. "Thanks, Papa! This is such a nice surprise. Shall we eat outside?"

"Lead the way." Ezio followed Terza to one of the sidewalk bistro tables.

Terza opened the breakfast sandwich and took a bite. She swallowed and said, "You make the best sandwiches, Papa."

"Thank you." His smile grew. "I think so, too!" He laughed.

Terza laughed along with him. Father and daughter enjoyed each other's company while Terza gobbled her breakfast. When she finished her sandwich, Terza cleaned up her table and kissed her father on the cheek. "Thanks, Pop! I have to run."

"Are you working today?"

"Just on paperwork. Last week was such a busy week of catering I have yet to start on my growing pile of paperwork." Terza peered through the Mercato plate glass window. "I see mom is still busy. Would you please tell her goodbye for me?"

"I will tell her."

"Great." She kissed him again. "I love you! Ciao."

"I love you, too, my little gnocchi."

Instead of going to work through the Mercato *secret entrance* as they called it, Terza walked around the corner and entered her company through her front office. She sat at her desk and stared at the foot-high stack of paperwork.

"Where to start?" To her delight, Terza's phone rang, and the screen read *Nico Garza*.

"Good morning, Nico."

"Is it morning? I've been working so hard I've lost all track of time."

"It is just about eleven," Terza told him. "Since you've been hard at work does that mean you have made an arrest?"

"It's coming soon. That's why we are so busy."

"Can you tell me who?"

"Not quite yet."

Then why did you call? "Then why do I have the pleasure of your call?"

"Can't I just call to say hello?"

"Of course, but that's not the real reason."

Nico laughed. "And who is the detective?"

233

"Just tell me," Terza prompted.

"Okay, I called to tell you that Alan Mann did not go into the McCool's garage."

Terza sat up straight. "How do you know that?"

"We brought him into the station yesterday, and he emphatically denied going into Doctor McCool's garage. Fortunately for him we were able to locate another camera that showed Mann walking around the side of Henry Follett's house instead of entering the garage as we first thought."

"What was he doing walking around the side?"

"Mann said he was just going for a walk, but I think he was really spying on Follett's house," Nico told her.

"Caroline Mann told me she saw Henry Follett look out the window on the night before the party."

"I remember that."

"I bet she asked her husband to go and snoop," Terza guessed.

"Maybe she did. That makes more sense than Mann supposedly going for a walk in the back alley rather than along the bayside boardwalk." Nico paused. "I better get back to work."

"What about Rose McCool and Henry Follett?"

"What about them?"

"Stop teasing me," Terza said. "Aren't you going to give me a hint about which one you are going to arrest?"

"I did give you a hint, and it's not Alan Mann," Nico said.

"That's it?"

"That's it. Before I can say anything else, I still have something I need to check out."

"Okay," Terza relented.

"Ciao, Terza."

"Ciao, Nico."

Before returning to the massive pile of paperwork Terza lifted the receiver of her company phone and punched in her code to stop the calls from forwarding to her cell. She then began the tedious task of the accounts receivable and accounts payable portion of Macaroni on Wheels. *Cooking is much more fun.*

Terza took a lunch break around 2:00 p.m. After making a simple salad and enjoying her lunch while reading her current book club mystery novel, Terza returned to her desk and the shrinking stack of papers. Right about 4:00 p.m., the office telephone rang.

"Macaroni on Wheels."

"Good afternoon, Terza," Nico said. "You don't usually answer by saying 'Macaroni on Wheels.' Did I call a different number?"

"No, it's the same. Since I'm in the office I took the phone off of forwarding."

"I don't get it," he said.

"When we first met I gave you the Macaroni on Wheels number, right?"

"Yes, it is on your business card."

"When you call my company number it either rings on this phone in my office, or on my cell. If I am in the office, I take the phone off call forwarding. When I am out of the office, all of the calls come directly to my cell. When that happens I can tell it's you."

"Basically you are telling me that I only have your work number?" he asked with a mischievous tone in his voice.

"Would you like my personal cell phone number?"

"Yes, please."

Terza laughed and then recited her number. "Now you can send me a text, too."

"I just might do that."

"Please tell me you have finally made an arrest."

"I'll save that answer for later. Actually, I was thinking about that gelato," he said. "I'm sorry for the late notice, but are you available after dinner tonight?"

Terza wondered why he specifically had stressed getting together *after* dinner.

"About what time?"

"Is eight too late? I'm going to have to work through dinner."

Terza's smile beamed into the receiver. "You can't just have gelato for dinner. Do you want me to make you something here?"

"Oh no, but that is so sweet of you," Nico said. "Thank you very much. We'll all just send out for burgers or something."

"Okay, then. I'll see you around eight. Did you want to stop by here, or shall I meet you at the restaurant?"

"I'll stop by your company. But, before you hang up, I have a message for you from Jacob Radovan."

"You do? What kind of message?"

"Hang on," Nico said. "I need to flip through my notepad. I wrote it down because he insisted that I tell you his message word for word."

Terza held her breath in anticipation.

"Okay, here it is. He said to tell you that Number Three is Number One in his book."

"Wow! He said that?"

"Word for word. I take it you're pleased?"

"Very, but what made him ask you to tell me?"

"You will know soon enough."

"Soon enough?" Terza whined. "I still have to wait almost four hours."

"Four hours is nothing. See you at eight?"

"See you at eight," she confirmed. *And I can't wait.*

Terza arrived home by 5:00 p.m. and changed three times before returning to her company at 7:00 p.m. She had finally decided upon white jeans with a black sleeveless sweater. Fortunately, the summer nights remained warm. She stalled by plumping a few pillows on her office sofa and then alternated between putting her hair back and allowing it to fall loosely.

Finally, she opted to pull the sides up, away from her face, with the back left long and shiny.

"What to do now," she mumbled softly. Terza suddenly gasped when her entertaining nature took hold. She raced into her catering kitchen and withdrew a pastry-wrapped brie wheel from one of the refrigerators. Then, after baking it to perfection, Terza centered the puffed pastry on a flat, porcelain plate and added a semicircle of sliced green apples. She cut a lemon in half and drenched the apples with the lemon juice to prevent them from browning. Terza also sliced a fresh, sourdough baguette and carried the brie and bread basket into her waiting area. Minutes later, the loud buzzer sounded.

Terza opened the door to an unexpected surprise. "What's all this?"

Nico handed her a bouquet of flowers.

"Oh my goodness, Nico, you brought me Stargazer lilies. They are one of my favorites!" She inhaled their sweet aroma. "I love them! Thank you."

"I think they will look better when the flowers bloom," Nico said, seeming to apologize.

"They are beautiful now. I am so glad you bought them with the flowers still closed. They will last much longer. Thank you again, Nico."

"It was my pleasure." He handed her a gold box.

"You brought me chocolates, as well? I am overwhelmed!"

"I don't know you well enough, or if you even like chocolate. So I decided to bring both."

Terza inhaled the chocolate smell through the package. "Oh yes!" She turned the gold box over to read the bottom label, and noticed he had selected a nut-filled assortment. "I especially adore chocolates with nuts. How did you know that I'm not allergic?"

"Because of the pistachio gelato. It has pieces of nuts."

Terza smiled. "Great detective work. To me, chocolate is not chocolate without a nut."

"Then, you'll have to fight me for them," he warned. "I adore nuts, too."

Terza raised an eyebrow. "It's on." Both of her hands were full when he extended a bottle of champagne. "Are you kidding? You brought champagne, too? Nico, I can't believe all of this!"

He smiled. "Good. That's what I was hoping. Do you drink champagne?"

"I certainly do." Terza eyed the label. "Especially when the champagne is Pol Roger. You have good taste, Detective. Is it chilled?"

Terza shivered when he touched the icy bottle to her bare forearm. "It's definitely chilled! Would you like to open it now? It should go great with the baked brie."

"You baked brie?"

Terza nodded. "I did, and I hope you like brie. It is nice and gooey inside of a homemade puffed pastry shell."

"Now I'm the one to be impressed."

Terza laughed. "Don't be. That's what I do." She walked toward the kitchen. "Please make yourself at home. I'll place these gorgeous flowers in water and bring us some glasses."

"Great. I'll open the champagne."

Terza returned carrying the vase and two champagne flutes. Then, after stopping to place the flowers on her desk, she walked toward Nico while taking note of his muted coral golf shirt. *He sure looks great in pastels.* Terza handed him the glasses. "You pour, and I'll be right back."

Seconds later Terza returned with the box of chocolates and a look of mischievous excitement. "Shall we open these, too?"

"Sounds good to me." Nico handed her a glass. "I'd like to make a toast."

Terza accepted the liquid-filled flute and then sat next to him on the small sofa. She held her glass up as an explosion of bubbles floated to the surface.

"To Terza. To the woman who solved my case and made me a hero."

Her glass barely touched his. "You made an arrest?" Terza took a quick sip before returning her glass to the table. She inched forward on the cushion, and turned her body toward his. "Don't just sit there, Nico! Tell me what happened."

"Thanks to you, I have a full confession."

Terza's mind clicked off her evidence. Her eyebrows lifted. "It was Rose McCool, wasn't it?"

"Yes, it was."

"And she confessed?"

"That she did."

Terza tapped the sofa. "Tell me everything."

Nico took another sip of champagne as Terza waited impatiently. "As you know," he finally said, "Rose basically stewed the evidence. According to Doctor Radovan, the constant simmering would completely erode the original shape. It doesn't matter though because we never located the actual bone."

Terza's eyes widened. "Did you find the particles?"

He nodded. "Thanks to you, Detective Tiepolo, we found trace evidence on two places in Rose's garage."

"Two places?"

"Why don't you take a guess," he prompted her.

She rubbed her chin in thought. "First on a saw."

"That's one." Nico raised his index finger.

Terza wrinkled her nose. "The second would have to be either on a workbench where she held the bone or perhaps on a vice."

"That's two choices," he said. "Which is it?"

Terza thrived on solving mysteries. "If I have to pick one, I would choose a vice."

"Final answer?" he teased.

She laughed. "Yes, final answer."

"Ding, ding, ding!"

"I got it right?"

"Yes, we found trace evidence on both the saw and on the vice that held the bone. Rose remembered to destroy the bone but forgot about the bone particulates. After we found the evidence, it was easy to get a confession from her."

"Was the murder premeditated or an accident?"

"Neither," Nico said. "It wasn't premeditated because Rose McCool never planned to kill her ex-husband. But it was also not an accident. She did it. Rose was the one who smacked her ex right on the head."

"What did she say happened?" Terza pressed.

"Do you remember when Rose stopped by the beach house unannounced?"

"Do you mean when I was there on that Friday afternoon?"

"Yes, on the Friday."

Terza nodded. "Of course I remember."

"According to Rose," Nico continued, "she went over that day and originally intended just to pick up all of the frozen beef that was stored in the freezer."

"Then why didn't she take it?"

"Rose said she was too angry and too upset."

Terza brushed a few stray hairs from her face. "Do you mean about the party?"

Nico nodded. "Rose McCool told me that hearing about the party was the last straw for her. It made her realize their marriage was over and that Mitchell was moving on without her."

"But she was the one who originally asked for the divorce," Terza reminded him.

"That she was. But you and Moheenie had it right from the start. The ex-Mrs. McCool could not stand the fact that Mr. McCool was finally moving on. So, she decided to ask him for a reconciliation."

Terza's mouth opened in surprise. "She did?"

"Yes, according to Rose, she asked him the very next day on the afternoon of the party. First, she called on the pretense that she wanted to simply empty the freezer. But when she got there, Rose told me she asked her husband if they could work on reconciling their marriage."

"And he said no," Terza commented.

"He said no to the reconciliation, and no to the party."

Terza placed a palm over her heart. "That is so sad. Rose also asked him if she could come to his party?"

"She asked, he said no, and I guess the rejection caused her to snap. Rose told me that she had already put all of the beef packages into a large canvas bag and was just about to place the bone on top. But before she did, Mitchell picked up the bag and said that he would carry it to her car. The next thing she realized was that he had been whacked on the head and had fallen to the floor."

"So, instead of calling nine-one-one, she went home and made stew?" Terza felt outraged. "Don't tell me she is going to plead temporary insanity!"

"I'm sure she'll try. But I don't think the fact that she went home to cook the murder weapon will go over well with a jury."

"I certainly hope not." Terza sipped her champagne. "I do kind of feel sorry for her though."

"I kind of do, too."

"I don't understand why you never saw film of her car in the driveway."

"We asked Rose that exact question," Nico told her.

"What was her explanation?"

"Rose said she parked down the street in the parking lot of the local grocery store."

"I know that parking lot well," Terza said, laughing. "Moheenie and I used it when we did our trash bin diving!"

"Please don't remind me," Nico said, laughing with her.

"But why did she park in the lot instead of behind the house?"

"Rose said she wanted to surprise him."

"That doesn't make any sense," Terza commented. "You told me Rose had already called, and Doctor McCool knew she was on the way."

"That just goes to show how a jealous mind works. Rose called to say she was coming over in two hours, but she purposefully arrived an hour early. She parked in the grocery store lot and then walked along the front bayside sidewalk. She hoped to catch Mitchell off guard when she knocked on his front door."

Terza looked up in thought. "She knocked on his front door that Friday, as well. I bet Rose parked in the grocery store lot that day, too."

"I'm sure she did."

"Were you surprised that Rose confessed?"

"Not when we showed her the evidence. Thanks to the information you gave Doctor Radovan about the bone, we were able to obtain a search warrant."

"But you really did not have much evidence. I'm surprised it was enough for a warrant," Terza said.

"We had the information that a bone was used as the murder weapon. We had confirmation of a bone missing from Mitchell McCool's freezer—"

"That would be from me," Terza interrupted him.

Nico smiled. "Yes it would."

"We also had the evidence of Rose cooking stew on the day our officer went over."

"The judge went for that?" Terza asked, surprised.

"He did," Nico answered. "I guess we just got lucky with the warrant." Nico raised his half-filled glass. "So again, to you I toast!"

"Thank you," Terza said, followed by a ping of the crystal. She looked down at the table. "We haven't even touched the brie." Terza poked through the puffed pastry and scooped generous dollops of cheese onto two baguette circles. She handed one to Nico. "Enjoy."

"I could get used to this," he said, with obvious implication. Nico held his bread as if making a toast. "Hats off to the chef. *Buon appetito.*"

"*Buon appetito.*"

They bit in unison. "Yum," Nico hummed through a full mouth. His eyes then filled with mischief. "You know, for this particular occasion, I can think of a more appropriate saying."

"And what might that be?"

"We could always say Bone appetito. You know"—Nico pointed to his elbow—"like a bone. Get it?"

Terza laughed. "Trust me, I got it! And I agree."

Nico looked at his watch. "It's nearing nine. How late do they serve gelato?"

Terza shrugged. "I'm not sure, but they may be closed. Are you hungry?"

"Not anymore," Nico said. "Plus, we still have chocolates to eat."

"Yes, we do," Terza agreed. "Nothing goes better with champagne and cheese."

"Chocolates go with everything, don't you think?"

Terza handed him the box to open. "Absolutely."

"If we are skipping the gelato tonight then we will have to take a rain check," Nico told her.

"Are you suggesting that we might see each other again even though your case is solved?"

"Would that be alright with you?"

She pretended to think about it. Finally, Terza smiled. "Yes, I believe it would."

Nico extended the opened box of chocolates so Terza could make the first selection. After analyzing several pieces, she chose the one that appeared to be filled with almonds. Nico then made his selection. "Bone appetito," he said before taking a bite.

"Bone appetito!"

CHAPTER NINETEEN: ANOTHER DAY— ANOTHER DOLLAR

Tuesday Evening

At 4:00 in the afternoon Terza and Moheenie stood around the expansive concrete island in the Macaroni on Wheels kitchen. Exhausted from a busy day, but anxious to finish the task at hand, they both stared at the murder board resting on the counter.

Terza opened one of the top drawers and withdrew a gray, rectangular chalkboard eraser. She first looked at the whiteboard, and then locked eyes with Moheenie. "Shall I erase Henry Follett's name?"

Moheenie nodded. "He did have a motive."

"Yes. There is no doubt that Henry Follett was in love with Rose McCool. When he came to scare me off I now know he was just being extra protective of her."

"Now that Doctor McCool is dead, do you think Rose and Henry will get together?"

Terza shrugged. "I don't see how they can. She will probably be in jail for quite some time."

"I don't know, Tee. If Rose has a good lawyer she could plead temporary insanity."

"Have you been talking to my sister? That is exactly what Angeline said."

"No, I haven't, but it makes sense," Moheenie answered.

"You're right. It does."

"So let's say Rose gets out soon, or never even serves time," Moheenie said. "Do you think they will get together?"

"I'm not sure. Do you?"

Moheenie shrugged. "I'm not sure either. He really doesn't seem like her type. But then, what *is* her type? Do we really know?"

Terza slowly erased each phrase under Henry Follett's column and then erased his full name. "I guess time will tell."

"Yes, it will."

Terza again looked at Moheenie. "Shall I now erase Alan Mann's name?"

"Alan Mann had a motive, as well."

"Even Faulkner Baine thought so," Terza added.

"Do you think Alan was really upset about losing his job?"

"It's hard to say." Terza paused in thought. "The online articles made it sound like he was upset, but Caroline painted a different picture."

"Maybe she was just trying to cover for her husband?" Moheenie suggested.

"I thought so, too, at first. But, since we now know Alan had nothing to do with the murder, we also know Caroline had no reason to cover for him."

"You are right, Terza. I bet Caroline was telling the truth."

"Maybe Alan was upset at first and then later realized everything turned out for the best." Terza waited for Moheenie's direction.

"Okay, then, erase his name."

Terza moved the eraser until all signs of Alan Mann and his possible motives were no longer visible. She then read the list of possible motives under the name of Rose McCool.

"We did it, Moheenie. Do you realize that we solved a true-life murder mystery?"

"You solved the mystery, Terza. I just helped a little along the way."

"No, Moheenie. We solved it together. Shall I now erase the last name?"

"Not until you tell me every single part of the story. I still have tons of questions."

"Okay, where to begin?"

Moheenie laughed. "At the beginning, you goof!"

"You already know part of it."

"Then start with when you borrowed the bone from your dad."

Terza began her story with the butcher shop bone. Her father never did get it back. To Terza's knowledge Jacob Radovan still had it in his possession.

"Do you think your father really wants the bone?"

"I doubt it," Terza answered. "Maybe I will wait until we need another favor and then go ask Jacob about it."

"You mean as an excuse?"

"Exactly as an excuse," Terza confirmed. "Now, shall I finally erase Rose McCool's name?"

"I guess so, but it seems sad."

"What does?"

"It's sad that our mystery is over."

"I agree, but erasing the board may be a symbol," Terza said. "If we have a clean board we will be ready for another mystery."

"Are we being morbid?" Moheenie cringed. "I feel like we are anxiously waiting for another murder to solve."

"It's not the murder," Terza explained. "We like the mystery."

"But we attend a murder mystery book club."

"That's fiction, Mo! Don't worry, we are not sinister. We are just two young ladies interested in solving mysteries."

Moheenie shot Terza a huge smile. "If you say so, my friend."

Terza returned the smile. "I say so! Now, we must say goodbye to our crime-solving and focus on our real jobs."

Moheenie chuckled. "Do you mean catering?" She asked, knowing the answer.

"Yes, catering." Terza wiped a clean damp cloth over their now blank murder board. "Let me put this away." She slid the whiteboard next to the refrigerator. They then both looked up at the catering board on the wall.

"I see we only have three jobs this week," Moheenie commented.

"Yes, but don't think we have an easy week," Terza said. "Do you see the wedding rehearsal dinner?"

"Does that really say thirty people?"

Terza nodded. "Thirty plus. There is no time to waste. Tomorrow we focus, big time!"

"What are you doing tonight?"

"Not one thing. How about you?"

"Ranger and I don't have any plans either. I think it will be a kick back kind of night."

Terza hugged her friend. "Ciao, ciao then. I will see you tomorrow."

"Bye, Tee. Love you!"

"Love you, too."

CHAPTER TWENTY: ENCOURAGEMENT FROM THE WORD OF GOD

After Moheenie left for the day, Terza stood frozen in place and stared out her office window. She felt overwhelmed from mental exhaustion. Before closing up, Terza decided to take a moment and read from the Bible.

She walked to her desk and retrieved a Bible from her top drawer. Terza opened to the book of Psalms, chapter 150, and read aloud from the New King James version. "Praise the Lord, Praise God in His sanctuary; Praise Him in His mighty firmament! Praise Him for His mighty acts; Praise Him according to His excellent greatness! Praise Him with the sound of the trumpet; Praise Him with the lute and harp! Praise Him with the timbrel and dance; Praise Him with stringed instruments and flutes! Praise Him with loud cymbals; Praise Him with clashing cymbals! Let everything that has breath praise the Lord. Praise the Lord!"

Terza closed her Bible and looked to Heaven. *Thank you for my life, Lord. Thank you for always taking such good care of me.*

EPILOGUE: THE NEXT MURDER

Terza returned her Bible to the desk drawer and lifted her computer tablet. She made a few notes before forwarding her company phone to her mobile. It rang the moment she finished.

"Macaroni on Wheels."

"Is this the catering company in Little Italy?"

"Yes, it is," Terza replied, instantly taking note of the man's British-sounding accent.

"Is it the one right next door to the Tiepolo Mercato?"

Terza chuckled. "Definitely yes, right next door. Who referred you? Was it Ezio or Benedette Tiepolo?"

"It was the butcher. I'm not sure of his name."

"That is Ezio Tiepolo, my father."

"Well, your father says you are the second-best chef in San Diego."

Terza's laughter continued. "Did he say that my mother is the first best?"

"As a matter of fact, he did. My name is Joshua Kamoze. I'm calling to see if you would consider catering a birthday party for my wife. Her name is Sloan."

"Of course," Terza said. "Birthday parties are my favorite. I will first need to check my calendar. When are you planning to have the party?"

"On the thirtieth of October, the day before Halloween," Joshua told her.

While Terza clicked on her calendar she asked, "Are you planning a Halloween theme?"

Joshua groaned. "Oh no! I'm planning just the opposite. Sloan complains that every year her birthday coincides with Halloween. This year I wanted to surprise her with a normal birthday."

"Good to know it is a surprise." Terza's calendar filled the computer screen. Using her mouse, she advanced the months to October. "You are in luck. I am booked for the thirty-first, but open on the thirtieth. How many people are you expecting?"

"Around forty. Is that too many?"

"No, forty is perfect. Will the party be at your home or another location?"

"At our home. It shouldn't be too far from you. We live in one of the historic homes close to Presidio Park."

"Oh, I love those houses. Is it a one, or two-story?"

"Two."

"Then, I bet you have a gorgeous staircase," Terza commented.

"Yes, we do. Sloan's favorite part of Christmas is decorating the wooden railing with garland."

"It sounds beautiful. Okay, I have you down for October thirtieth. I just need your contact information to get started. Then, I can send you menus and all the information you will need to plan the perfect party."

"That sounds great. I am glad I met your father, Terza."

After ending her conversation with Joshua, Terza telephoned her father.

"Tiepolo Mercato."

"Hi, Papa. I called to thank you for the referral. The man's name is Joshua Kamoze, although I forgot to ask him when you met."

"Hum," her father mumbled while obviously thinking. "Does he have a British accent?"

"Yes, yes he does. Well, it sounds British, but I caught the sound of another place."

"Jamaica!" Ezio announced with great enthusiasm. "He is a nice man."

"How do you know he is from Jamaica?"

"Because we had an enjoyable talk while I was making his sandwich. I think he walked over during his lunch break. If I remember correctly, he was at a business meeting downtown."

"Papa, you are a very special man. I adore how kind you are to absolutely everyone!"

"We're all God's children. Right?"

"You are correct." Terza paused a beat. "Guess what? He lives in one of the historic houses by Presidio Park."

"Your mother would love that," Ezio said. "Maybe he lives in one of the homes on the tour your mother took."

"He might. I cannot wait to see the staircase. They always look so beautiful decorated for Christmas with garland. Mr. Kamoze said that decorating the staircase is his wife's favorite part."

"I can imagine. It must be a grand staircase," Ezio said. "You know the ones that curve from the second floor down to the first."

"We'll know soon enough, thanks to you. Mr. Kamoze hired us to cater a surprise party."

Look for the second book in S.K. Derban's Macaroni on Wheels series.

Case of the Curved Staircase—A Macaroni on Wheels Mystery

TERZA'S COOKING TIPS
Straight from the Macaroni on Wheels Kitchen

How to Properly Cook Pasta / How to Properly Salt Your Pasta Water

It is not like the ocean!

It has been suggested that one should salt pasta water so it tastes like the ocean. I don't know about you, but personally, I do not like the taste of the ocean! You are eating your pasta water, not swimming in it. This is how we prepare our pasta water and cook our pasta in the Macaroni on Wheels kitchen:

- Bring a large pot of water to boil. Please make certain the pasta has room to dance. You should never overcrowd your pasta.
- Add one-half tablespoon of kosher salt for each quart of water just when the water begins to boil.
- Never ever add oil to the water. Your goal is to season the pasta. Adding oil will prevent the pasta from soaking up the salt, and will also prevent the sauce from adhering to your pasta.
- Add the pasta only after the water comes to a full boil. Be prepared to stir whenever necessary.
- Check by tasting, not by tossing pasta to the wall! Your pasta should be cooked al dente.
- Before draining your pasta, use a large measuring cup to scoop out at least two cups of water. Set aside.
- After your pasta is drained, pour the entire batch onto a serving platter. Depending on the type of sauce you prepared, you may now add a cup of sauce to your pasta to prevent it from sticking.

- You may also add a touch of pasta water to enhance your dish. Skip this step if your pasta water is over salted. (Like the ocean!)

Buon appetito,
Terza Tiepolo

SMOKED ITALIAN MEATBALLS BY SAM RHODES

Terza's good friend, Sam Rhodes, was kind enough to share a special recipe. Join in the cooking fun by following his Instagram Handle @Sams_Smokehouse

Smoked Italian Meatballs:

Introducing a mouthwatering culinary adventure: Smoked Italian Meatballs! Perfectly tender and full of savory goodness, these meatballs will become a family favorite. Whether you're a seasoned pitmaster or just looking to impress at your next gathering, these Italian meatballs infused with smoky perfection will not disappoint. Let's fire up the smoker and get cooking!

Ingredients:
- 1 pound ground beef
- ½ cup chopped onion
- 1 tablespoon Italian seasoning
- 1 teaspoon ground mustard
- 1 teaspoon paprika
- ½ tablespoon Worcestershire sauce
- ½ cup breadcrumbs
- ½ cup freshly shredded parmesan cheese
- 2 eggs
- 1 large jar marinara sauce

CASE OF THE BAYFRONT MURDER

Instructions:

1. **Prepare Your Smoker (or Oven):** Preheat your smoker to 225°F (107°C). If you prefer to use an oven, preheat it to the same temperature (225°F/107°C) and place a cast iron skillet inside.

2. **Mix Ingredients:** In a large mixing bowl, combine all ingredients except for the marinara sauce. Mix until all ingredients are well acquainted.

3. **Form Meatballs:** Take the mixture and shape it into meatballs, about 1.5 inches in diameter. You can adjust the size to your preference.

4. **Arrange in Cast Iron Skillet:** Place the meatballs in a cast iron skillet. If you're using an oven, make sure to have the skillet preheated inside the oven.

5. **Pour Marinara Sauce:** Pour the marinara sauce evenly over the meatballs in the skillet. Ensure that the meatballs are fully covered with the sauce.

6. **Smoke (or Oven Bake):** Place the cast iron skillet in the smoker and smoke at 225°F (107°C) for about 2.5 hours. Check the internal temperature of the meatballs using a meat thermometer; they should reach 165°F (74°C). If using the oven, bake the meatballs in the preheated oven at 225°F (107°C) for approximately 2.5 hours, or until they reach an internal temperature of 165°F (74°C).

7. **Serve:** Once the meatballs are done, remove them from the smoker or oven. Let them rest for a few minutes, then serve hot with additional marinara sauce, over pasta, or even make a meatball sub.

We hope you enjoy your delicious smoked Italian meatballs! Remember to follow Sam Rhodes @Sams_Smokehouse on Instagram for more mouthwatering recipes. If you try this recipe, we would love for you to take a picture and post it, tagging @Sams_Smokehouse!

Olive's Friends - Meet the Fabulous Felines

Olive's winning personality is a mixture of many past and present feline friends:

Cocoa; The beautiful feline who started it all! She was an award-winning, purebred, Seal-Point Siamese.

Alyssa; This delightful diva ruled the house. One might say she was a total snob!

Buddy; It was difficult to admire this good-looking guy, as he always hid whenever company arrived. He was a true scaredy-cat!

Jedi; This magnificent male always came running when he heard his owner open the pop-top on a can of wet cat food. He was a hunter extraordinaire!

Patches; She fancied shoes, and would sit right on top. Both adorable and athletic, she could catch a fly between her paws!

Pokie; This beautiful boy was an architect at heart. He often climbed on the drafting table when his owner was drawing plans!

Rusty; He had the funny habit of pushing his empty bowl back and forth. It was his cute way of requesting more food!

Sookie; It was difficult to admire this gorgeous girl, as she also hid whenever company arrived. She adored bags!

Wappo; This good-looking guy also adores bags. An empty bag will keep him occupied for a very long time!

My Extraordinary Readers

Thank you very much for reading *Case of the Bayfront Murder*. I sincerely hope you enjoyed this first book in my Macaroni on Wheels series. My readers mean the world to me! I would be extremely grateful for an extra moment of your time:

Rating – Simply select the number of stars. It's that simple!

Review – After you select the number of stars, feel free to share your thoughts. A review can be as short as a single word.

Ratings and/or Reviews can be posted on Amazon, Goodreads, and BookBub.

There are two more books in this *Macaroni on Wheels* series. I hope you will also enjoy reading *Case of the Curved Staircase*, and *Case of the Paella Party*.

Blessings beyond blessings!

—S.K. Derban

ABOUT THE AUTHOR

    S.K. Derban resides with her husband in Southern California. Although born in the United States she moved to London within the first three months, and remained in England until the age of five. Her father, an American citizen, was a decorated veteran of the Second World War. Her British mother was involved with the London Royal Ballet Company, and a great fan of the arts.

    After returning to the United States, Derban's life remained filled with a love of the theatre, and a passion for British murder mysteries.

    S.K. Derban's personal travel and missionary escapades are readily apparent as they shine through into her characters. Readers are often transported virtually across the globe. She has traveled to Hong Kong on five separate occasions to smuggle Bibles into China, and has been to Israel on seven missionary trips. Derban's other adventures include visits to Bangkok, Greece, Egypt, Italy, and the Caribbean.

Beginning with her faith in the Lord, S.K. Derban relies on all aspects of her life when writing.

She hopes her books will allow readers to go on holiday without having to pack!

Visit S.K. Derban at https://childofthecarpenter.com/

OTHER BOOKS BY S.K. DERBAN

Uneven Exchange

A brave woman confronts mortal danger
with faith that reminds:
"For the battle is not yours, but God's..."

For No Apparent Reason

A calloused murder, a chance discovery—
two unplanned events become the catalyst that proves:
"in all things, God works for good..."

Circumvent

When perfection turns to panic,
an isolated couple must learn:
"For we walk by faith, not by sight..."

Milton Keynes UK
Ingram Content Group UK Ltd.
UKHW030240190324
439698UK00014B/907

9 781963 188028